Unlikely Date

A CALLOWAY BROTHERS NOVEL

samantha christy

Athena Books Publishing Group

Copyright © 2022 by Samantha Christy

All rights reserved, including the rights to reproduce this book or any portions thereof in any form whatsoever.

This is a work of fiction. Names, characters, places, and incidents are either the product of the author's imagination or are used fictitiously, and any resemblance to actual persons, living or dead, business establishments, events or locales is entirely coincidental.

Cover designed by Coverluv

Cover model photo by WANDER AGUIAR

Cover model – Thiago Lusardi

Unlikely Date

A CALLOWAY BROTHERS NOVEL

Samantha Christy

Chapter One

Tag

"I don't get it," Jaxon says, sinking his teeth into a foot-long chili dog. He studies the impressive ass of the busty blonde waitress who just tucked her phone number into my breast pocket. "We have the same DNA. Share the same parents." He glances down, eyes sweeping over his jeans, Doc Martens knockoffs, and standard-issue Nighthawks fan tee. "Is it my clothes?"

"It's my charm," I deadpan.

"Charm?" He chokes down another bite. "Brother, you couldn't charm the deuce I took this morning back into my asshole. Seriously, how do you do it? I mean, you're such a dickwad."

My left eyebrow spikes at his choice of words. "Dickwad?"

"I teach teenagers all day. What do you expect?"

The suite roars when the Nighthawks score a run, putting them up 7-2 over the Indians in the eighth inning, all but ensuring a win.

Cha-ching!

The more the Hawks win, the better my job security. They're my biggest client. And as owner, president, and CEO of a sports marketing firm, every run they score is more money in my pocket.

Brady Taylor, the former Nighthawk who still holds the team record for pitching the most perfect games, crosses the room. "You see my kid pitch that fastball in the fifth inning? He's pushing one hundred miles per hour. That's Hall of Fame territory."

"Sure did. Stryker is the reason the stands are packed."

He smiles proudly. "Hell yeah, he is."

The inning turns over, and the Hawks take the field. Brady thumbs to his wife who's sitting in the front row biting her nails. "Better get back to Rylee. She can't watch him pitch without squeezing all the blood out of my hand."

"Give her my best."

"Will do. Catch you later, Tag."

A pair of kids duck around Brady and bump into me as they zoom by. I check my tailored pale-gray Hugo Boss dress pants to make sure they didn't smear food on them. Fucking kids. They shouldn't be allowed in here. I get out a smoke and nod to the door. Jaxon shakes his head but doesn't say anything. He gave up years ago on trying to get me to quit. I step outside the suite and find the nearest designated smoking area. A semi attractive woman talks to me as we puff away. I oblige her, proving my point that despite my dickwad tendencies, I can still charm the pants off a snake.

I toss her number into the trash can, then look back. Yeah, she saw me do it. She shoots me the bird and turns in a huff. *That's right, honey. Mentioning your seven-year-old when you want to ride my cock all night is not how to get me into bed.*

Unlikely DATE

As soon as I'm back in the suite, Dylan Graff crosses the room with two drinks in his hands. I lean into Jaxon, eyes still on Dylan. "Here it comes."

"Here what comes?"

"Just wait."

A fresh beer is placed before me as if I can't snap my fingers and have Miss Hotpants appear with one in ten seconds flat. Probably with her address this time. And maybe the key to her place. Yeah, it's happened.

Dylan is an intern for the New York Nighthawks. Someone who wipes noses and asses if he's told—of adult baseball players. He's got his head so far up my butthole that it must be hard for him to breathe. I get it. He's young. A recent grad who's trying to make connections with anyone and everyone. But he's taken his suck-up-ness to a whole other level.

He wipes the wetness from the beer off his palm and onto his Old Navy chinos before extending his hand. "Mr. Calloway," he says.

I hate it when people call me Mr. Calloway. Unless said person is a stacked woman with tits that stand at attention when she's flat on her back, and I'm driving into her like a jackhammer.

"Tag," I say with my handshake.

He nods to the stadium below. "Looks like it's going to be another good day."

"I guess you get to keep your job."

He laughs a little too loudly. *Fucking suck up.* Jaxon chuckles beside me.

"So, hey." He wipes both palms now, hesitating.

"Spit it out, Dylan."

He looks nervously across the room. I follow his gaze to the attractive brunette leaning against the wall chatting with another

3

familiar Nighthawks staffer. Her cheeks pink when she sees three pairs of eyes on her.

"My cousin Ingrid was wondering if you'd like to, um…" His palms run down the side of his pants again. If the guy doesn't change soon, I could wring him out like a sponge. "Meet her?"

I shamelessly appraise her from thirty feet away. I pride myself on assessing the fuckability of any woman from afar. It's one of my best qualities.

The rounded globes of her tits, which scream push-up bra, are squished together by her tighter-than-spandex V-neck T-shirt. Her honey-brown hair falls loosely, a chunk of it trapped in her cleavage as if asking to be pulled out. *By me.* "She seems nice."

He smiles like a kid who's been given a silver dollar and a pat on the head. "She is."

"And by nice, I mean her brunette curls would look amazing bobbing between my legs."

Jaxon spits beer onto the table. Dylan stiffens. He's probably trying to decide if standing up for his cousin is worth burning bridges with me. I meet his gaze, challenging him. *What's it gonna be, kid?*

"I, uh…" He fumbles in his pocket, pulling out his phone. "Damn, I just got a text from the boss. I'll catch you later, Mr. Calloway. Uh, Tag."

"Your assholery really knows no bounds, does it?" my brother says.

Ignoring him, I finish my beer and start on the one Dylan gave me, focusing on the guy on third and hoping the Hawks can get him out before he scores.

Someone clears his throat. "Tag Calloway?"

Unlikely DATE

I love that I get invited to watch the game in a suite and all, but sometimes I just want to watch the fucking game. I turn and paste on my CEO face. "You found him."

His hand juts out. "Stu Richards. We met at a convention last year in Stamford. You were on a panel of business entrepreneurs that I found quite interesting."

And I went back to my hotel room with the bleach-blonde keynote speaker who made me forget you and *my own name.*

"Right. Stu. How are you? Enjoying the game?"

"Immensely. I come to the city whenever I get the chance. I'd love to move here, but Lisa—that's my wife—has a boutique in Southbury she just won't part with."

Is there a point to this conversation?

"It's interesting," he says. "Last week I ran into someone who knows you."

"Small world."

"Hunter McQuinn. No Mickaid. Wait, what was it?"

Hatred spews from my pores. "McQuaid."

"Yeah. That's it. Hunter McQuaid. When he said he was from Calloway Creek, I remembered your name." He laughs. "When I did, he looked exactly like you do now. Like I'd said the name of the devil himself. What's with the two of you?"

"It's not just the two of them," Jaxon says. "It's our families. They hate each other. Always have. Always will."

"Is that so? What happened? Someone kill somebody or something?"

Jaxon and I share a look. We're tired of regurgitating the same story over and over about the Calloway-McQuaid feud.

"Or something," I say. "Hey, look at the time. I have another obligation I need to attend to." I shift as if I'm going to stand. "Nice seeing you again, Stu."

He hands me his business card. I barely scan it before shoving it into my pocket. When I do, I feel the napkin the waitress wrote her number on.

Stu leaves and I toss the napkin to my brother.

"I don't need your hand-me-downs, Tag."

"I believe, in fact, that you do. When is the last time you tossed the hotdog down the hallway?" The waitress across the room holds my stare as she runs her tongue across her lower lip. "We look enough alike. Call her in a few days. She won't remember who she gave her number to."

"Thanks. I'll pass. And not that I want you to take her home, which would result in my having to suffer through yet another play-by-play on how you made a woman come, but isn't it unlike you to turn her down?"

"I have a thing. And I'm already late."

Gotta go fuck some flower girl.

"A thing? Is that why you made me drive? Normally, you won't be caught dead in my Honda. You seem to have an unnatural attachment to your Range Rover."

Because women cream their panties over it.

"I'm staying in the city this evening."

"For?" He lounges back in his chair as if awaiting some breaking news.

"It's nothing. Something Amber did. Signed me up for a dating service."

"No shit? Which one?"

I pick up my phone and swipe it. "After Dark."

He fingers the edge of the napkin with the phone number on it. "I'm confused. Why would your best friend, who recently found her soul mate and wants everyone else to do the same, sign you up for the most popular one-night-stand app? Enlighten me, please."

"She met Quinn on a one-nighter. Some shit about finding love when you least expect it."

"Love?"

"Hey, who the fuck cares what Amber thinks will happen? Thanks to her, I'm about to be balls-deep inside FlowerGirl529 while you go home and rub one out to reruns of Baywatch."

"Not fair. Getting divorced does not mean I'm dating my right hand. Besides, I met someone. Technically, we've known each other since high school, but she recently moved back to town. She's a teacher at the high school."

This conversation is starting to bore me. I stand. "I'm late."

"You're coming to dinner at Mom and Dad's tomorrow, right?"

"Mom won't let me forget," I say on my way out.

I flash one last look at Ingrid, part of me bummed that I won't be living out my fantasy. Then again, I'm on my way to a sure thing. Dylan, at Ingrid's side, gives me the stink eye. I lift my chin to him.

Outside the stadium, I have trouble finding a cab. The game is almost over, and people are pouring from the stands. I decide to walk a few blocks to see if I have more luck.

New York City is bustling. It's Saturday night, after all. Not that there's ever a night the city isn't alive. And while I'm no stranger to the area, I'm still a visitor. The place I call home is a thirty-minute train ride north of here, twice as long by car. So unlike native city dwellers, it's harder for me to ignore the sounds. The incessant honking, as if cars think that will move traffic along any quicker. The chatter of people on their cell phones. Heels clacking on the sidewalk. Buskers playing music. Construction noise—even at this hour.

There's not an available cab in sight, and I'm getting later by the minute. FlowerGirl529 will be pissed. Then I realize I don't care.

Still, in an effort to show I'm trying, I descend the steps into the nearest subway tunnel, cringing when I sidestep a puddle of stagnant water, or worse, urine.

A train stops and I step in, careful not to touch anything. My bare dick inside a hundred women would be safer than what I might pick up from one of the poles on the subway. Case in point when I see a meth head lick one.

My nose turns up. It smells like feet and cheap perfume.

I should have waited for a cab. Even the stained seats, the smell of bad Chinese takeout, and the mindless chatter from the driver about his ten snotty-nosed kids would be welcome over this eclectic mix of strangers who are doing their best not to make eye contact with one another.

A woman bumps her baby stroller into me as she struggles to get off the train. She shoots me a venomous look as if I'm here for the sole purpose to help her unload.

Finally, I reach my destination, climb the exit stairs, and turn the corner, arriving at the agreed-upon location, albeit twenty-seven minutes late.

I come to the city frequently. Business meetings. Guys' nights with my brothers. 'Dates.' I air quote that in my head because I don't go on dates. Oh, the women might think they are. They aren't. Sure, we eat and drink and sometimes even talk about crap I couldn't care less about, like their jobs and their families. But in reality, it's all a show. A game. A choreographed dance I learned a long time ago that always ends the same way: with me on top of, behind, or below a gorgeous woman. If all goes well, all of the above.

I enter the restaurant. It was her choice. Nice place. Doorman. Impeccably dressed hostess. White linen tablecloths. I wonder if she thinks I'll be paying. I will, of course, because it's all part of the dance.

I wait behind a couple as the hostess speaks with them. She notices me and eye-fucks me even as she taps something on her iPad. The couple is escorted away by another über attractive female in a pencil skirt tighter than a rubber on an elephant's dick. I step up to the stand. "I'm—"

"Here on business? Meeting friends?" she spews hopefully. The phone rings. "Excuse me, Mr…"

"Calloway."

She answers the phone, scribbling on a notepad while speaking to whoever's on the other end of the line like she's kissing ass in a job interview, then hangs up. "Sorry. You were saying… Mr. Calloway, was it?"

"Tag."

She playfully pushes two fingers into my bicep and giggles. "You're it."

For fuck's sake.

"My name. It's Tag."

She giggles again, louder this time, and throws her hair back. "Mel."

"I'm meeting someone in the bar, Mel."

She sighs as if I delivered the worst news since the toilet paper shortage of 2020.

"It's right through there." She points with a manicured fingernail longer than Hunter McQuaid's cock. Then she rips a piece of paper off her pad and tucks it into my pocket. "Just in case."

I nod my thanks and walk into the bar. I spot my next dancing partner immediately. Black dress with red stripes—exactly as her description stated. We followed the rules of the dating app. No names. No pictures. You just fill out a questionnaire about your likes, dislikes, and personality (or Amber did on my behalf) and are matched with others their algorithm deems compatible.

News flash: having a vagina and a face that doesn't repulse me are the only qualifications.

FlowerGirl529 is flirting with a bartender. Her body bounces with laughter. I can hear it all the way across the room. It's the throaty kind that belongs in a seventies porn movie. I can already see how this night is shaping up, and it's giving me a semi.

Her strawberry-blonde hair flows in waves down her back, which is bare from her neck almost to her waist. Points for no bra. Her legs are long, her thighs disappearing halfway up her leg under a tight dress that she tugs on every so often so it doesn't ride too high.

That's right. I'm the only guy here who will see what's underneath it tonight.

Her dress is a contradiction in itself. While there's not much room for imagination when it comes to her legs, her arms are entirely covered. All the more for me to discover later.

If her face is anything like the rest of her, I'm done for. In the most hellacious, dirty-talking, pile-driving, pussy-eating kind of way.

Damn, I love my life.

Chapter Two

Maddie

Derek refills my drink. We're on a first-name basis now that I've been sitting here for almost an hour. I arrived thirty minutes early, knowing I'd need a bit of liquid courage to go through with this. And although I refuse to be *that girl* who stares at the entrance to the restaurant, I do take a peek at my phone.

Derek notices. "How late is he?"

"Twenty minutes, but who's counting?"

He wipes the bar. "You, based on the incessant tap-tap-tapping of your thumb on my bar."

I put my hands in my lap.

"So you have no idea what he looks like?" he asks.

"After Dark." It needs no explanation. Everyone knows what the app is. I should be embarrassed. I *am* embarrassed and completely overrun with crippling anxiety. But I hide it well. I look down at my thumb, now tapping a hole into my knee. Well, maybe not.

"There's no shame in that. Tried it myself a few times if I'm being honest. And hey, if he doesn't show, I get off at eleven." His friendly smile tells me he's kidding. *Maybe.* I'm so bad at reading men.

I laugh. "Willing to take his sloppy seconds, huh?"

"Screw that. I'm willing to be yours."

I self-consciously shift the V-neck of my dress to make sure it's covering all the right places. I move it too far to the left, almost exposing my left boob. Derek's eyes zero in.

"Oops. Sorry." I flush.

"Thought you might have been giving me a preview." He flashes me an award-winning smile and moves down the bar to serve another patron.

It's nice to be getting attention from an attractive man. It's refreshing to flirt. Although rusty, I *have* done it recently. Regan and Ava took me to a bar here in the city last week as a dry run. I tried to practice on Patrick, but flirting with my gay best friend just wasn't the same.

Derek winks at me, giving me attention even though he's having a conversation with a man at the end of the bar. Would he really take SportsFan601's place if he doesn't show? Surely he's just being nice. I look down at my cleavage, once again making sure my dress is hiding what it needs to.

The hem rides up, and I tug it down. I should have worn tights.

He's going to see you, dummy. All of you. Tights have to come off before sleeping with a man. Everything does.

Suddenly, my mouth goes bone dry despite all the liquid I've been consuming. Am I really going to do this? Sleep with a stranger? It's been a long time since I've been with a man. Since anyone but my barrage of doctors, plastic surgeons, and dermatologists have seen me without clothes on.

Unlikely DATE

It's time. I'm doing this. I'm ripping off the Band-Aid like Regan said. If things go south, I'll never see the guy again. If he rejects me… What am I thinking? Of course he's going to reject me. It's expected. Maybe even welcomed. Then I can go back and give a big fat 'I told you so' to my friends.

"Want another?" Derek asks, spying my empty glass.

"I probably shouldn't."

He pours anyway. "On the house. And just so you know, any guy who stands you up is an idiot."

"Thanks."

I don't go into the whole spiel I told myself earlier. A pep talk, really, in case he didn't show. *He doesn't have a picture of you. He hasn't seen you. If he doesn't show, he either chickened out or was hit by a bus.* Oddly, both scenarios are a bit too appealing because each ends up with me leaving alone, buying a bottle of wine I can't afford, and watching reruns of *Friends* all night. The point is, he wouldn't be rejecting me personally. Just the nameless, faceless woman he was going to hook up with tonight. Rationally, I know this. Emotionally, him not coming feels like another blow to my already-fragile ego.

"They never work, you know," Derek says. "Believe me. I see it all here. Lots of hookups. Very few happy endings. Even fewer happily ever afters." He thinks on it. "Unless you count my sister's friend Julie, who actually just married some guy she met on Tinder. I take it back. It can happen. I suppose it could happen to you."

"I'm not looking for a happy ending."

"Huh." He sighs like a psychiatrist trying to shrink me.

I trace the rim of the glass. "What does that mean?"

"It's just, I meet very few women who don't want it. You know, the white picket fence and all."

I throw my head back and laugh. "So not in the cards for me."

"Then I guess it makes sense."

"What does?"

"Why a gorgeous woman like yourself would want to use a dating app."

"You're sweet."

And totally judging a book by its cover. Its perfect, unmarred, glossy cover like it was just shipped hot off the printer. Little does he know that once the book is opened, its pages are tattered and torn. Wait, wrong analogy. Old books are often coveted, sought out by collectors, revered as works of art even with torn and dog-eared pages. I rack my brain for the correct parallel. When Derek looks at me like he thinks I'm taking a dump on his stool, I stop.

"Maddie?"

I raise my eyebrows.

"Don't look now, but a guy is staring at you."

My stomach does flips, and butterflies migrate all the way up to my brain. "Is he…"

"Good-looking? I hate it when women ask me that. I mean, yeah, I guess. You two look like you'd make a good couple. My roommate, Leah, would even say you'd be hot together."

"Not helping," I say, grateful my stomach is empty. Otherwise, its contents might be working their way up for an encore.

He traps my hand under his, a reminder of my anxious thumb tapping. "You got this, Maddie. And if not, my offer stands."

I breathe in through my nose and blow it out. Calm down. He's a stranger. A nobody. This is no big deal.

I turn and I swear everything that happens next is in slow motion. Is it too late to back out of this? Pretend I'm not the girl he came to have sex with? Perhaps there's another woman here wearing a black-and-red dress.

Hint: there's not. I already looked.

I see him. Tall. Dark. Gorgeous. *Him.*

The butterflies are gone, dead from the blood that boiled them. Because I know all about this tall, dark, and gorgeous guy. He's a monumental prick. The town playboy. The bosshole CEO. And, press release: *my* blind date.

What are the odds that Tag Calloway and SportsFan601 both prefer crisp white dress shirts underneath black bomber jackets? That was the description he gave of what he'd be wearing. I tell myself it can't be him. It's a coincidence.

But when his jaw drops as his eyes work their way from my cleavage to my face, I know it's not. And I feel like the stupidest, most desperate girl on the planet. The unwelcoming grimace on his face says it all. I spin my stool back around and down the rest of my drink.

Seconds go by, but they seem like centuries.

"Is he still there?" I ask.

Derek shakes his head.

He left. Of course he left. And I'm here, the desperate outcast from Calloway Creek. As if things couldn't get worse for me. I'll never live this down. The rumor mill will feast on this juicy tidbit.

"Wait," Derek says. "He's coming back."

I freeze, cemented to the stool, convinced Derek must be joking.

"The least I can do is pay for your drink," a low, rumbly voice says behind me. Then a twenty is tossed on the bar, a slip of paper along with it.

Tag reaches over me and picks up the piece of paper before I can, but not quickly enough. I read it. It says 'Mel' and has a phone number scribbled on it.

I spin back around and face him. "You really know no bounds, do you?"

"Is it my fault women everywhere want to fuck me?"

I'm speechless. Derek chuckles behind me, and I want to slap him. It's like there's a gorgeous guy code all of them stick to. "Not everyone wants to sleep with you."

"I said they want to fuck me, not sleep with me. And"—he motions to my dress—"you signed up for the app. *You* want to fuck me, Flower Girl."

"I do not want to fuck you."

We've now said *fuck* so many times that we're garnering the attention of other patrons.

"Now that would make you a liar."

He's right. I did sign up for the app. "Not you in particular," I clarify.

"But you want to fuck *someone*, am I right?"

"Would you stop saying that?"

"Whiskey neat," he says to Derek.

It takes a lot of willpower to keep my jaw from dropping. "You're *staying*?"

"I already paid for your drink. Might as well use up the rest of the money."

I push his twenty back to him. "I don't want your money. Besides, it's not enough."

Tag laughs. It's a low, boisterous, cocky laugh. Like Santa on steroids. For the moment, I pretend like I hate Santa.

"I see." He looks into my eyes as if searching for something, getting far too close for comfort. I can smell his breath. Cigarettes and… *chili*? "You drunk?" he asks.

I push him away and hold up the fresh glass Derek poured. "Almost." I cringe. "And your breath reeks."

Unlikely **DATE**

"Yeah, well your—"

"My what?" I put my hand over the scars that threaten to peek out near my cleavage. "My *what*, Tag? I dare you to finish that sentence." *Whoa, where did that come from?*

He tosses back his drink and throws a fifty on the bar.

"Wise man," Derek says quietly.

I snap my head toward him. "You. Shut it."

"See you around, Flower Girl," Tag says.

I refuse to turn and watch him leave, holding back tears and taking a sip of my drink. The night ended exactly the way I knew it would.

Chapter Three

Tag

I pace outside the restaurant, pissed. At whom, I don't know. Me—for agreeing to this. Maddie—for being my match. Amber—for putting me in this position.

Lighting a cigarette, I settle on Amber. I pull my phone out of my pocket so quickly it almost drops on the pavement.

"Aren't you supposed to be on a date?" she says without even a hello.

"Not a date. A hookup. Whatever. And it's not happening."

"Did she not show?" Muffled laughter. "Oh, please tell me she didn't show. Tag Calloway stood up. We might have to alert the evening news."

"Shut up. She showed."

Silence.

Then her angry voice berates me. "If you looked at her and left because she wasn't pretty enough, I will single-handedly tie you up by the balls and torture you with hot wax, and not in a good way."

"It's not that. She was pretty enough."

Gorgeous.

"Then what?"

I stop walking and lean against the hard brick siding of an apartment building. "I know her."

"You mean you've *slept* with her."

"No. I definitely have not slept with her."

"Don't tell me it was Nora."

"My assistant wouldn't be caught dead on an app like After Dark."

"Says you. I think there's a lot you might not know about the people who work for you."

"And I'd like to keep it that way."

I snub out my smoke on top of a nearby trash can. When I look up, I see Maddie exiting the restaurant. She walks in the other direction, not even noticing I'm standing twenty feet away. A homeless woman on a bench speaks to her. Maddie fishes in her purse and hands her some bills. The change from my fifty, perhaps?

A bleeding heart. Makes sense, I guess, considering what happened to her. I'm surprised, though. I've heard rumors that her shop is barely in the black. Seems she'd need all the extra cash she could get her hands on.

Not that I care what she does with ten bucks. I turn away. Because I don't care. I don't care what she does with her money. Her time. Her life.

"Tag?" Amber says.

"Did you say something?"

"Where'd you go?"

"Bad connection."

"So who was she?"

"It was Maddie."

"Maddie Foster? Oh, my god. Of course. FlowerGirl whatever whatever, right? It makes sense now." Her voice turns cold, like a mother scolding her child. "She didn't see you, did she? You must know her story. The woman hasn't dated in like forever. She's self-conscious enough without having a man turn her away."

"I… well…"

I spin around. The black-and-red dress disappears around the corner. I tap another smoke out of my pack and light it. Then I follow.

"Tag Calloway, that's even worse than seeing a stranger and leaving. This is Maddie Foster. I don't know her all that well, but she's friends with Ava and Regan. They tell me she hasn't been out with a man since the fire. Do you know how long that is?"

"I dunno. Ten years?"

"Four. Four years. Seriously? It was all Calloway Creek talked about for six months. How can you not remember that?"

I reach the corner where she turned. She's only about twenty paces ahead of me. Her heels are a mile high, making her legs look even longer. Her toned calves contract with every step. How does a flower shop manager get such ripped calves? I've never seen her at the gym.

"Your point?" I say, passing my favorite NYC pizza hole. And by hole, I mean greasy-ass plastic booths with tables sporting chipped corners that came right out of a fifties diner. But their pizza tastes better than Leigh Kilgore's pussy after douching with strawberry-flavored champagne.

I almost stumble at the memory. She lives in the city. I think of calling her after I hang up with Amber, until I remember she found me fucking her sister the following Friday and almost punctured my lung with her stiletto. In my defense, they were twins. I *had* to see if the rumors were true, and everything about them was identical.

"My point is, she's fragile."

"Right. Because her husband died or something."

"Boyfriend."

"Still, four years is a long time. I wonder why she waited so long."

"How can you be so obtuse, Tag?"

"Obtuse?"

"Uncaring. Lacking emotion. A total fucking prick."

"Easy there. You're supposed to be my best friend."

"And that gives me the right to tell you when you're being a total dickwad."

"Have you been talking to Jaxon?"

"What? No. All I'm saying is the girl has scars. Emotional and physical scars."

"You've seen these scars?"

"Not entirely. Just one on her forearm. Sometimes her sleeves ride up. How have you never seen it? You live in the same town, minutes from each other. She works on McQuaid Circle, where we spend half our time. You really are completely oblivious, aren't you?"

Her sleeves. I stare ahead. It explains the outfit. Skirt short enough to give a passing toddler some thrills. Sleeves like my grandmother at a funeral.

What Amber said is right. I'm oblivious. I never gave Maddie a second glance. Ever. But not because she isn't gorgeous. Because she lives in a goddamn shell. She rarely comes out of the shop. When she does, she never makes eye contact with anyone. She's invisible.

Or maybe she just wants to be.

Then why the hell is she on After Dark?

"I think I'm beginning to get the picture."

"Which is?" Amber asks.

"Maddie. She comes to the city for hookups. I guess I can't blame her. Calloway Creek has zero privacy. Hasn't been on a date, my ass. You should see her. Short dress. Ass wiggling like she's teaching a goddamn hula class. Hair loose and bouncy, sure to make any red-blooded man's cock dance in the wind."

"You're looking at her?"

"No."

Yes.

"Are you still in the restaurant?"

"The street."

"Are you *following* her?"

Busted.

"I'm not a total douchebag, Amber. I'm just making sure she gets to the train okay."

"Or you could offer her a ride."

"Don't have the Range with me. Jaxon drove us to the game."

Maddie jerks to a stop. I slow, slinking behind a light post like a creepy stalker. Her heel got caught in the sidewalk. She struggles to work it free.

Help her, asshole.

I don't, of course. It would blow my cover. Besides, I'm not the kind of guy who rescues damsels in distress.

Apparently, though, there are plenty of others who are. A kid in a hoodie stops and helps steady her. He leans over and frees her shoe from the crevice. I can see her thankful smile from here. Then her smile falls, her face contorting in horror when the kid forcefully tugs her cross-body purse, breaking the strap and throttling her to the ground before he sprints away.

Right toward me.

"Gotta go," I tell Amber and shove my phone into my pocket.

I step out from behind the pole and trip him. He plummets face-first into the unforgiving metal, smacks his face on it, and falls right onto a fresh pile of dog shit.

Strike one up for karma. I've never been more grateful for lowlifes who think they're above picking up after their stupid fucking pets.

The purse tumbles a few feet away, and I pick it up. He scrambles to his feet, blood streaming from his nose, and tries to swipe it from me.

"Unless you want a broken rib to go with that broken nose, I suggest you get the fuck out of here." I step forward and puff out my chest, getting close but not so close that dog shit gets on my hundred-and-forty-dollar button down.

When he doesn't make a move either way, I step around him and go to Maddie. On my way, I find it amusing that nobody stopped to look. In Calloway Creek, had anything similar happened, there would be an audience of dozens. If not to help, at least to see the excitement.

She's as white as a ghost when I hand her the bag. "Th-thank you." She cranes her head around me to make sure he's gone on his way. I don't even glance back. I know he has. Either that or I'm about to get a bullet in the back of my skull because he was packing.

Thankfully, she looks relieved. But extremely shaken.

Fuck. Now I'm goddamn responsible for her. I should have just let it be. How much could she have had in the small purse anyway?

"My life is in here," she says, clutching it. "I can't believe he did that." She slumps onto a nearby bench. "Of course he did. I'm so stupid. Everyone has ulterior motives."

"Way to be cynical."

My phone vibrates with a text. I know it's Amber. I ignore it.

Maddie tugs on the V-neck of her dress and then fiddles with her right sleeve, almost like a nervous tic. I remember what Amber said about her having scars on her arm. I wonder how bad they are.

Why the hell do you care?

Morbid curiosity?

No. That's not it.

Human nature?

Strike two.

"What are you doing here?" she asks, pulling me from my internal conversation.

"Going to the train. Same as you."

She points. "It's in the other direction."

Way to look like an ass.

"Were you following me?"

I contemplate telling her I'm going to meet my backup After Dark match, but she already caught me in a lie, so there's no point in feeding her another. "Just making sure you got home okay. The city can be dangerous." I nod to her purse. "Case in point."

"I'm not going home."

Maybe *she* has a backup After Dark match. "Swiped right on another so quickly? Didn't waste any time, did you?"

Her head moves from side to side in irritation. "Hardly. Regan and Ava made me do it. You were my first and last swipe."

I sit, having been proven wrong. I was sure she did this on a regular basis. The female equivalent of Dr. Jekyll and Mr. Hyde. Demure, shy little Maddie in Cal Creek; slutty, face-riding

FlowerGirl529 in the city. "Same. Well, first. Who knows, I may give it another shot."

"Of course you will. Are you going for the record in Guinness? You've already dated half of Calloway Creek, White Plains, and Yonkers. You have to tap out After Dark too?"

"Is that a nice way of telling me you think I'm a player?"

"There was nothing nice about it."

"Ouch."

"Somehow, I think your ego can take it." As I light a cigarette, she sneers in disgust, scooting further away. "You *so* lied."

"You're going to have to expand on that. I've lied about so many things in my life."

An incredulous puff of air akin to an eye roll exits her lungs. "Your After Dark profile. You lied. I'd have never swiped right on a man who smokes."

I blow the toxic sludge in the other direction. "Didn't fill it out. Amber did."

"Amber?"

"You think I'm lying?"

"It makes no sense. It's no secret she's made it her mission to marry you off. Seems like kind of the opposite signing you up for a hookup app."

"She's twisted that way."

"Still, she lied."

"Wishful thinking on her part."

"Why do you do it?"

"Lie?"

"Smoke."

"I like the taste."

More frustrated puffs of air. Lots of them this time. "Impossible. How could anyone enjoy the taste of smoke?"

"You ever tried?" I hold it out to her. She bats my hand away like the cigarette might burn her.

Burn her.

Fuck.

I am a dickwad.

I snub it out on the underside of the bench and toss it in the street.

"That's littering," she says. "The world is not your ashtray."

I eye the fallen light-post flyers, half-empty fast-food wrappers, and the old shoe lining the gutter. "Whatever you say."

After fishing around in her purse, she comes out with a stick of gum and shoves it at me.

"No, thanks."

"Take it. You truly have no idea how disgusting cigarette breath is, do you?"

"Nobody's complained until now. And Amber doesn't count."

"Women tend to put up with things to get what they want."

"You're saying they overlook my halitosis to sleep with me?" I lean back and stretch out my legs. "Man, they must really like what they hear from those who went before them."

She stands. "There are no limitations to your cockiness, are there?"

"Believe me, Flower Girl, my cock has no limits."

Maddie storms off as fast as her Jimmy Choo knockoffs can take her. She walks down the block right into Gordo's Pizza Joint.

I light up and head back for the train station, stopping ten steps past Gordo's.

Keep going and go the fuck home. Or go to Leigh's and hope she's forgiven you long enough to get your rocks off. Call Cooper and see if he made it to town yet. Hell, go find Jaxon and see if he's up for a late-night game of pool at Donovan's. Anything but opening the red-and-black checkered door.

Someone exits, and smells waif out and swirl around me like a smoke monster with gravitational pull, urging me in, causing my mouth to water and my taste buds to crave the doughy, cheesy, meaty heart attack on a cheap plastic platter that makes Gordo a culinary god.

My stomach growls, arguing against the logic that the chili dog I ate earlier will sustain me until breakfast. Which will be my usual: coffee and a Marlboro.

I flick my butt toward the gutter, earning me some colorful curse words from the guy it strikes along the way. I don't bother saluting him back with the same finger he waved at me.

I open the heavy checkered door and step through, telling myself I'm going in for the pizza.

But everyone who knows me knows I'm a goddamn liar.

Chapter Four

Maddie

A gust of air rushes in at the same time as the bell over the door rings. Not turning away from the menu, I narrow down my choices. Pepperoni is a must. Do I want meatballs?

"One large meat extravaganza with a side of dipping sauce, Gordo," someone says behind me.

I don't have to look. The stench of cigarettes mixed with something I can't put my finger on—spring rain?—invades my nostrils. It overpowers the smell of the beef. The garlic. The spices as they cook into the cheese of the pizzas in the oven behind the counter.

The cigarette funk could be anyone. The spring rain—that narrows it down. I tried not to inhale when he leaned over my shoulder in the restaurant. Then again when he gave me back my purse. Then there was the bench. *Why are you chronicling all the times you were close to him?*

It's probably his laundry detergent. He doesn't strike me as a guy who wears cologne. To him, that would seem like he's trying too hard. Tag Calloway barely has to lift a finger to get women to fall at his feet. All he has to do is exist. I find it pathetic that we live in a world where a man with a pretty face, skilled tongue, and bad reputation make him as sought after as the latest E L James novel.

And then there's the voice. If his smell didn't give him away, that would have. It's low. Rough around the edges. Throaty. If sex could talk, it would sound like him.

"Excuse me," I say, irritated and refusing to justify his existence with eye contact. "Mind waiting your turn?"

"And two beers, Gordo."

My hair gets moved aside. Fingers brush my neck. *Intentionally?* Rows of goose bumps ripple up and down my flesh.

"You like beer, don't you, Flower Girl?"

His hot, smoke-laced words flow over my ear like lava on a glacier. I swallow. My shaky hand finds my purse, blindly searching before it reappears with the stick of gum he rejected earlier. I hold it over my shoulder, still refusing to look at him.

He laughs.

My stomach flips over.

He takes it. "I tell you what. I'll chew this stick of gum, but you have to split my pizza."

Someone behind us clears their throat. We're taking far too long in line.

"You think my wife should split the pizza with me?" he asks. I turn to see him talking to the woman behind him. "You see, we had a fight earlier. I'm trying to make up with her." He shoves the stick of gum into his mouth and awaits her response.

"I, uh…" The woman looks at me, clearly at a loss for words. Does she want to side with me? Or will she fall for his charm like every other creature with a vagina? The woman cocks her head. "I guess I'd need more information."

"Of course," Tag says. "Well then, it goes like this: I found her using her vibrator ten minutes after we…"

I cough, mortified. I go to speak, but he puts a finger to my lips. "Shh. You'll get your turn, babe." Back to the woman. "So to me, that means she faked it, because I was sure she, you know… *had*. But the question is, why did she fake it? I mean, I get it if she wanted to get it over with because she had cramps or some shit like that. She is expecting her monthly curse soon. But then to find her finishing herself off? So I got mad. I took her vibrator and threw it across the room. She stormed out and went to her mother's."

Gordo and his employee are now fully standing at attention behind the counter, paying no mind to anything they were doing before Tag said the word vibrator.

He gives me a smirk. "Anything to add, sweet cheeks?"

I want the floor to swallow me whole. Do I walk out? Tell them he's crazy? But who would believe it? He's him. And I'm… me.

I shore myself up, refusing to look like more of a fool than I already am for the date that never happened. "Actually, you left something out, *babe*."

"What's that?" he says, a challenging glint in his eye.

"The fact that you called me Kiki." I turn to the woman and put my hands on my hips for emphasis. "My name is Lana."

The woman's jaw falls open.

Tag's mouth turns up into a half smile. He likes this game. "An honest mistake, honey cakes."

"And it's not the first time," I say. "He's called me the names of all his previous wives at one time or another. All four of them. Kiki was the last straw. So I didn't go to my mother's place." I turn to him. "I went to Cooper's."

He feigns surprise. "Cooper… my brother?"

"Mmm," I say like I've just licked the most delicious ice-cream cone dipped in melted chocolate. I run a fingernail down the cord of my neck for effect.

"You fucked my brother and didn't bring me? We've been begging you for a threesome for months."

"Uh…" The woman looks at her phone and mumbles something about being late. She scurries out the front door.

Tag bends over laughing. It's hard for me not to follow his lead. The woman was utterly speechless.

"My apologies, Gordo." Tag pulls out his wallet and throws money on the counter. "To cover the lost sale."

Gordo and the kid working for him fist-bump Tag. "Worth it, my friend," Gordo says with a heavy New England accent. "That was very entertaining."

I glance between the two men. "You know each other?"

"This is my favorite pizza place in the city," Tag says.

"Hey, now," Gordo warns.

"Sorry. It's my favorite pizza place period."

"That's more like it like. Go find yourselves a seat. I'll have Ricky bring your drinks over."

Tag leads us to a table by the front window, which I find amusing. What if someone sees him with me?

"You have an interesting way of getting a woman to have dinner with you."

He pulls out a chair for me, his minty breath rolling across my cheek. "And you have quick wit. I like that."

More tingles.

There isn't a world in which this man's words should cause such a visceral reaction. He's a toad. No, he's pond scum. Worse, he's the amoebas that feed on the pond scum.

"Why are you here?" I ask. "Really?"

As if on cue, his stomach rumbles, and he belts out another laugh.

I pinch my thigh to keep my body from reacting.

"Any other questions?" he asks.

"Why SportsFan601? I get the sports fan part, but what is the significance of 601?"

He shrugs. "It's just a number. It doesn't have to mean anything. Anyway, Amber is the one who made my profile, remember? I could ask you the same thing. Why FlowerGirl529?"

"Same. Just a number."

"You're lying."

"Am not."

"You just asked me the significance of my number, which clearly indicates the number you chose must have significance. Plus, it doesn't go to reason that you'd be allowed to ask me about my number without being willing to disclose the meaning of your own."

"I, uh—"

"Your drinks," Ricky says, placing them on the table on top of coasters that have definitely seen their better days.

The alarm on my phone sounds. "I'll be right back. I have to make a quick call."

"It's my brother, isn't it?"

I laugh.

Stop laughing at his jokes.

I thumb to the door. "I'm just gonna…"

He raises his beer. "Sure. Whatever."

Outside, I go out of sight from him, down the block a ways, and lean against the wall. *What are you doing?* I should have stuck with the original plan. Wine. *Friends.* At least there I know the score. I'm in control. Why do I have the feeling no woman is ever in control around Tag?

I get out my phone and dial home.

"Mommy!" Gigi sings. "You didn't forget. You called right on time. The little hand is on the eight and the big hand is pointing straight up."

"Told you I would, baby. I made you a promise. What are you and Patrick doing?"

"Making bracelets."

"For me?"

"One for me. One for you. One for Paddy."

The funny thing is, he'll probably wear it. Around Gigi anyway. He'd do anything for my daughter.

"I can't wait to see it. Don't stay up too late, okay?"

"I won't. Paddy says I need my beauty sleep so I can be as pretty as you one day."

That man. "I'll let you in on a secret. You're already prettier."

She giggles. "That's not true, Mommy. You're the most beautiful girl that ever lived."

My heart expands right here on the spot.

"Thank you, baby."

"Paddy wants to talk. Kisses?"

I make kissy noises into the phone, hoping nobody is looking or listening. She does it back.

"Hey," Patrick says.

"I should come home."

"Don't start that, Maddie. You deserve a night away once in a while."

"Yeah, but it's pointless now."

He sighs. "What happened? Was he a dud? Did you leave?" His voice grows more concerned. "Did he try anything?"

"Nothing like that." I step over and crane my neck to see inside Gordo's. Tag is glued to his phone. "He's still here."

"Then what are you doing talking to me? Go have fun."

"It's not like that. It's *so* not like that."

Part of me wants to tell Patrick it's Tag. He'd insist I come home. I *should* go home. Therefore, I should tell him.

But I don't.

"What's it like?"

"Nothing. I guess I should get back."

"Relax, girl. It's just a date. Just because you met on After Dark does not mean you have to do anything you don't want to. And remember, I've got buddies in firehouses all over the city who can be there in minutes if anything goes south. Tell me this. Is the guy attractive?"

"Very."

"Muscles?"

I sigh. "Lots."

"Then just do it. I know I resisted the idea at first, but Regan and Ava are right. You've waited far too long. It's time someone cleans out those cobwebs between your legs before you become an old lady with seventy-five cats."

"Fine."

And by fine, I mean I'll go back inside, split a pizza with Tag, and then go do the whole wine and *Friends* thing. Patrick doesn't need to know how pathetic I am just yet. I'll keep that to myself until tomorrow.

I slip my phone back into my purse and open the door to Gordo's. When I sit, Tag doesn't even look up at me. He continues tapping on his phone like I don't exist. Because I don't. Not to guys like him.

Chapter Five

Tag

When I finish answering a work email, Maddie is sitting across from me sipping her beer. "How's my brother?" I joke. "Did you set a time for our ménage?"

"Very funny. I promised Gigi I'd call her before bedtime."

Gigi. Right.

Her kid.

I swallow the bitter taste in my mouth and try to analyze if Maddie just became a whole lot less attractive. She's a mom. She squeezed a human out of a place nothing bigger than my cock should occupy.

"How old is the little rug rat?" I ask like someone who might care.

I've seen the kid around with her. In fact, it's hard to remember any times when they haven't been joined at the hip. The kid's gotta be ten. Cut the umbilical already.

"Five," she says proudly. She holds her phone up, showing me her home screen. The girl is sitting on a swing laughing.

"You want to compare home screens?" I turn my phone over and show her mine.

Earlier this year, I'd driven the Range to the highest place in the Smoky Mountains. Cooper snapped a pic of me in front of it.

Maddie appraises it. "Your home screen is a picture of yourself? And your... *car?*"

"My most prized possessions."

"Touché."

A text pops up on my screen before Maddie looks away.

Amber: Will you please call me back? Maddie Foster? Really???

I flip my phone over, but not soon enough.

She looks horrified. "You told her?"

"She is my best friend."

"When did you even have the time?"

"Outside the restaurant. And come on, are you going to sit here and pretend you didn't call or text any of your friends when you found out it was me?"

"That's what I'm telling you."

Her thumb taps against the table. I've been with her a total of twenty minutes and already know that's her tell. "You're lying."

"I'm not lying. Okay, so Patrick asked about the date, but I didn't tell him it was with you."

I raise a brow. "Patrick?"

"Patrick Kelsey. He's Gigi's babysitter."

"The firefighter?"

"Yes."

"Why didn't you tell him it was with me?"

"Because he probably would have called one of his buddies in the city to come get me and take me home."

"But he knew you were meeting someone from the After Dark app?"

She nods.

"Then why would it matter who it was? A hookup is a hookup."

"It matters."

"Why?"

"You think he wants me to be another one of your conquests? A notch in your bedpost?"

The hypocrisy.

"Maddie, you were going to be *someone's* conquest tonight."

"It's different if it's a stranger."

"Yeah. Strangers are *so* much safer. Just ask your bag." I pull out my pack of smokes and thumb toward outside. "I'm going to step out for a sec before the pizza gets here."

"Doesn't it get old? Having to go out in the cold, or the heat, or the rain? Having to sneak out while people talk about you behind your back?"

"What do they say?"

"Mainly that you're a huge dick."

I heard her correctly, but I paste on a smirk anyway. "They're not wrong. It is huge."

Her eyes roll. "I said *are*, not *have*."

Gordo puts the pizza on our table and hands us plates. Guess I'm staying put.

Maddie uses a napkin to blot the grease on top of her slice. My slice is history before she even takes a bite.

"Hungry much?" she asks.

"Very. Now tell me what else you lied about on your profile."

"Unlike you, I didn't lie."

"Again, it wasn't me who lied, it was Amber. And yes, you did. I never would have swiped right on a woman with kids."

"You really are an ass."

"I've never denied it. But the fact that you lied indicates you know there are a lot of guys like me out there. Asses or not, most single men don't want a woman with baggage."

"Baggage." Her lips curl in disgust. "Charming."

"I'm just saying, now that we both know you lied, what else did you lie about? No way did we get matched by coincidence. We're complete opposites."

"Did you ever stop to think that maybe that's how they do it? You've heard the phrase opposites attract, right?"

"So you're attracted to me?"

She coughs and wipes her face. "No."

Her pinking cheeks reveal another lie.

"Let's test your theory. What did you put for your favorite food?"

Meat topples off her slice as she lifts it into the air, revealing her answer. She takes a bite. When she pulls the slice away, melted cheese spans a trail between the pizza and her lips. Her finger twirls around the blend of mozzarella and provolone until it breaks free, then she eats the gooey cheese off her finger.

My dick really likes the show. I shift in my seat. "Fine. But that's easy. Probably more than seventy-five percent of people our age said it. Favorite band?"

"Reckless Alibi."

"No shit? Amber's cousin Maddox is friends with them."

Excitement crosses her face, then wanes. It's like she thought she had an in to meet the famous musicians but then realized it would entail asking a favor of *me*.

Unlikely DATE

"Okay, so we're two for two," I say. "Let's see… Favorite movie?"

"*The Martian.*"

I choke. "Nobody's favorite movie is *The Martian.*"

"What's yours?"

"Okay, fine. *The Martian.*"

She laughs and my cock twitches like it's auditioning as a backup dancer for J.Lo. I try to douse my lower half's excitement with a swig of beer. Women laugh at me all the time—my wit, my charm—but junior never seemed to care. Until now. Maybe it's the way she laughs. It's not seductive. She doesn't throw her head back and expose her throat like a woman who wants to ride the sausage train. And unlike at the bar, it's soft. Reserved. Genuine.

She sees me staring and tugs on the neckline of her dress. Another nervous tic perhaps.

I wipe grease from my mouth. "For a dating service that specializes in one-nighters, you'd think they wouldn't ask the same old compatibility questions."

"What should they ask?"

My thumb and forefinger work my jaw. "I'm thinking something along the lines of 'Do you like it on top or from behind'?"

Her face slackens. Her cheeks pink. Her hazel eyes sparkle.

Then she surprises me with "Or maybe 'Do you swallow'?"

Now I'm the one throwing my head back and laughing.

"And did you read their fine print?" she asks.

In my best drug-side-effect TV-commercial voice, I say, "Not responsible for failed encounters, sexually transmitted diseases, pregnancies, stalking, criminal activity, or other unintended outcomes not withforseen."

"Withforseen?"

"Whatever. I was on a roll. So what made you choose my profile?"

"Honestly? Because you sounded exactly like the kind of guy who sleeps with women and doesn't call the next day."

At least Amber didn't lie about that.

"It's like all the other profiles had a hook. Like when you're looking for a book to read on Amazon, you browse them until something catches your eye. They all screamed, 'I'm rich. I have a great body. I'll give you the night of your life.' But yours seemed honest."

"And that's what you're looking for? A guy who doesn't call the next day?"

Instead of answering, she eats.

I motion for her phone. "Lemme see the others. The ones you didn't choose."

She opens the app and hands it over. I page through a dozen or so. She's right. All these imbeciles do is talk about how great they are. Truth is, I'd have probably done the same had I written it myself.

My eyes fixate on one bio. "Did you see this one?" I turn the phone and hold it out to her. "Claims he has a souped-up El Camino, the biggest hands west of the Mississippi, and the best anchor beard goatee you'll ever see. Sound familiar?"

Her eyes scrunch in thought as she chews on her lip.

More chair shifting.

Her brows shoot up. "Oh, my gosh! It's Denny Janson from the movie theater."

"I'd bet on it. The guy is more attached to his El Camino than I am my left nut. I'll never understand why he hasn't aspired to be anything more than the assistant manager of the only movie theater in Cal Creek. His only claim to fame is the enormous size of his hands. In high school, he'd go around waving his clown hands, reminding the ladies of what the size of a man's hands meant to his other anatomy. I've seen him in the locker room. Believe me, it's just a myth."

"And he prides himself on the goatee," Maddie says. "I had no idea what an anchor beard was until he explained it ad nauseam to Ava and me one day when he was waiting on his coffee." Her smile falls. "How many other people from Calloway Creek do you think use this app?"

"Beats me."

"I knew this was a bad idea. And I'd like to get back to the fact that you told Amber. I'd rather nobody know about this if it's all the same to you."

"Amber won't say anything."

"It's not Amber I'm worried about."

I point to myself. "Me? I can keep a secret."

She covers her mouth before beer spews from it. "Oh yeah? Tell that to Regan Lucas, Jennie Straight, Karla Lohan, Izzy Peterson, Chrissy—"

I hold up a hand. "Fine. I get your point. Anyway, why would I say anything? This isn't a date. We're not hooking up. It's nothing."

Her gaze falls to the weathered linoleum tile. I suppose I should apologize. Any half-decent guy would.

"I won't say anything, Maddie. I mean it when I say I can keep secrets."

"Tell me one you've kept."

"Now see, there's the catch-22. If I told you, it wouldn't be a secret."

"Then there's no reason for me to believe you."

"Amber and I were fuck buddies for ten years."

It just came out, and I'm not sure why. I wasn't lying when I said it was a secret. I've never told anyone. Not even Jaxon and Coop. I instantly want to take it back. What do I care if she believes me or not?

I've stunned her into silence. When she recovers, she lays into me. "You've just proved my point. You can't keep a secret. And Amber should know what a crappy friend you are."

"She told someone, too. Quinn."

"Her husband? That hardly qualifies as a breach of trust."

"She told him the day after they met."

"You mean she told a complete stranger from Texas who lived two thousand miles away and didn't know anything about you or Calloway Creek?"

"Can I not win with you?" *Why do I need to win with her?* "Besides, and not that I'm going to say anything, but would it be the worst thing in the world for people to find out we shared a pizza?"

She stares out the window. "Well, there's the fact that it's *you*." She sighs. "And also the fact that it would be the first pizza I've shared with anyone since… Well, in a long time."

I sit back in my chair, astonished. "Wait, are we talking about pizza or sex?" Her silence gives me the answer. I'm rarely surprised when it comes to women. This surprises me. "You haven't…?"

Her head moves from side to side.

"Since…?"

Her eyes close.

I'm speechless. I thought Amber was exaggerating. "Damn, Maddie. How long has it been?"

"Over five years."

"But Amber said the fire happened four years ago. You and Cody lived together, no?"

"We did. But only because I was trying to make my grandmother happy. She's old fashioned. Doesn't believe in having kids out of wedlock. So I tried. For her. But Cody and I weren't… intimate much after I got pregnant. Listen, can we not talk about this?"

For someone who wasn't in love with the guy she was shacking up with, she sure does seem torn up over it. Then again, he is dead. And he is her kid's dad.

I start to put two and two together. "Are you telling me this night was meant to bring your vagina back from the land of the dead?"

"Must you be so crude?"

"Was it?"

"I suppose. But this information falls under our NDA."

I chuckle. "Non-disclosure agreement?"

"The one you verbally agreed to a minute ago when you said you'd keep it a secret. You're a businessman. You know what it means."

"You're right. I am. And I do." I cock my head to the side, studying her. She's practically a virgin. Over five years? How can a woman as beautiful as she is go that long without being with a man? My eyes lock on her cleavage. She again pulls on the material and then steeples her arms on the table as if to shield her chest from my X-ray vision. "So let's take this NDA one step further."

"Meaning?"

"Meaning let's do what we came to do."

Shock overtakes her. Her mouth opens and closes as she reaches for words. "I… just… *no!*"

"Why not?"

"Because it's *you*."

"That's exactly why we should. I won't call the next day. Won't stalk you either. And now you know I can be discreet."

The sleeve on her right arm rides up. I see the scar she's trying to cover before she pulls it down. Suddenly, it hits me like a ton of bricks. Amber's words about Maddie's scars echo in my head. She hasn't slept with a man in years. When men pass her on the sidewalk and look at her, she looks at the pavement. I've noticed. She's been hiding. From men. Hell, from life.

"It'll be quick and easy. Rip off the Band-Aid."

She stands. "I'm not ripping off anything with you, Tag. Thanks for the pizza. I'm leaving."

"Suit yourself."

She makes it to the door. "Remember your promise."

I bring my fingers to my lips and twist an imaginary key.

Then she walks out the door and doesn't look back.

Chapter Six

Maddie

Well, this was a bright idea.

I should have at least looked outside before storming out. The nighttime spritz of rain quickly turns into pellets, beating against my skin as I rush to the hotel four blocks away. I contemplate stepping inside a diner or pawn shop as I pass them. But what would be the point? My dress is already soaked through and plastered to my skin. Damn these heels. Why I borrowed them from Regan is beyond me. I haven't worn heels since senior prom in Lincoln, Nebraska. But Regan and Ava insisted on dressing me up like Gigi dresses up her Barbie dolls. And I stupidly let them.

This whole night has been a disaster. I can't even stop to get the bottle of wine I want. I'm not sure what's more pathetic, a grown woman sitting in a hotel room drunk while watching mindless TV after a failed hookup—or a sober one.

I turn the corner, and my feet come out from under me when my foot slips. I brace for the feel of the hard concrete meeting my ass, but instead, arms come around me and hold me steady. Instinct has me clutching my purse.

Back on my feet, I turn to thank the stranger. But it's not a stranger.

Torn between embarrassment, anger, and some other emotion causing my insides to tumble, I ask, "You're following me again? What was it you were just telling me about *not* being a stalker?"

"I may be an asshole, Maddie, but I do have a conscience. One: you left in the rain. And two: not in the direction of the train station."

"So you took it upon yourself to make sure I wasn't swiping right and having a little soiree with someone else? I see. You're jealous that you won't be the one to deflower the born-again virgin. That's it, isn't it? I'm a challenge. And Tag Calloway never backs down from a challenge, does he?"

"You're soaking wet." He removes his bomber jacket and puts it over my shoulders. "Let's get you inside somewhere."

"That's exactly where I was going until you stopped me."

"Stopped you? I *saved* you. Probably from a broken tailbone from the looks of it. You can barely walk in those shoes. I've been trailing you for four blocks. Exactly where are you going?"

"My hotel."

The amusement in his eyes makes me stiffen.

"Your hotel?" Rain soaks through his white dress shirt, outlining every ripple of his chest. "You really did mean business tonight, didn't you?"

I don't dignify that with an answer. "I'm leaving." I walk away. Even through the heavy sheets of rain, I hear his footsteps behind me. I turn, hands on hips. "What do you want?"

"You're wearing my jacket."

I shrug it off my shoulders and throw it at him, then start walking again.

Unlikely DATE

"Wait," he says behind me. The jacket comes over my shoulders again. "You'll freeze."

I spin and eye his drenched clothes. "It's June. I doubt it."

"Help a guy out? Let me come with you to dry off. Your hotel room will have a hair dryer."

"First off, it would take hours to dry your clothes with a hair dryer. And secondly, you're not stepping foot into my hotel room."

"Come on. I'm soaking here."

Rivulets of water come off his hair, which—*damn it*—is still sexy, even when matted to his head.

His lower lip juts out, making him look nothing like the CEO he is. "Please, Flower Girl? I promise I won't try anything."

I roll my eyes and start walking, already regretting the words that haven't yet left my mouth. "Are you coming?" I say over my shoulder.

The doorman of the hotel sees us approaching and steps forward with an umbrella as if that will help. In the lobby, I note the sleek marble tile, hoping I don't make even more of a fool of myself by slipping on the mess I'm making as I drip my way to the elevator.

As if reading my mind, Tag takes my elbow. "Not bad," he says, appraising our surroundings. There's a bar off to one side. A clothing and sundries shop on the other. And a few bellmen waiting for guests to arrive.

It's not the Waldorf, but it's far better than anything I could afford. Patrick won a night's stay at a fireman's charity auction last summer. He never used it, and it was going to expire, so he gave it to me when he found out I was coming to the city. He asked for it back when I told him why. He's protective of me. Has been ever since the night of The Incident. It took some convincing, but in the end, he said I deserved a night away. And he was all too happy to watch Gigi.

As I step inside the elevator, I try not to let my intense fear of them show. The floor pools with water underneath us. I think Tag is going for the jacket, but instead, he gathers my hair and wrings it out, adding more water for the poor housekeepers to mop up. I should pull away. Having a man's hands in my hair is so intimate. But it feels unexpectedly good.

In the twenty seconds it takes us to travel to the sixteenth floor, he does it three times. And I find myself melting into a pile of mush along with the liquid surrounding my feet.

The doors open. He releases my hair. I draw in an uneven breath.

"Watch your step," he says. This time, he doesn't take my elbow. Guess he only does that when others are watching. He walks ahead of me. "What's your room number?"

"1605."

"Here we go." He quickly takes the jacket off me and drapes it over his forearm in front of him.

I open the door. He glances around.

"It's not the penthouse suite," I say. "I'm sure you aren't used to seeing the regular rooms."

"You must be mistaking me for a McQuaid." His jaw twitches when he says the name.

"You're a CEO. You own your own company. You drive a Range Rover. You wear Armani shirts."

"I wear expensive clothes because I'm a CEO and need people to think I'm more powerful than I am. It's all about appearances. I do okay, but I'm not rich, Flower Girl."

"And the Range Rover. Is that for appearances?"

"Yup. But not necessarily business related." He winks.

"What is it about men and their need to have cars that appeal to women?"

"All part of the game."

"What game?"

"Life."

"You think life is a game?"

"It *is* a game. Think about it. People compete to have the best grades or go to the best colleges. Get the best jobs and then the fastest promotions. Women compete to have the prettiest faces or the most adorable kids. Businesses compete to have the best clients. Billionaires compete to have the largest portfolio."

"And men compete to have the most conquests."

"Some of them, yeah. My point is, life is a series of competitions, and what are competitions? Games."

I grab a towel and run it over my hair. "My life isn't a game."

"You're wrong. You may think it's not, but it is."

"How?"

"You run a flower shop. How many other flower shops are in Cal Creek?"

"Two."

"Do you do anything to make people want to come to your flower shop over the others?"

"Yes."

"And there's the game."

I pull my small suitcase onto the bed and retrieve the outfit I'd brought for tomorrow. Tag shuts the lid. "Oh, no. If I don't get a change of clothes, neither do you."

"What? How is that fair?"

"It's all about playing the game, Flower Girl. Leveling the playing field is half the battle." He goes to the closet and pulls out two plush robes. "We'll wear these until my clothes dry."

"This is a stupid game." I eye the robe. "I'm not sleeping with you." I grab a bra and panties from the suitcase. "And I'm wearing these."

"I believe you when you say you won't sleep with me. But it doesn't mean I'm conceding the game."

Something in the way he looks at me when he says it makes my skin pebble. He's a lion. I'm the zebra (stripes and all). I should be scared that he's going to devour me.

But I push the voice of reason away, grab one of the robes from him, and head into the bathroom.

Chapter Seven

Tag

She comes out of the bathroom, hair still damp, robe wrapped tighter than a burrito from Taco Bell. She self-consciously tugs on the hem of the three-quarter length sleeve.

She walks by me, pretending not to care that I'm sitting on the couch in a robe, a tuft of chest hair exposed between my pecs, looking like Hugh Hefner. She grabs her phone and says something about the hair dryer. She thinks she's hiding it—the look in her eyes that tells me what I'm doing to her. The hitch in her voice that lets me know she's wet between the legs.

I haven't yet met a woman who hasn't creamed her panties for me. Why would FlowerGirl529 be any different?

When she catches me staring, her forearms cross in an unnatural pose, attempting to hide the scar that peeks out from her sleeve.

"That right there. What you do to hide your scars only brings more attention to them. I don't get it. You know you're gorgeous, right?"

A childlike snort escapes her. "You think I'd be trying to get out of this rut I'm in if I did?" She looks at her right arm, still hiding it. "This is just the tip of the iceberg."

"How bad is it?"

"Bad."

"Everyone has something they try to hide." I lift my foot off the ground. "Look here, my second and third toes are partially webbed together. People teased the shit out of me in gym class. Called me Aqua Man before he was even a thing."

She steps closer, examining them. "You freak," she says, heavy on the sarcasm.

"That's not all. My knees are knobby, and I have an ungodly number of freckles on my back."

"How can you show yourself in public?" She's still joking, but now she's looking at my knees, which are exposed courtesy of the short robe and the fact that I don't care to cover myself up like a little Amish girl. And by the slow controlled breath coming out of her lungs, I'd say she thinks they are anything but knobby.

Seeing just how far I can take this, I turn and drop the robe to my waist, showing her my back. I look at her over my shoulder as her eyes rake over me.

"They're not that bad. Some might even say..." She stops talking and pulls the tie of her robe even tighter.

"Some might say what?" I shift back around. Now she's staring at my chest. My nipples.

I watch her slender throat as she swallows. "You have nipple rings?"

I flick one.

"Doesn't that hurt? And when things get caught on them, it must sting."

"When things get caught on them, it zaps right to my dick."

Her eyebrows jump in wonderment. "Really?"

"Men's nipples are just as sensitive as women's are. They're a major erogenous zone."

She tries not to stare at them but fails miserably, the luminescent centers of her eyes blazing with unspoken desire. "I… I didn't know that."

"Well, then there you go," I say. "You've already learned something new about sex. I've been told I'm a great teacher."

"Nothing like a side of cockiness to go with your assholery."

"They do go together nicely. Like a tight-fitting condom."

Her head shakes with a pinched expression. I pull the robe back over my shoulders because, well, it seems way too desperate to sit here half-naked. And I'm anything but desperate.

She crosses the room and sits on the bed, putting a buffer between us. She lays her left forearm across her right one. I'm not even sure she's aware she's doing it. She's probably done things like that for so long that it's become second nature.

"You're doing it again," I say. "You make too big a deal out of it. It's just a scar. Why do you feel like you have to cover it?"

"People stare."

"Because they are curious. It's human nature. You actually call attention to yourself by wearing sleeves when others are sweating their asses off in hundred-degree heat." I nod to the bathroom. "Or by wearing a dress that almost shows your ass but hides your arms like a cloistered nun. It's your behavior that's freakish, not your scars. Yeah, people will look. Some will even stare for a while. Like if you have an abnormally large nose. People may be shocked for a beat, then they get over it, and it just becomes a part of who you are."

She covers her face. "You think I have a big nose?"

I push myself off the couch and cross the room, removing her hand and leaning over her, well aware that my robe is gaping open. "Your nose is perfect." I take her arm in mine and inspect the sliver of her scar. "Let me see it."

She pulls away. "No. Shouldn't you be drying your clothes?"

I gather my things and go into the bathroom. I run the hair dryer for a few minutes on my pants. They're still soaking wet. This could take all night. I hang the pants from the shower curtain, then use one of the clips from a hanger to secure the hair dryer in place and keep it aimed at the pants. I turn it on and leave it, admiring my genius contraption on the way out.

My pack of cigarettes is damp, but I tap one out anyway.

"This is a non-smoking room," Maddie says. "And you cannot just leave the hair dryer on. It's a fire hazard."

"It won't start a fire."

"It will." She stomps across the floor, goes into the bathroom, and slams the door behind her.

On my way into the hallway, I grab a Coke from the minibar, wishing there was some whiskey to go with it. I stand outside the room, light up, and chug half the Coke. It burns my throat, but I need an ashtray. A guy comes out of the elevator and walks past, giving me a lift of his chin. I'm standing in the hallway wearing a hotel robe. He probably thinks I'm having a post-coital smoke.

When I'm done, I realize I don't have any way of getting back into the room. I knock and try to see through the peephole. I still hear the hair dryer. *Fuck.* I'm stuck out here until a) a sympathetic housekeeper comes by, or b) she's done drying my goddamn clothes.

I sink to the floor, wishing I'd brought my whole pack of smokes with me. I don't even have my phone. Minutes go by and I'm getting bored as shit. I almost take a drink of the Coke. A woman and child pass. The woman chuckles. Must think I was kicked out. She's carrying a bag with the hotel's name on it. It gives me an idea. I sprint to the elevator, not caring who sees me. I've worn less while playing a pickup game of touch football with my brothers.

Down in the lobby, I ignore the stares as I enter the gift shop/convenience store/clothing corner. I laugh at the selections. Why do hotel gift shops only sell tennis outfits and 'I heart New York' tees? But it's better than nothing, so I pick out a white polo and navy-blue shorts. Then I spy a rack of women's clothing off to one side and wander over. This is stupid. I've never bought clothes for a woman. Ever.

The cashier comes over, an enormous smile on her ebony face. "I see you have a clothing emergency."

"What gave it away?"

She bats her lashes. You'd think I'd be used to it by now, the ogling of females young and old. How they trace my muscles with their eyes and bat their lashes at me.

Her fingers brush mine when she takes the clothes from me. "Shall I ring this up for you?"

"Can you charge it to my room? It's 1605."

"No problem."

"Mind if I duck into your changing room and ditch the robe?"

Her eyes blink repeatedly. Yeah—she's picturing me naked. She coughs. "Go right ahead." She puts a hand on my arm, guides me to the changing room, and hangs up the clothes.

I emerge a minute later looking like a yuppy at Wimbledon.

"I'll be needing one of these as well," I say, returning to the rack of dresses and running a finger along the tips of the hangers. "But I have no idea what size."

Disappointment saddens her features. I almost say she's welcome to give me her number anyway, but I don't.

And then I stand here and wonder why.

I pick one of the dresses off the rack. It's short. It'll show off Maddie's amazing legs. It even has sleeves.

Why am I not buying her a T-shirt and stretchy pants?

Realizing she's similar in size to the cashier, albeit taller, I ask, "My friend is about your size. Would this fit you?"

Friend. Well, what should I have said? Date wouldn't describe it, even if the night *had* been a success. Acquaintance? Some girl I know from Cal Creek?

The cashier looks at the tag and puts it back, choosing another, much different dress. "This one is my size."

I study the dress. Maddie would never wear it.

Boisterous laughter echoes across the solarium from the bar, where a group of men are celebrating.

I look back at the dress, getting an idea. "I'll take it."

The woman sends me on my way with the dress and my robe packed neatly in a bag, and a pair of flip-flops on my feet—for a lack of anything better.

Back on floor sixteen, I listen at the door. No sound of the hair dryer. I knock.

Maddie answers, trying not to laugh at my chosen attire. "I wondered where you went."

"Stepped out for a smoke. Got locked out."

"That'll teach you."

"To leave without the key card?"

"To not smoke. It's disgusting and inconvenient."

"So you've said."

She opens her purse and throws me a stick of gum.

"Just how many pieces do you have in there?"

"Gigi likes gum."

I unwrap the stick and pop it in my mouth.

"Are you going home like that?" She giggles. "You'll get mugged for sure. I can't believe they sell that stuff in the hotel." She covers her mouth. "Oh, my gosh. You had to go downstairs in your robe."

I shrug.

Her lush, kissable lips form a thin line. "What am I thinking? You probably loved every second of it."

I hold out the bag. "I got you something."

She reaches for it, but I pull it back.

"Well, what is it?" she asks, a trace of nervous curiosity flitting across her face.

"An experiment," I say.

She narrows her eyes. "Did you buy me a tennis outfit? Wait, do they even have a court here?"

"Not that kind of experiment."

She grabs the bag and pulls out the dress. The *sleeveless* dress. It gets crumpled up and thrown back at me without a word.

"Come on, Maddie. Put it on and let's go down to the hotel bar."

"The *bar?*" she squeals in horror as if I asked her to descend the stairway to hell with me. "I thought you just wanted me to put it on. No way am I going anywhere wearing something like that."

"Why not? You don't know anyone down there. They don't know you. I'm willing to bet men will come on to you."

"Until they see me."

"That's the point. They *will* see you. They'll see your scars. And yeah, they'll look. And they'll still come on to you."

"No."

"Look at me. I look ridiculous and I'm still willing to go down there."

"That's different."

"You don't think people will stare at my hideous attire?"

"Hideous." She flinches. "See, even you use that word to equate your clothes to my scars."

"Bad choice. I didn't mean it as a comparison. You are not hideous. You're fucking hot."

Silence floats between us. And as my words sink in, the unease in her eyes turns into something else. I can almost see her resolve wavering.

"Be sensible. Your end goal tonight was to sleep with a man. You can't sleep with someone without them seeing you naked. You were willing to let a stranger see you naked, so what's the difference? There are strangers down in that bar who will see your arm. Just your arm."

She sits heavily on the couch. "Why are you doing this? Why is this so important to you?"

Yeah, Tag, why?

"I don't know."

"Everyone has an ulterior motive. Like the guy who helped me with my shoe and then tried to steal my purse."

"You really think that?"

"Yes."

"So what's mine?"

She studies me and shrugs. "Pity? Redemption for past indiscretions? Bargaining power to help you get past the pearly gates?"

I bend over laughing. "Flower Girl, you read way too much into everything. And you care too much about what others think of you. Just put on the damn dress, and let's go have a drink. Why do you have to be so fucking difficult?"

She snatches the dress from me, furious. "Fine. But you'll see what always happens and then I'll win." She storms out of the room for the second time.

"See? I told you. It's all about winning the game."

I stand and gape at the bathroom door, not sure what I'm more excited about: winning the argument or seeing her in that dress.

My cock is all too happy to answer the question.

Chapter Eight

Maddie

I stare at myself in the mirror, surmising that I haven't had nearly enough alcohol to do this. My eyes are trained on the patchy, discolored skin up my right arm. Gigi calls my scars my *quilt*. In all her innocence, she's coined the perfect term. I'm sure had my last name been McQuaid or Montana, the richest families in Calloway Creek, I'd have been able to afford the best plastic surgeons money could buy. But Gran was already on Medicare, and Cody was only able to get Gigi on his (totally inadequate) medical insurance plan since we weren't married, leaving me without. Public hospital. Less-skilled doctors (interns, I remember them being called). And when I got insurance after The Incident, nothing related to The Incident was covered. Pre-existing condition, they called it. Even today, years later, if I have an issue with anything related to my scars or grafts, I pay out of pocket.

Two surgeries. Eight skin grafts. Four weeks in the hospital. Not to mention outpatient procedures, hyperbaric treatments, follow-ups, and the laundry list of medications and creams I needed for years. I'll be paying off my medical bills until the day I die.

The more I stand here scrutinizing myself, the more I realize Tag was right. Had I gone through with what I'd originally intended tonight, some guy would have seen me naked. Yes, I could have turned off the lights. *I would have.* But in all honestly, would that really have made a difference when he'd be able to *feel* my scars, too?

I run my fingers down my arm. Some of the skin is smooth. Some leathery. Some wrinkled in a mesh pattern from the grafts. All of it is discolored in some way—parts of it white as if from an albino, some pink like in a constant state of blush.

"Quilt is right," I say to the pathetic girl in the mirror. "A quilt made by a blind person."

"Today!" Tag shouts from outside the bathroom door.

I go for the door handle, wondering why I'm agreeing to this. He's an arrogant bastard, yet *he's* the one I'm going to let see me for the very first time? It makes no sense. This whole night has been one big series of unlikely events. I shore myself up and open the door.

I walk into the room and gaze out the window. We're up high, so there's nothing to see but other buildings. It's better than watching his reaction. Even so, laughter is not what I expected. My head snaps back in his direction. He's staring at my arm, *still laughing.*

I cover it as best I can, holding back tears that burn my throat. I won't give him that satisfaction. "You're a real prick." I spin and head for the bathroom.

He catches my arm and yanks me back. "No you don't. I mean, Jesus, Maddie. You built it up so much I expected you to look like something out of *Night of the Living Dead*. I've had sunburns worse than this."

I give him the stink eye. We both know he's lying.

"Okay, fine. So it's worse than my sunburns. But it really isn't *that* bad."

"It's not the worst part," I say, crossing my arms over myself, my left one covering my right.

He pulls them apart. "Quit doing that. You'll draw attention. I promise if you act like it's no big deal, others will too."

"But they'll stare."

"They might. Get used to it. You're hot. Men stare at hot women."

Another lie, but it's useless to fight with him. "That's not why they'll stare."

"Get over it, Flower Girl. Feeling sorry for yourself is not an attractive quality."

"I don't feel sorry for myself."

More arrogant laughter. "Wow. And here I was starting to think you were smart."

"Being embarrassed about the way I look is not me feeling sorry for myself."

"Keep telling yourself that."

"And you keep telling yourself you're not an asshole."

"I *am* an asshole. At least I admit it. Are you ready to go?" He grabs his pack of cigarettes off the table.

"Wait a minute. I'm doing something for you, so you have to do something for me."

"Sweetheart, us going to the bar so men can hit on you is most definitely not *you* doing something for *me*." When I don't speak, he rolls his eyes. "Fine. What?"

I nod to the pack. "Don't smoke for the rest of the night."

"That's ridiculous. It doesn't affect you. I go outside."

"But it does. You smell."

"I chewed the gum."

"It's in your hair. It oozes from your pores. How can you not realize that?" He holds the pack like it's his most prized possession. "You can't do it, can you? You can't go one night, a few hours even, without having a cigarette."

"I can do whatever the hell I want."

"I'll bet you can't go the rest of the night without smoking."

"You'll *bet* me?"

"Well, you do seem to like games."

He chuckles. "See—I knew you were bright. Okay, I'll accept your bet. What are the stakes?"

"I'm not actually betting anything."

"What's the fun in that? The whole point of the game is that someone wins."

"If you win, so do your lungs. There."

"That's the stupidest thing I've ever heard. There have to be stakes."

"Fine." I pace and think. "If you light up before the night is over, you have to buy flowers for every female at Calloway Sports Marketing."

"You know I'll never live that down."

"Why do you think I chose it?"

"Okay. But those are pretty high stakes. I've never bought flowers for anyone."

"*Anyone?*"

He offers a pompous shrug, his expression of extreme satisfaction annoying me to no end.

"How old *are* you?" I ask.

"Almost thirty."

"Wow. I think you may have just set the record for the most inconsiderate man alive."

"Sweet. What do I win? Medal? Trophy? Blow job?"

I pick up a shoe and throw it at him.

"I'm serious. Buying flowers, even for employees, will severely damage my reputation. People will say I've gone soft. If I agree to that, you have to agree to something equally as risky."

"I can't wait to hear this."

"If I go all night without smoking, you have to kiss me."

The instant the words come out of his mouth, my body reacts. Tingles run down my spine. Inside me, curiosity does a dangerous dance.

"You're tapping," he says with a shameless grin.

"Huh?"

He motions to my thumb. "You do that a lot. I'm just not sure if it means you're nervous or pissed."

I trap my thumb inside my fist. "I'm not kissing you."

Except in my head. Right now. I'm kissing you in my head right now.

Why am I doing that?

He plops down on the floor in the middle of the room like a petulant child. "Then it seems we're at an impasse. I guess we'll just stay here, play finger violins, and feel sorry for you all night."

"You are infuriating, you know that?"

"You're not the first woman to say so," he says with a stubborn burn in his eyes.

I huff my annoyance. "Fine. Let's go."

"Fine?"

"You heard me."

He springs off the floor, looking very much like the tennis pro he's impersonating. Leaving his cigarettes on the table, he opens the door for me. I hesitate, then walk through. While waiting for the elevator, Tag removes my left hand from my right arm. "Every time you do that, you owe me an extra kiss."

My hand falls to my side. "That wasn't part of the deal."

"Seriously, Maddie. Don't do it. Leave your arm alone."

"I'm not sure I can. I've been covering it for so long."

"If you hear me cough, it means stop touching your arm. Got it?"

The elevator doors open, and we step aside to let a family out. A little girl looks at me. She's about Gigi's age. I smile and she waves. She sees my scars and keeps looking as they pass.

"Mommy, what happened to that lady's arm?"

The woman glances back, looking as horrified as I did when Gigi and I were in line in front of an obese woman last year and Gigi asked her if she was having a baby boy or girl.

The girl gets scolded as they scurry away.

"Ignore her," Tag says, urging me inside the elevator. "She's just a child."

"Children are honest. They tend to say what everyone else is thinking."

His head shakes. "When you get to the bar, order yourself a double so you can chill the fuck out."

"*You* order yourself a double."

"Planned on it."

"How is this supposed to work? Are you just going to sit there and watch me from across the bar?"

"Planned on that too."

"For how long?"

"As long as it takes to prove my point."

We reach the lobby and cross to the bar. Echoes from my high heels clacking the marble tile contradict the flip-flopping of his casual footwear. We must look like quite the pair.

Unlikely DATE

"Tag?" someone shouts behind us. "Tag Calloway?" It's a high-pitched nasally voice that I just know belongs to a stick-thin woman with supermodel looks.

Both of us turn. If Gisele Bündchen and Chrissy Teigen had a love child, this woman would be it. As she approaches, I feel about as inadequate as a snowball at a bonfire.

"Jassinda," Tag says, all too happy to receive the air kisses she's planting near both cheeks.

Jassinda? Even her name is pretentious.

"What's it been?" she asks. "Three years?"

"If you say so."

"I've been traveling abroad. Just got back last week. We should get together for a drink." She finally notices me, as if an afterthought. "Oh, you have a friend." As expected, her eyes stop on my right arm. She doesn't even try to hide her cringe.

"This is Maddie," Tag says.

"Nice to meet you." I offer my hand. She eyes it, hesitating as if she thinks my scars are contagious.

Finally she shakes, her palm as soft and supple as the rest of her flawless skin. "What a lovely, um… dress."

"Thank you. Tag bought it for me."

I hear small puffs of air escape Tag's nose in a silent chuckle.

My comment seems to have the intended effect, as now she's looking at me less like a lame duck and more like the competition. She straightens her back, which makes her appear even taller. She, too, is sporting a sleeveless dress that, with the length of her torso, barely covers her ass cheeks. Men walking through the lobby don't fail to notice. Just as the women checking in can't tear their eyes from Tag, even in his absurd outfit.

I stand to the side, examining my un-manicured nails like I don't have a care in the world.

They make quite the couple, these two. Him with his striking dark hair, meticulously trimmed in all the right places beard, and Greek godlike chiseled features. Her with her mile-long legs, perfect skin, and blonde hair I can't even pretend came from a bottle. They're gorgeous together. And although there is no part of me that wants anything to do with Tag Calloway, I find myself confused by the sharp stab of jealousy piercing parts of my anatomy.

Laughter comes from the bar, catching my attention. There's a group of men in the corner watching a baseball game. Determination engulfs my entire being, and suddenly, as ridiculous as it sounds, I want to make Tag Calloway feel the very same emotion I felt just a moment ago.

Chapter Nine

Tag

As soon as she walks under the archway into the bar, heads turn. The lighting isn't bright—a few muted lantern chandeliers overhead and the flickers from the TVs. She's doing a good job keeping her arms at her side. However, I don't fail to notice her thumb twitching against the fabric on her hip.

If the men notice her scars, they don't react. Then again, it's not her arms they're looking at.

The dress has a plunging neckline, though she's discreetly covered by lace. It's worse than being able to see her cleavage clearly because you know it's there, just under the surface, but you can't quite get to it. Like your favorite candy bar encased in a semitranslucent wrapper. The back of the dress has a deep *V* going almost to her waist, her exposed skin creamy white as if never touched by sun. A birthmark the size of a quarter and roughly the shape of a crescent sits to the inside of her left shoulder blade. It's fucking sexy. I have the sudden urge to put my lips on it.

I don't even make it as far as the bar. I quickly take a seat on the couch so I don't look like a horny stalker.

Four of the five men in the corner have all but forgotten about the baseball game on the television above their heads. I surmise the fifth is gay. Either that or a much bigger sports fan than I am.

"Is this seat taken?"

A pretty brunette wearing a business suit stands next to the couch.

"Yes." I look at the four empty seats surrounding me. Ordinarily, I'd just leave it at that. But Maddie's voice rolls through my head, telling me what a scuzzball I am, so I add, "I mean, no. But I'm just here to watch the game. Some other time. You understand."

"No problem," the woman says and moves to the bar.

Men notice her, too, but only for a fleeting moment, as if regarding a paper bag floating in the breeze. Their attention is fully on the self-conscious strawberry-blonde currently ordering a double shot of Patrón, who I know for a fact would rather have them looking anywhere but at her.

Maddie tosses back the shot and turns to see if I'm watching. I wink. She pushes her glass across the bar for another.

Two of the men stand at the same time, then seem to verbally fight over which of them will approach her. The Black man wins. I can see why. He looks like Shemar Moore, with Will Smith's award-winning smile and Mamoa's forearms.

Maybe this wasn't such a good idea after all.

He walks to the bar with a swagger. He doesn't bother pretending he's there to get a napkin or order a drink. He goes right for the kill, sidling up next to her and leaning close. She's startled, but then laughs at whatever he says.

Fuck. I may have met my match with this young Denzel.

He plants his ass on the barstool next to hers. She doesn't seem to mind one little bit, though she does absentmindedly cover her arm.

She glances my way when I cough. I shake my head, scolding her. She leans back with false confidence, crossing one bare leg over the other, pastes on a seductive smile, and goes back to locking eyes with Michael B.

I force myself to stay glued to the couch, but what I really want to do is walk over there, grab her hand, stake my fucking claim, and whisk her back to the sixteenth floor.

Stake my claim? I've never staked anything, business world aside. Not that she'd even go for it. She's made it all too clear she wouldn't. But even my asshole brain knows someone like me would be toxic for someone like her. She's fragile. She doesn't need a man who would use her for her body and then barely give her a passing nod on the street.

Still then, despite how badly I want to smoke right now, why does the thought of getting to kiss her completely douse the need to satisfy my craving? I still have a craving. Just not for cigarettes.

She's covering her arm again. I cough. We do this dance so much that people probably think I have Covid.

Then, he leaves, shooting me an incredulous stare before returning to his friends. He says something to them, and the lot of them peer over at me. I lift my chin because, what the hell else do I do?

I have to know what just happened. I go to the bar, finally ordering the double I wanted. "Mind sharing what that was all about?"

She giggles. Maybe she should go easy on the tequila.

"He noticed how I kept looking over his shoulder at you. He thought we were swingers or something."

"And?"

"And I didn't bother correcting him."

I laugh, and it occurs to me that I can't recall laughing in the presence of any other woman as much as I have with her. "Is my point proven?"

"One brief interaction doesn't prove a theory," she says. "Besides, it's dark in here."

"He didn't notice your scars because there are plenty of other things about you worth noticing." I down my drink and realize nature is calling. I stand. "If you're ready to go up, I have to hit the head."

"I'm not ready. This is fun."

"Fun?"

"We need more data."

And by data she means more guys ogling her breasts. The unique color of her hair. The sensuous, delicate structure of her cheekbones. Her fuck-worthy ass.

I motion for the bartender. "Another." He pours it and I retreat to my couch, bladder be dammed.

My phone vibrates with a text.

> **Cooper: Not going to make it to dinner. Give my apologies.**

My gut twists. I'm surprised he didn't cancel on us earlier. He's done it the past two years. Understandably. But still, I try.

> **Me: Dude, it's your birthday party. You can't bail.**

> **Cooper: Sorry, bro. Can't.**

Unlikely DATE

Me: You know Mom has gone all out.

Cooper: There's a Cessna 182 with my name on it. Got a jump scheduled for tomorrow. Seeing the Grand Canyon from the air will be spectacular.

Part of me wants to remind him to open the chute. Because tomorrow isn't just Coop's birthday. It's also our dead brother's.

Me: Mom will be sad.

Cooper: She'll get over it.

Me: You're not the one who has to deal with her. It's still hard for the rest of us, you know.

Cooper: Gotta jam.

Me: Okay. Happy birthday, brother.

He doesn't reply. Mom has been so excited that this might finally be the year he's able to celebrate his birthday again. He's stayed away, keeping his distance from the family when any special occasion arises. Their birthday. The anniversary of Chaz's death. Pretty much any holiday. Those occasions hit all of us hard, but especially Cooper, given they weren't just twins. They were identical. He literally lost half of himself.

I glance over at Maddie. She's suffered a loss too. The loss of her boyfriend. The loss of her beauty (according to her). She deals with it through denial. Or work. Or maybe her kid. Cooper deals with it by trying to join Chaz. Jumping out of planes, off buildings, antennas, and bridges. He jumps at any and every risky opportunity. Even has sponsors who fund his excursions as long as he promotes them on his YouTube channel.

A guy in a three-piece suit walks past me, sits at the bar, sees Maddie, and immediately changes seats, taking the one to her left. She shakes his hand. Her smile falters and she covers her arm. I clear my throat loudly, even though I know he just noticed her scars. The biting glare she offers me is as good as a middle finger.

Good-natured, fun-loving Maddie from five minutes ago has left the building, leaving withdrawn, reluctant Maddie in her place. I want to thump the guy for whatever he did to make her uncomfortable. She tries to get up, but he puts a hand on her arm and says something to make her sit back down. She nods as he talks, left arm covering her right. I cough. She ignores me. I cough again.

"Will someone get that man a glass of water?" she says loudly.

My lips twitch in amusement. *She's back.*

The bartender rushes me a glass of water. I don't even look at him when he sets it down in front of me. I'm too busy watching her flirt with the man who, thirty seconds ago, almost had her running away. With Denzel, she was pretending. This guy, however, has her glowing like the goddamn north star. She doesn't even seem self-conscious anymore. Her mannerisms change. She leans into him. She tucks a wisp of hair behind her ear. And there is no thumb tapping whatsoever.

From *her*.

My thumb, however, is tapping my glass so hard that it starts traveling across the table. I pick up the glass and take it to the bar for a refill, never taking my eyes off the happy goddamn couple.

This time, I don't go back to the couch. I observe from my perch at the end of the bar.

"You okay, man?" the bartender asks.

"Fucking peachy," I reply, not bothering to make eye contact. I toss the drink back in one swallow.

"You don't plan on driving anytime soon, do you? You're staying here, right?"

"I am, so keep 'em coming." I pull a twenty out of my pocket and slide it across the bar. "And there's another one of these in it for you if you cut off the redhead at the other end of the bar."

"Whatever you two got going on here, I'm not getting involved, buddy."

He walks away before he can hear my derogatory musings about his ancestors and homeland.

Maddie's laughter dances across the bar. I should just go. Problem is, all my shit is upstairs, and she's got the only key card. And then there's the fact that I know I won't leave this stool unless a goddamn earthquake riddles New York City.

The guy picks up a chunk of her hair and rubs it between his fingers. Then he runs a hand down her arm.

It must be an 8.2 on the Richter scale, because I disappear from my seat faster than a donut at an AA meeting.

"Helen," I say, running over like a madman. "Finally! I've been looking all over for you."

The guy looks between us. "Don't tell me this is your husband."

"He's not." She gives me a look I can't quite decipher. "You can be done with babysitting duty."

I can't tell if she's amused that I intervened, or mad.

"Then maybe you should back off, man," the guy says. He cocks a brow at her. "Helen? I thought your name was Maddie."

I throw my hands up dramatically. "You're Maddie today?" I turn to the guy. "You're lucky I found her. Do you know how close you came to being arrested for soliciting a mentally incompetent woman?"

"Mentally what?" His eyes bounce between the two of us.

Now Maddie looks pissed. And totally hot, temper flaring in her eyes, coloring her cheeks.

"Right now, she's Maddie, the slutty girl you find on the street corner who's willing to spread her legs for any sorry sap who looks her way. But in ten minutes, who knows which one of her fourteen personalities you could end up with. Dude, you could have been balls deep in Maddie when the light switch flips and she turns into Kiki, who will chop off your nuts and fry them up for dinner."

"Are you for real?" the guy says.

"Do you want to chance it?" I say, getting in his face. "Because I'm very protective of my sister."

His hands go up in surrender before he throws money on the bar. "Whatever. I'm outta here."

I slide into the seat he vacated.

"Multiple personalities," she says with a brooding stare. "Really?"

"He was making you uncomfortable. Had to do something." I raise my glass, asking for another refill. The bartender complies, shaking his head at me. I'm sure he's seen it all working at a hotel bar.

"He was nice."

"He said something that made you frown."

"He asked about my scars. But only because he has a niece who got severely burned by a pot of boiling water when she was just two years old. He could relate. He was someone I could have gotten to know. Someone who understands my pain."

"Oh, *he* understands?" I take a sip, completely aware the dickhead bartender watered down my drink. "You don't own the rights to having shitty things happen to you, Flower Girl." I turn to the bartender. "Pour a real fucking drink next time, will you?"

He ignores me.

"Oh, my gosh," she says, guilt overtaking her soft features. "You're right. I wasn't even thinking about Chaz. I'm sorry."

"Are we done here?" I stand. "Because I could really use a goddamn smoke."

"Nuh-uh. No smoking. You promised."

"I didn't promise. I bet."

She gathers her purse. "Go ahead, then. I'm thinking a dozen long-stem roses in crystal vases with gold-laced foil for each of them would run you about seven hundred dollars."

"Might be fucking worth it."

It's a goddamn lie. It wouldn't be worth it. No amount of money and no rush from nicotine could possibly feel better than having my deceitful lips on her soft, pink, pouty ones.

"I'll just run up and get your pack," she says, walking out of the bar.

And I follow like an obedient golden retriever. And not for the pack of smokes.

Chapter Ten

Maddie

He catches the cigarettes I throw at him and tosses them back on the table. "You're not getting off that easy," he says.

There's a look of intense carnal need in his eyes. He stares at my lips, making me remember the bet. Involuntarily, my tongue swipes across my lower one. I need this man's kiss like I need a hole in the head. He's dangerous. Toxic even. One taste of him could do me in. And still, I crave him, despite knowing it's all a game. I'm the mouse to his cat. The moth to his flame.

"You okay?" he asks.

I shift in the dress. "This outfit is a little itchy," I lie.

"Then take it off. What did you bring to sleep in?"

Heat crosses my face. "Nothing."

"Right. You weren't planning on sleeping."

I sit on the arm of the couch and scrub my hands down my face. "Honestly, I don't know what I was planning. This whole thing was a stupid idea."

"It doesn't have to be a complete waste, you know. My offer still stands. I'll rip that Band-Aid right off your pussy anytime, anywhere."

"Poetic."

"All part of my charm."

"You saw me drinking tequila, and you think I'm drunk and will be an easy lay."

"You were an easy lay the minute you signed up for After Dark, Flower Girl."

I open my mouth to argue, to spit venom in his direction, but what is there to say? He's one hundred percent right. I march into the bathroom, collect his still-wet clothes, push them into his chest, and nod to the door. "You know what they say. Don't let it hit you where the good Lord split you."

"These are still drenched," he says.

"They're barely even damp."

His clothes aren't dry, but they're not dripping wet. They'd be uncomfortable at the very worst. He might end up with chafing down there. *Down there.* My insides get all twisty when I think of that part of his anatomy.

He walks the clothes back into the bathroom and hangs them up again.

"Fine," I say. "Leave them. You can go home like that."

"Not a chance." He shuts the door to the bathroom, and then I hear him pee.

I try to ignore it, because when did the sound of a man peeing become so intimate? So weirdly sexy?

When the door opens again, he's wearing the robe from earlier, the breadth of his wide shoulders barely allowing the two sides to meet. He plops down in a chair. "I'm staying."

"But it's *my* hotel room."

"It's *our* date."

"Date? You were just downstairs pawning me off on other men."

"To prove a point, which I did. Any one of them would have happily followed you up here."

"I'll agree they probably would have. But they wouldn't have stayed long."

His eyes travel up my chest, where my arms have crossed, and I've tucked my left hand into my right armpit as if to camouflage the scars all along my right side.

"You're doing it again," he says, standing and forcing my hands down. "You think they would have left when they saw you naked?"

My gaze meets the floor. "I know they would have."

I'm not looking at him, but I can feel him staring at my arm. He's closer than we've been all night. He no longer smells entirely like cigarettes. More like tequila and spearmint. Did he chew more gum? To appease *me*?

He touches the shoulder of my dress. I flinch. I haven't felt the touch of a man in a very long time.

His throat clears. "You're right. It's scratchy." He picks the other robe up off the bed and hands it to me.

"I'm not wearing that. I have clothes."

His head shakes slowly from side to side. "We're still playing the game."

"If the game is you trying to get me to sleep with you, I can assure you, that ended the second you walked into the restaurant."

He sits. "You're wrong. We've been playing all night; you just don't realize it." His robe falls open slightly. Just enough for me to see his muscular right thigh. My gaze travels along his inner leg from his ankle, where dark, thick leg hair covers his skin, up to where the sparser fuzz disappears under the robe. I momentarily wonder if the hair under his skivvies is thick or thin. Then I wonder if he's even wearing skivvies. I get it now—the hot sexuality he exudes that has women begging for more.

I make the mistake of meeting his eyes. They're raw with sensual heat, and strikingly possessive. "I, uh...what?"

I turn away so he can't see my blush. Too late. His low chuckle tells me he noticed.

I refuse to be his pawn. His conquest. And I swear to myself I won't sleep with him, but I take the robe anyway as if to prove a point. What point, I have absolutely no idea.

He makes a call when I'm in the bathroom changing. Who could he be calling after ten o'clock on a Saturday? Probably Jassinda, or Chrissy, or Kayla, or any one of his past hookups.

I stare in the mirror after I change. Then I play with the robe, putting it in different positions, trying to make myself look sexy while still covering the parts I need to cover. It's fruitless. This is pointless anyway. I pull it snugly around me and join Tag.

His gaze lingers on my legs before moving north. "You should show me."

I tighten the long cotton belt. "Show you?"

"You know, get naked."

"I—"

He shuts me up before I can get in a word. "I'm not going to touch you, Maddie. I just think you should get comfortable taking your clothes off in front of a man. You need to realize it's not that bad."

"You haven't seen it."

"I've seen your arm."

"That's not the worst of it. And seeing it is just half of it. The way it feels…" I look away, knowing exactly what would go through a man's head if he touched me. Disgust.

Tag laughs. *Again. At me.*

"Did you see the couple at the back of the bar by the window?"

"The one who was kissing?"

"That's the one. He was a beanpole. And she was…"

"Overweight?" I say, knowing there must be twenty derogatory terms he's dying to use.

"Overweight?" He chuckles. "That's putting it mildly. Let's just say when she decides to sing, *everything* will be over."

"Your point?"

"Do you think he gives a shit about her fat rolls when he's glazing the donut? You think when she's tugging on his dick, and he's knuckles deep in her lady garden, that he's thinking how she's so huge he can't even wrap his arms all the way around her? Hell no, he's chasing the moon. Seeing stars. Praising the very ground she walks on."

I ignore all his crude euphemisms. "Are you telling me you'd date that woman?"

"Me? No."

"See?"

"Yeah, but I'm a vain asshole."

"My point exactly."

"I'm just saying, you need to show someone eventually. Why not me?"

"You. The vain asshole. Right. There may not be enough alcohol in the world to make me open this robe."

There's a knock on the door, and I stare in the direction. "What's that?"

He hops off the couch and goes over, offering me a smirk along the way. "All the alcohol in the world."

Chapter Eleven

Tag

She eyes the bottles of wine, whiskey, and tequila. Her brows draw together in a scowl, and her cool, cynical eyes appraise me. "I'm not getting drunk with you."

"But you're halfway there."

"I had the bartender water down my drinks. I didn't want to do anything stupid."

"I was sitting right there, Maddie. I wouldn't have let you."

Her eyes meet mine. There's a moment of… something. Then they flicker away. Oh, she was talking about *me*.

I get some paper cups from beside the coffee maker. "What'll it be?"

"Why are you still here, Tag?"

"My clothes are wet, and I don't want to get jock itch. And I'm sure as shit not riding the train looking like I just came from the U.S. Open. Most importantly, I've got nothing better to do right now. Now tell me which drink you prefer, or I'll choose for you."

She rolls her eyes. "Wine."

Plenty of women roll their eyes at me. All of them do at one time or another. It's expected. Hell, I'd be disappointed if they didn't. Means I'm off my game. But when Maddie rolls her eyes, it makes me want to cup her face in my hands and kiss the shit out of her. Which is a strange feeling considering I don't prefer kissing over all the other nocturnal activities.

I pour us each a cup of wine. Slowly, so my half chub has a minute to wane.

Sounds from the television fill the room. She's flipping through the channels until she finds one to settle on. I hand her a cup. "*Friends*, huh?"

She raises it. "This was my original plan all along. Monica, Rachel, Phoebe, Chandler, Joey, Ross, and wine."

"You mean it was your plan B."

She shrugs and takes a sip.

I sit on the other end of the couch, leaving an empty cushion between us. "You really like this show?"

"Sure, what's not to like? I guess you can say I'm envious. I grew up watching it and thought that's how everyone's friendships went."

"You have friends."

"Yeah, but not like these. The ride or die friends you know will be with you until the grave. Don't get me wrong, Patrick, Regan, and Ava are great." She nods to the TV. "It's just not on this level."

"Very few friendships are. That's why they call this entertainment. It's fiction, Maddie."

"Are you and Amber like that? Is she your ride or die friend?"

"Used to be. She's got Quinn now."

"There's no one else back home? My friends say they see you out all the time."

"With family mostly. My brothers or cousins. Or Amber's husband. There's no one else in Cal Creek I'd call a close friend."

"Cal Creek? Why do you call it that?"

"Isn't it obvious?"

"You don't like to share your name with the town?"

"It'd be different if the Calloways actually had something to do with the founding of it."

"Right. The infamous bet. So it's true what happened between your ancestors and the McQuaids?"

"You've heard the nauseating stories."

"Only some of them. I didn't grow up here, remember. I moved here when I was twenty."

"I forgot. Where are you from originally?"

"Lincoln, Nebraska."

"Ouch. Good call moving here."

"There's nothing wrong with Lincoln, Nebraska."

"Not if you like watching corn grow."

"Tag, you're one to talk. You've lived in Calloway Creek your whole life. It's got, what, twenty thousand people? Talk about a town where you watch corn grow. Lincoln can be exciting. There's a huge university there, much larger than CCU, and no corn in sight. We had to travel way out of town to pick corn."

"You picked corn? From an actual cornfield?"

"A lot of high school students did. It was our summer job. Hard work and hot as heck because we had to wear long sleeves and pants. But it paid well."

"Still, at least in Cal Creek, the city is close."

"We had Omaha. It's less than an hour's drive."

I almost spit my wine all over the couch. *"Omaha?"*

"It's not as country as it sounds."

"You moved here with your grandmother to help her in the flower shop? What did your parents think about that?"

"I have no idea. They aren't in my life."

"Sounds heavenly."

"Seriously, Tag? I know your parents. They're wonderful. You think growing up without mine was *heavenly*?"

I hold up a hand. "Jeez, sorry. Didn't mean to start World War Three. So why did your grandmother raise you?"

"Isabella, that's my mom, got pregnant as a teenager, and Colin, the guy who knocked her up, wanted nothing to do with them. Colin's parents were religious and forced him to marry her. But he started beating her. Gran could see the signs, so she took in Isabella and me and told him to take a hike, which he had no problem with. But Mom was messed up. Gran tells me she was suffering from depression. She left before I was even as old as Gigi, and I haven't seen her since. We have no idea what happened to her. It's been over twenty years and not one birthday card or letter."

"Maybe she died."

"Gran hired an agency once to look into it. They couldn't find anything. No death certificates. No job history. Nothing. She simply disappeared."

"And your dad?"

"Gone with the wind."

"Dang. Sorry."

"Tell me about the McQuaids and the Calloways. Fill in the blanks for me."

I cross the room and bring the wine bottle back with me. When I hold it out, she lifts her cup.

"Lloyd McQuaid and Samuel Calloway immigrated from England in 1860 as twenty-year-olds. They were best friends.

Unlikely DATE

Samuel was my great-great-great-grandfather. While he got a job in a button factory to earn a living wage, Lloyd took up boxing. He became well known as a prize fighter in New York City. Eventually, he earned enough money to buy his own land. So in 1867, the place we now call Calloway Creek was founded as McQuaid Plat. But twelve years later, he lost a bet to Samuel, and Samuel got to rename the town."

"And you all hate each other because of that bet?"

"I suppose. But not always. The story goes that all was well for years after the bet. The McQuaids and the Calloways co-existed peacefully. It was Lloyd's grandson, Norman, who stirred the pot. He thought his grandfather had been duped and fought to rename the town. But by then, it was the 1930s and a post office had already been established, which in itself makes renaming a town nearly impossible. Not to mention by then, the town was incorporated, so it failed to pass the needed votes to rename it. It would have cost millions, even back then. But Norman never let it go, and it got so much worse when he lost his half of Lloyd's inheritance."

"How'd that happen?"

"So Lloyd McQuaid owned more land than what became Calloway Creek. His only son, Chester, inherited the land, and then when he passed, the land was divided and split equally between his two sons, Clarence and Norman. Clarence sold his land to a New York City land developer in 1950 and used the money to open car dealerships, which you know have made his family one of the richest in town."

"Along with the Montanas."

"And that's where it's gets interesting. Norman saw what his brother had done, but he got greedy, holding on to his land, asking astronomical prices and turning down deal after deal. He was determined to double what his brother had gotten. But what he didn't count on was land prices going back down. He finally sold to Andrew Montana's father, long before Andrew married into the Calloway family."

Maddie holds out her cup for more. Although I've told the story a dozen times and it's lost its luster, she's glued to every word. "Wait, so that's how the Montanas came into the picture? But why would Norman be bitter? He must have gotten millions."

"He did. But he lost most of his money in bad investments and gambled the rest away before he was found face down in a pile of cocaine, leaving nothing but bad debts for his two daughters, one of whom died young, and the other married into the Cruz family."

"Let me get this straight. So the Cruzs are part of the McQuaid family and the Montanas are part of the Calloway family, and that's why you all hate each other? It makes so much sense now."

"What does?"

"Why Blake Montana and Lincoln Cruz never want to work together. I always thought it was over a girl or something."

"Work together? For *you*?"

"They both work at the shop part-time while they go to college. Blake works summers and holidays while Lincoln works year-round while attending CCU. They deliver flowers and sometimes watch the store if I need to be away. They're great guys separately, but together… There's a lot of bad blood there, I guess."

"Blake is my cousin. Well, first cousin once removed if you're keeping track."

"What does once removed mean?"

"It means we're separated by a generation. His great-grandfather is my grandfather. Distantly, I'm related to Lincoln, too. We share a great-great-great-grandmother. Not that the Calloways and the Cruzs consider each other family. Chances are decent we don't even share DNA."

"I may need you to draw me a family tree."

"Oh, it gets way more complicated. Some time ago, two Calloway women married McQuaids. Technically, the McQuaids are my third cousins; again, not *really* family. And not only that, a McQuaid wife dumped her husband and married my uncle."

"Hawk's mom, right?" She laughs. "I knew you were all distantly related somehow, but wow… your family tree sounds more like a Sequoia. Mine's barely even a twig."

I pick up the bottle and empty it into my cup. It only fills it halfway. I chug it back and go for the tequila. "After all that, I could use this."

She downs the rest of her red liquid and extends her arm.

I raise a brow. She's getting drunk. And she wants more. This could go so many different ways. But being the guy I am, I happily fill her cup—way more than I should.

We drink and laugh at the television. She pulls her legs up onto the couch and wraps her arms around them, intently watching "The One Where Ross Got High." Her robe falls to the side, revealing a good portion of her upper thigh and a sliver of her butt cheek. Like the predator I am, I stare. The skin is discolored slightly, a lighter shade than the rest of her. A scar? But it's her left side. I thought she was only burned on the right.

She stops laughing when she catches me staring. She pulls a blanket over her legs. "Skin grafts," she says with a wounded grin before motioning for the bottle.

Who am I to deny her? I hand over the bottle. "Believe me, Flower Girl, that's the last thing on my mind when I was looking at your ass."

Her cheeks pink. She pours tequila into her cup and focuses back on the television. She slowly lifts the cup to her lips and tips it back. I can tell she's not watching the show. The pad of her thumb is drumming on the side of the couch. Is she thinking about what's on my mind? Because *I* sure as hell am. And what's on my mind is ripping that goddamn robe off her, tossing her over the end of the couch, and driving myself into her until she screams my name with the dirty mouth of a long-haul trucker.

I throw back a shot, unable to remember a time I felt this wrought with need. It's almost midnight and she's drunk. I should go. But hell if I will before I collect. Drunk or not, she's paying up.

"I'm ready to collect my winnings."

"Winnings?" she asks, brow lifted as if she doesn't know exactly what I'm talking about.

"You heard me. Have you seen me light up since our bet?"

"I have no idea what you were doing while I was talking with Nelson."

"Nelson? What kind of name is Nelson?"

"Says the guy named after a label on a piece of clothing."

"Are you saying you're the kind of girl who doesn't make good on her bets?"

She straightens. "I live up to my bets."

I stand. "Prove it." My voice is rough and deep and full of arrogant demand.

She inhales a shaky breath I'm sure I wasn't supposed to hear. "Here? Now?"

I look at my wrist, devoid of a watch. "We're not getting any younger."

She goes to stand and falls back to the couch.

I reach out to steady her. "You good?"

"Fine. I'm fine. Totally fine."

The tension tightening the delicate features of her face tells a different tale.

"In my opinion, someone who says they are fine—three times, no less—is most definitely the opposite of said word."

Rising again, more steadily this time, she takes two steps and plants herself directly in front of me, never losing eye contact. It's the most confident thing I've seen her do tonight, and I fail to hide my country-boy grin.

"Let's get it over with then," she says, as if completely uninterested. "The next episode is one of my favorites."

My eyes fall to her lips. The lips I watched spew words to two other men I wished were me. The pouty pink lips I've been imagining running up and down my cock for the last four hours. The lips I'd trade the Range for if they'd just whisper my name.

"Well?" she says impatiently, her mouth waiting like a question.

Fuck. I'm almost thirty goddamn years old. I've never been nervous about anything. I started my own business on a loan that could have bankrupted me. I double majored in college even though it meant pulling all-nighters and hiring tutors. I've slept with models, television actresses, and Brazilian beauties. Yet, right here, right now, in front of FlowerGirl529, my entire body wound like a bow string, I have fucking stage fright.

I clear my throat and set my drink down. I crack my knuckles and shift my weight. Her hazel eyes peer up at me. Waiting. Wanting. Maybe even challenging. And Tag Calloway never backs down from a challenge. I put a hand on the back of her neck and close the gap between us.

"Time to collect," I say, just as my lips find hers.

Her eyes close, as do my own. This is a one-time thing and both of us know it. After today, this moment, this kiss, she'll go back to being the sheepish flower shop owner, and I'll continue being the CEO asshat everyone thinks I am.

Our lips brush together tentatively, the warmth of hers consuming me instantaneously. It's nothing like I expected. Her lips don't form a firm line, a barrier against which I'm not allowed to pass. Her mouth doesn't stay shut. My tongue doesn't have to force an entrance. Her lips part willingly and invite me inside. And when our tongues meet, it's fervent, greedy, explosive; each of us fighting for something we don't even know exists. Neither of us wins. Or we both do, it's hard to tell.

I've never been a big fan of kissing. Now I feel it's landed in my top ten and is quickly moving its way up the list. My cock protests to the order change and is reminding me painfully that he will steadfastly hold on to the number one spot.

She tastes of wicked temptation and sinful delight, and it has every cell in my body erupting with desire. With the way I'm panting, I pray the taste of cigarettes is no longer on my breath. It's an invocation that's never crossed my mind before now.

A mewl escapes her. My cock thinks it's all for him and thickens further. I tell him to fuck off, her lips are all mine. He can wait his turn. It's a turn he knows he'll never have, and he's pissed. He throbs against my boxer briefs, begging to be seen. Felt. Paid attention to.

I give into him, but only so much as I walk her back to the wall and press myself against her. There's no way she doesn't feel my hardness through our robes. She doesn't protest. She does the opposite and deepens the kiss, exploring my mouth and sucking on my tongue. My cock thinks it's a preview and is happy with this. For the moment anyway. And this time, a sound escapes *me*.

She holds me against her, hands running across my shoulders, my back, even the top of my ass as she kisses me with toe-curling determination. I move her head to the side, exposing her neck, and let my lips devour her jaw, the supple skin below her ear, her collarbone. The peachy scent of her hair invades my nose, driving my want for her.

My hands cup her face and move along her jawline back into her hair as I pull her lips to mine. I expect her to pull away, say the kiss is over. One kiss is all we bargained for. She doesn't. Her swollen lips part for mine, and once again, our tongues engage in battle. I fear it's a fight that's going to leave both of us in ashes.

I suck her lower lip. She bites mine. Our chests mash together, leaving me unsure if the thud I feel is her heartbeat or mine. Maybe it's both and they're beating in sync. Her breathing is heavy and ragged, her chest rising and falling as if she's running a marathon. I should know. I'm running the same race.

I taste her again, sucking her tongue. Needing more. Needing everything she'll give me.

There's a loud noise in the hall, and Maddie pulls back. I want to go out there and kill the fucker who put an end to this. I take half a step back, staring down into her eyes as I wonder if the kiss rendered them glassy, or the alcohol.

"I, uh…" She ducks under my arm and walks to the mini fridge. She downs a full bottle of water before sitting on the bed.

My balls remind me they're so blue they're about to explode. I thumb to the bathroom door. "I'm gonna…"

Whack off? Take a cold shower? Fucking cry?

I close the door behind me and shake my head, bringing myself back to reality. But reality has changed. I'm not going to lie to myself and make this out to be something it wasn't. Less than fucking perfect. It was the perfect goddamn kiss.

I stare at the stranger in the mirror as I splash water on my face. It takes ten minutes for the blood to drain from my dick. Ten minutes of me wondering what the hell just happened.

What's next? What happens when I emerge? Do I thank her for my winnings and watch the next episode of *Friends?* Chug the bottle of Patrón so I can get rid of the taste of her along with whatever this feeling is that's making me have some out-of-body experience? Buy her breakfast? What's in the fucking rule book for doing what we just did and then pretending it didn't even happen?

But when I open the door, I find I have to do none of the above. Maddie is passed out on the bed. And her robe has fallen open, exposing all of the scars she never wanted me to see. I can't look away. She's right. People stare. Her scars are a patchwork of grafts coming down from her armpit, which is still covered by the robe, weaving around the top and right side of her bra, down the side of her rib cage and then ending partially across her stomach.

I hold my side, imagining the pain she must have gone through. Both of her thighs, inside and out, are lightened with scars from the skin they must have used to cover her burns. The cruelty of it. They had to create more scars on her to fix the original ones.

I sit on the bed, careful not to wake her, and trace the roadmap of her horror with my eyes, not believing anyone could be so strong to live through what she did and come out of it the way she has. She's a mom. A business owner. A friend. She's kind. Not bitter. Her only fault is her timidity, her reticence, her self-doubt.

And as I sit here, up close and personal with her flaws, another unexpected pang of longing shoots through me. But I know Maddie Foster is way too good for a prick like me. So I cover her up. Then I do what I do best.

I leave.

Chapter Twelve

Maddie

Something feels wrong. I roll over in bed. *Something sounds wrong.* I wipe the sleep from my eyes. *Something* smells *wrong.* A whooshing sound echoes outside my bedroom door. I sit up in bed and turn on the light, horrified to see smoke sliding in under the door and drifting to the ceiling. "Gigi!" I yell, springing out of bed and sprinting across the room.

I pull back when my hand touches the doorknob. It's too hot. I slip on a pair of shoes and then use a dirty shirt from the floor to open it. Then I press the shirt to my face. I know there could be fire on the other side. I also know I have to save my daughter.

I throw the door open to the screaming shrill of the smoke detector. I cover my sobbing mouth when I look down the hall toward her room. Flames lick the wall by the bathroom between us, spreading across the ceiling in rippling sheets. They dance as they crackle the wood beneath them, producing an acrid smell that assaults my nostrils.

The table in the hallway collapses with a crash, its legs reduced to charred stumps. The glass in the picture frame splinters. It's a picture of Gigi. And now it's a scorched piece of curled plastic quickly disappearing before my eyes. The long, wavy hair of the doll left on the hallway floor shrinks into frizz and burns away; the plastic face drooping as it melts into the floor. Oh, my god. Gigi. I've never been so terrified. So utterly helpless.

Flames turn toward me, a monster looking at me as its next object of prey. Paint bubbles on the wall, the light from my bedroom flickers then shorts out. Small explosions come from the bathroom, and sharp chemical odors mix with the campfire smell. My chest burns with every breath I take through the balled-up cotton pressed against my mouth and nose. Even through the shirt, I taste ash. Thick phlegm collects in my throat.

The window at the end of the hall cracks, then explodes. The flames that were coming for me shift and move toward the open air—toward Gigi's room. Her doorframe warps. The door moans as fire eats away at it. Flames disappear into her room as I watch in abject horror. "Gigi, baby, I'm coming!"

I run but instantly fall, my foot going right through a floorboard. Walls cave in around me. My vision goes blurry. Pain sears my side as screams bellow out of me. I curl into a ball, knowing I'm going to be with my baby soon. Just not in the way I had planned.

Wetness surrounds me, a waterfall pours on me from above, pooling under me. The glow of orange succumbs to the darkness. A light down the hall shines toward me, outlining the silhouette of a firefighter. He's coming for me. *Save her! I* try to scream but can't. I can't even lift my head and turn toward her room. But I don't have to see it to know it's gone. Destroyed. Engulfed. Leave me. Leave me here with her.

My head swirls. The pain overtakes me. I sink into blackness just as arms come around me.

I jolt awake, breathing heavily. Sweat pools between my breasts as jagged pieces of my nightmare slice through my brain. I sit up, pull my legs to my chest, and wrap my arms around them. It takes a minute for me to get my bearings, but soon it all comes rushing back. The *not* date. The rain. The sleeveless dress. The alcohol. *The kiss.*

Unlikely **DATE**

I search the room for clues. No sign of him. Just a robe draped over the end of the couch.

The last thing I remember is the kiss. We didn't…? I open my robe to see my bra and panties intact. I had sheets on when I woke. Did he cover me up and leave? Or did he stay the night and go to get breakfast?

I cross to the bathroom. His clothes are no longer hanging in the shower. I peer back into the room. His cigarettes are gone. There are no shoes on the floor.

I sit on the edge of the bed, feeling a fool. He left. Of course he left.

Did you think he was going to kiss you and fall in love? Ditch his playboy past and get down on a knee? Look beyond your scars and see if there's anyone there worth knowing?

I shake my head. Tag is not the kind of man who's capable of doing any of that. I'm just the gullible girl who let him worm his way into my heart over the course of one incredible night. The night he'll laugh about with his buddies. The night he'll forget as soon as a pretty woman turns his head.

The night I fell in love with Tag Calloway.

~ ~ ~

"I'm sorry," the man behind the lobby counter says. "Your card on file was declined."

"Declined?" I say, embarrassed. "But I thought there weren't any charges. I paid with a gift certificate. They said the debit card was just for incidentals. Of which there should be none."

He pushes a piece of paper across the counter. "Here's the list of everything charged to your room, ma'am. Do you wish to dispute?"

I scan the list, and my heart sinks. The son of a bitch stuck me with the bill. My dress, his clothes, the liquor—it's all here in detail. All four hundred and twelve dollars of it.

I know full well what's in my bank account, and it isn't even half that. "No. I don't wish to dispute." I get out my wallet and hand over my one and only credit card. The card I save for emergencies.

We'll be eating Ramen for weeks.

I scold myself for allowing it to happen. All of it. I should have pushed him away, made him leave me alone right after he gave me back my purse. Leave it to him to stick me with the bill *and* a broken heart.

To be fair, the broken heart isn't his fault. Not entirely. I let it happen. I played his game. And I lost. Spectacularly.

Stupid, stupid girl.

"Perfect," the staffer says, handing me my receipt. "We hope you'll be staying with us again very soon."

Or never.

I pull my small bag behind me and make my way through the lobby. Everywhere I look holds a memory. Tag taking my elbow and escorting me to the elevator. Jassinda making me so jealous I flirted unnecessarily hard with those men. Me leaving the bar, knowing I'd made him want me—if only for the kiss I owed him.

Refusing to let the tears fall, I sniff them back and hold my head high, walking out into the morning sun.

On the train, conversation buzzes around me. I feel like there's a sign over my head. A marquee that flashes: LOSER.

I lean against the window and watch the passing landscape as the rail car takes me further away from the best, albeit weirdest, night I've ever had.

Unlikely DATE

~ ~ ~

"Mommy!"

Gigi jumps into my arms the second I enter the apartment. She smells like coconut—her shampoo scent of choice—and pancakes.

I squeeze her extra tight as memories of the dream and The Incident are still fresh. "I missed you, baby."

Patrick appears. His eyebrows raise in question. "Thought I might hear from you again sometime last night. I'll take the absence of communication as a good sign."

I carry Gigi into the kitchen-slash-family room. With peeling linoleum floors, chipped cabinet doors, and mismatched furniture, it's a far cry from the classy hotel I left an hour ago. But it's clean. And it's mine. Or the mortgage is anyway.

Three years ago, Gran retired. She said fifty years of trimming flowers had her arthritis flaring up on a daily basis. She was tired. So she signed the mortgage on the store, and the apartment upstairs, over to me and moved into a retirement community. There was one stipulation: I can't sell it until she's dead.

Gran is the healthiest seventy-five-year-old I've ever met. Which means I might be here for a long time. Not that I'd go anywhere else. Where would I go? And other than the memories of The Incident (I avoid driving down Marigold Lane at all costs) and the Jamisons (Cody's parents, who never let me forget I killed their son), I actually like Calloway Creek. Although I now have a third reason not to: Tag Calloway.

I pour myself a cup of coffee while Gigi finishes her breakfast.

Patrick is staring. "Something's up."

"Nothing's up."

More staring. I ignore him.

"Gigi." Patrick puts her plate in the sink after she finishes. He gets down on her level. "Be a sweetie and go wash up. Then be a big girl and pick out your clothes for the day."

"Okay. Thank you for the smiley-faced pancakes, Paddy." She plants a kiss on his cheek and happily skips away.

He turns to me. "Spill."

I sip my coffee, stalling.

"You know I'll get it out of you sooner or later." He pulls out a chair, points to it, then sits down on another. He crosses one of his thick, muscular fireman's legs over the other.

I roll my eyes and sink onto the chair. "You won't believe it. *I still don't believe it.*"

A slow smile spreads across his face. "You did it?"

"Not *it* exactly. But I did kiss him." My cheeks flush. Remembering that moment is something that will stay with me until the day I die. His lips were warm and inviting, his tongue forceful and teasing. The way his hands held me exactly where I needed to be held so our lips fit together to perfection. The soft groans percolating from his throat. It was like I had been standing under a cloud for years, and then his kiss parted them, allowing the sun to shine on me.

Then again, I was a bit drunk. Perhaps my mind is embellishing.

I run a finger across my lips. No. Everything I felt was real. It had to be.

Okay, so the jerk stiffed me with the bill, but maybe it was a small price to pay for the memory that will last an eternity.

"Girl, if that's the way you look thinking about a kiss, you'll melt the floor beneath your feet if you do the deed with this guy."

Sadness overcomes me, and I perch my elbows on the table, steepling my hands over my mouth. "That's never going to happen."

"Why not? Wait, what's not to believe? You said I wouldn't believe it."

"It's not the *what* you won't believe. It's the *who*."

"Are you telling me you kissed someone famous? Oh, please tell me it was a Nighthawk. Was it a Nighthawk?" He sits straight up in his seat, impatient for my revelation.

"It wasn't a baseball player. It wasn't anyone famous. Infamous is more like it. Around Calloway Creek, anyway."

His eyebrows shoot up and touch his hairline. "He's from Calloway Creek? Who is it, Maddie?"

"If I tell you, you have to promise it stays between us. You cannot tell the guys at the firehouse. Got it?"

"I promise."

"It was Tag."

Incredulous breaths puff out of his nose. "Calloway?"

"Do you know any other Tag?"

"Holy shit!" He looks behind him, realizing how loud he was. "Holy shit," he whispers, as if I didn't hear him the first time. "Tag Calloway? Sister, seriously?"

I tell him about my whole night. It feels good to get it off my chest, like I'm unburdening myself somehow.

He hangs on to my every word. Studying me. Scrutinizing me. When I'm done, he sits in silence for a beat.

"You like him." He searches my hazel eyes with his blue ones. "Oh, my god, you *more* than like him."

"I don't." I shift uncomfortably. "I mean, I don't want to. It's a stupid crush. I'll be over it by lunchtime."

"He stuck you with the bill, Maddie. He's a prick of colossal proportions."

"I know." I say the words. I even try to mean them. But beneath the surface, sorrow eats at my soul, aching in places I never knew I had. How could one night have affected me so brutally?

"You should make him pay you back."

I get up and wash out my mug. "Believe me, seeing him is not on my list of priorities. Avoiding him is, however."

"*I'll* ask him, then."

I spin. "You will do no such thing, Pat Kelsey. I'm serious. Swear to me."

He knows I mean business when I call him Pat. He hates the shortened name. In fact, the only person he lets use a nickname for him is Gigi.

"Okay, okay. I swear."

"And if you see him—*when* you see him—do not give him any indication that I told you. Just keep on walking and go about your merry way."

"So you're going to just pretend it never happened?"

"Yes."

Gigi comes into the room, ending the conversation. I take her hand. "Come on, baby. Let's go put together the flower arrangements for Mrs. Mahoney's party."

Patrick grabs his overnight bag and follows us down the stairs.

"And *you*"—I put a finger to his chest—"remember what I said." I lean in and kiss his cheek. "And thank you for watching her. I don't know what I'd do without you."

"Anytime. You know that."

Downstairs, pounding on the front door gets my attention. I peek out from the back room. Regan and Ava are standing outside looking like two starving puppies waiting on a treat.

I glance at Gigi and then say to Patrick, "I can't. I don't have the energy to regurgitate it all again."

"Want me to do it? I'll swear them to secrecy."

"Not only that," I say. "Tell them I forbid them from ever bringing it up with me. Regan has been with him. I'd never hear the end of it."

"Got it."

"*Ever.* I mean it."

"Calm down before you pop a vein already."

"Be sure to relock the front door with your key. I don't open for another few hours."

He tugs on one of Gigi's ponytails, which he so expertly fashioned. "See you later, squirt."

"Bye, Paddy." She hugs him.

He looks back at me before reaching the door. His head shakes in laughter. I really wish men would quit laughing at me.

"Come on, Gigi. Let's go make the world more beautiful."

"You do that all by yourself, Mommy."

I get on my knees and take her into my arms. My child. My biggest fan. My sole reason for living.

Chapter Thirteen

Tag

I park in the street, walk past the other cars in the driveway, and go through the heavy wooden front door of my parents' house. Boisterous laughter comes from the back porch. I look out to see that I'm the last to arrive and Josie, the one-year-old daughter of Amber and Quinn, is toddling across the deck giving kisses to anyone who will accept them. Which appears to be everyone.

I wait a minute until it stops. I don't need to catch whatever germs she's passing around.

My sister, Addison, sees me and moves to get up too quickly. Jaxon races over and keeps her from falling. She often forgets about her limitations. Quite frankly, though, it's those limitations that kept our family going after Chaz died. Her accident happened right after we lost him—the night of his funeral to be exact—in a drunk driving accident where *she*, at eighteen, was the drunk driver. Rallying around Addy became our sole cause for the next few months.

I run over to her and give her a hug. "Don't get up."

"Quit babying me."

"I'm not."

I am. But not necessarily because of the accident. Addy is the baby of the family. She'll always be the baby.

"Whatever. Did you see how well Josie is walking?"

"What's the big deal? Hasn't she been walking for like a month now?"

"You're such a tool, Tag," she says with a hint of sisterly love.

"Hey, guys." I greet everyone. "Mom, Dad."

Mom kisses me. I let her. I stopped turning away years ago—about the same time I stopped calling her Libby instead of Mom, like I had been since I was fourteen. She sighs. "He's really not coming?"

"Nope."

"I thought this was going to be the year. He's twenty-five. I got him a cake and everything."

"We'll take a picture of all of us around the cake and text it to him."

She wipes a tear. "Do I even want to know what he's doing today?"

"Probably not. He'll be fine. He's a big boy."

She runs her hand over the edge of one of his presents. "Guess I'll have to ship these to him. Is he still living in that barn down in Florida?"

"He left Florida in April, Mom," Jaxon says. "He bought a converted van and has been living out of it for the past few months. Mostly in Colorado, I think."

"Dude," I say. "Cooper did not want her to know about this."

She looks aghast. "I thought he was kidding when he mentioned wanting to get a van. He's really homeless?"

"He's not homeless," Addy says. "Van living has gotten huge. People have blogs about it and everything."

Unlikely DATE

Dad looks pissed. "He doesn't have a home. That makes him homeless. My son is homeless."

"Where am I supposed to ship his things?" Mom asks.

"He's got a post office box," Addy says. "And he uses Amazon lockers for his online deliveries."

Mom's jaw drops. "You *knew* about this?"

Addy glances around. "We all did. Well, except for you and Dad. He knew you'd react like this. But he's a grown man. He can live the way he wants."

"Where does he use the toilet?" Dad asks. "What if he has to—"

"Take a deuce?" I add.

"Well, yes."

"Most van dwellers have gym memberships. They use the gym bathrooms and showers."

"Like a homeless person," Dad says, shaking his head again.

"And Colorado?" Mom asks. "What'll he do in the winter?"

"He could drive south," Addy says. "But it's not necessary. Many still live in their vans even in cold weather. They use heated blankets and sleeping bags."

"But those require electricity."

"That's what the solar panels are for."

She gasps. "He's got solar panels? So this is for real? As in long term?"

"Makes sense for him," Amber says. "He moves around so much anyway."

"None of this makes sense. He should be home with his family."

Dad puts an arm around her. "It's okay, Lib. Cooper will come home sooner or later."

"It's not as if he never comes home," Jaxon says. "You saw him in March. And he was here for Christmas."

"The day *after* Christmas," Mom says, reminding us he's never here for the holidays.

"This day is harder for him than anyone," Addy says.

"Hey now," Dad argues. "That's just not true. Look at your mother. She gave birth to Cooper and Chaz. He isn't the only one who grieves on their birthday."

Addy wraps Mom in a hug. "I'm sorry. That was insensitive. Of course you're hurting just as badly as he is."

Mom pats Addy's hand. "Thank you, sweetie."

Josie toddles over to get in on the hug. Mom gladly pulls her on her lap.

"Anyway," Dad says. "No point dwelling on what we can't change. I might as well fire up the grill. Cooper or not, we can still celebrate."

"Let me help you with those," Quinn says, hopping off the wooden bench.

"So, Quinn," Dad starts. "What's keeping you busy these days? Are you still flying for that Landry fellow in the city?"

"Flying for Landry Enterprises was taking up too much of my time. I'm flying for the Montanas now."

"My cousins?"

Quinn nods. "Peter and Chris don't need me much. A few days a week. Gives me more time to spend with Josie."

"And count your millions," Addy says.

Jaxon playfully swats the back of her head. "That was rude."

"What?" she says. "He's probably got at least as much money as they do, and yet he's working for them. It doesn't make sense."

Quinn laughs. "It makes sense because I love flying helicopters. I don't do it for the money, Addison. I do it for fun."

She looks horrified. "They don't pay you?"

"They pay me. They pay me well. Amber and I donate the money."

"If you're looking for a charity case." Addy points to herself. "Poor college student here."

Everyone laughs.

Ever since I walked through the door, Mom has looked like she's mad at me. Maybe it's because I couldn't convince Coop to come home. During dinner, she finally breaks her silence. "I have a bone to pick with you," she says. "I heard a rumor in church this morning. Actually, it was all anyone could talk about. In fact, Pastor Nichols stopped the sermon at one point because there was so much buzz coming from the pews."

I want to ask her if, after all these years, she only goes to get back in God's good graces. But I don't want to bark up that tree again. "What did I do now?" I ask instead.

"Maddie Foster. Really, Tag? A clandestine affair in the city? Why did you have to choose her of all people? She's never been anything but a sweetheart. And after all she's been through."

Quinn coughs, sputtering beer onto his sleeve. "You hooked up with Maddie Foster?"

"Where in the hell did you hear that?" I ask Mom, shooting an accusing glance at Amber. But Amber's eyes tell me she's not the one who spilled the beans.

"Linda Lannister's sister's friend, Rhianna Dern, who contracts with Gigi's Flower Shop for her medical office's fresh flower arrangements, was in the city last night and ran into her cousin, Jessica or Malinda or something or other, at a hotel. She said she saw her cousin talking with you and Maddie, who then went into the hotel bar." She stares me down. "Do you deny it?"

"Jassinda."

"What?"

"The woman's name was Jassinda. Linda's sister's friend's cousin or whatever." I rub my brows, warding off a headache. "Anyway, that's not the point. So everyone knows about this?"

"Like I said, it was all the buzz at church."

"Fuck."

"Tag," Dad warns.

"It isn't what you think. We weren't having an affair. It was a mix-up. Some stupid blind-date thing that turned out to be her. It was nothing."

"That was your *thing*?" Jaxon says incredulously.

"How can you say it was nothing?" Mom's eyebrows hit the ceiling. "Is that why you were in a hotel with her?"

"*Bar.* Hotel bar."

Bar. Room. Robe. Whatever.

Oh, and I kissed her, too. I'll bet everyone in this room, and this town, would have a heyday over that as well.

"So you didn't...?" Mom waits impatiently for my answer.

"No, Mom. I didn't. *We* didn't."

"Poor girl," she says. "I'm afraid she might have some damage control to do. You know how the rumor mill goes around here." She cocks her head in thought. "There was something strange, though. Were you wearing tennis clothes? I wasn't aware you played tennis."

Motherfucker.

I push away from the table. "I have to go."

"We haven't eaten cake," Mom cries.

"Save me a slice. I'll catch you later."

Amber chases me out to my car. "What just happened?"

"Our clothes got drenched last night so I got some in the hotel shop for both of us. Then later, I ordered some booze.

Charged it all to the room. Then I took off late and forgot to pay the tab."

She covers her laugh. "She must really hate you."

"Yeah, no shit. They weren't cheap clothes either." I slide into the driver's seat of the Range.

"Were you being truthful back there when you said nothing happened?"

"Nothing happened, Amber."

She stares me down, something she's perfected after all these years.

"Fine. We kissed. But only because she lost a bet. Listen, it's no big deal."

"Then why did you run out of there like your pants were on fire?"

I don't answer. I start the car and put it into gear.

"You couldn't care less what anyone thinks of you." Brows lifted, she studies my face. "You don't want her to hate you. Tag Calloway, you *like* her."

"Back off or I'll run you over."

She gets out of the way but laughs all the way back to the house. I drive off knowing the people I left inside will never let me hear the end of it.

Chapter Fourteen

Maddie

I pluck a variety of different-colored roses from the hydration bucket, trimming the stems as I inhale the sweet smell. Even after all these years, I still love the powdery smoothness of the petals. I tear a sheet of florist paper from the roll and place the roses on it, then grab some greenery and baby's breath. Finally, I wrap a rubber band tightly around the base of the arrangement before securing it all inside the paper. It's something I've done a thousand times. I can do it in my sleep. But it still brings me joy.

I admire the bundle with its array of colors. If I had to pick the perfect arrangement, it would be this one, with each rose having a distinct separate meaning. Love, friendship, passion, admiration, caring. I can't think of a more perfect bouquet to give someone. Yet most people opt for those of all one color.

I thought we had made enough bundles of roses to get through a typical Sunday, but today hasn't been typical at all. The after-church rush was twice what it normally is. Mrs. Stanley was here, of course, picking up the usual white orchid she takes to her husband's grave every week. Only today, she was chatting with

Beverly Goodwin and Regina Henderson over by the coolers. They kept looking at me. I thought for sure one of them would offer to set me up with a grandson or nephew. It hasn't happened for a while because I always turn them down, but some of the ladies in this town have taken it upon themselves to find me a man.

Like right now, Mrs. Gregory is here. I've never seen her near McQuaid Circle on Sundays. Claims it's too busy and littered with kids who do drugs behind the bowling alley. She lingers, eyeing me from behind the display of greeting cards.

I take the newly bundled flowers over to one of the refrigerated cases and set them down. "Anything I can help you with, Mrs. Gregory?"

She hesitates, then picks up a floral wreath I made yesterday. "I need a centerpiece for my dinner party."

"Well, that's a wreath, Mrs. Gregory." I gather it from her and put it down before picking up a basket of sola wood flowers instead. "These might work. I dyed them different colors of earth tones and clipped them short. You'll be able to sit around the table and have a conversation without having to look around them. And they'll last a very long time."

She doesn't pay them much attention. "Sounds perfect."

"Shall I ring you up then?"

"Please. How's that beautiful daughter of yours?"

"Gigi is fine. She's playing with her dolls in the back room." I wrap the basket in cellophane. "That'll be thirty-eight fifty today."

She hands me forty dollars. "Keep the change. Buy Gigi a lollipop."

"Will do. Thank you."

She heads for the door, stopping before she leaves. "Are you doing okay, sweetie?"

I cock my head. She's about the seventh customer to ask me that. Not the usual 'How are you,' platitudes when people come to the shop. Their queries have been laced with concern. "I'm great, Mrs. Gregory. I hope you have a wonderful day. Enjoy your dinner party."

She smiles and nods but still has an air of apprehension.

Blake comes in from the back. He helps with the weekend deliveries. Gigi trails behind him. I think she's enamored with him. I get it. He's got that James Dean look that makes women weak in the knees. A bit young for me, however.

Ten minutes. I'd gone ten whole minutes without thinking about last night, and then I had to go thinking about weak knees and guys who look like James Dean. Because I swear, with his hair, which most women would kill to run their fingers through, those whiskey-colored eyes you can get lost in, not to mention his propensity for cancer sticks, Tag could be a distant relative of the deceased cultural icon. And the elder Calloway brother is definitely a rebel without a cause, only with more facial hair.

I run a finger across my still-tender lips, recalling the feeling of that hair rubbing against them.

"Finished the first run," Blake says. "How many more?"

"Gigi, can you please watch the register while I help Blake?"

She pulls over the stool and climbs up on it, looking very confident in her abilities to run the place.

I laugh and walk Blake back to the cooler that holds the afternoon deliveries. "Looks like seven or eight. I'll help you load."

Blake looks at me strangely. Just like Mrs. Gregory did. I put my hands on my hips. "What is it with everyone today? Do I have spinach in my teeth or something?"

He puts the last box in the back of the SUV his daddy bought him. Apparently, Chris Montana buys cars for his kids that make mine look like a junkyard model, but he makes them get jobs to pay for gas and insurance. Still, I have to credit the elder Montana with instilling a good work ethic in his children despite the fact that they'll probably never have to actually work, what with all their millions and all.

"I wasn't going to say anything."

My tongue runs along my teeth. "Do I really have something in there?"

"It's not that. It's, um… well, so like my sister's friend Carla overheard her mom and Mrs. Flanders talking about you and, um…"

I hear the bells over the door ring out in front. "Spit it out, Blake. I don't have all day."

He shifts uncomfortably from foot to foot. "So, like, they said you and Tag Calloway were together at some hotel in the city."

My jaw goes slack. My stomach balls into knots. Anger creeps up my spine like a slithering snake.

"Mommy!" Gigi calls from the front.

"Just a minute, baby!"

"How? Where?" I ask, certain all the blood has drained from my face.

"I don't know anything else, Maddie."

Rage percolates up from within. He promised. He stood there and lied through his lying bastard teeth. I swallow back tears, knowing how gullible I am to have trusted him. "That jerkhole."

"Jerkhole?" He chuckles. "Wait, so it's true?"

"It's not. I mean, it's complicated. Please don't say anything to anyone."

"Maddie, I hate to tell you this, but I think everyone already knows."

Unlikely DATE

I sink into the cold concrete wall by the back door, wishing for it to swallow me whole.

Gigi dances through the doorway to the front of the shop. "Mommy, someone is asking for you. It's rude to keep a customer waiting. That's what you always say."

"You're right. I'm coming."

I take a few deep breaths and vow to hold my head high no matter who else decides to stare at me today. But when I walk through to the front and see none other than Tag himself, I contemplate looking for the nearest thing I can use as a weapon.

"Hi, Flower Girl. Miss me?" he says, his lips curving into a dangerous smile.

My heart pounds through my chest at the sight of him, warring with itself over love versus hate. He's standing there, tall and muscular, looking all innocent, a hand in the front pocket of his jeans, shirt rolled to his elbows. Fingers rake through his hair, an indication of nervousness or frustration. Or maybe he just likes touching his hair.

Hate. It's definitely hate I feel in this moment. I thought I fell for the guy? The guy who, the second he left the city, told everyone and their dog what happened. And probably laughed about it.

I paste a smile on for my daughter's sake. "Give me a second, please," I say through gritted teeth. "*Sir.*"

While Gigi may not get that my head is about to explode, *he* does. And the guilt is written all over his face. I'm surprised he even has the decency to look guilty. Shouldn't he be basking in the limelight over the fact that everyone in Calloway Creek thinks he deflowered the florist?

I get my earbuds out of a drawer, plug them into my phone, and pull up Gigi's playlist. "How about you listen to this for a while, baby?" I say, putting a bud in her ear. I put the other one in mine and turn it up to a level just below blaring. Enough so she won't hear what I'm about to say to Tag, but not so much that it'll damage her hearing. Then I securely fit the other earbud on her. She starts humming.

I leave her at the counter and march to the far corner of the front of the store. Tag follows.

"You've got some nerve showing up here after what you did," I say, anger thickening my voice.

"I can explain."

"Explain all you want. There's no excuse. Do you know what I've had to endure so far today? What I'm going to have to put up with for weeks or even months to come?"

His brows dip in confusion. "Months? Maddie, it was only a few—"

"A *few*? So because it was only a few, you think that makes it okay?"

"But that's why I'm here. To make it right."

"There's nothing you can do to make this right, Tag. You broke a promise. Not that I should be surprised. You've proven yourself to be exactly the douchebag everyone says you are. Did you think it wouldn't get back to me? The looks. The whispering. As if people didn't feel sorry for me enough as it is, now they think I'm Tag Calloway's newest plaything." I close my eyes and pinch the bridge of my nose.

He blows out a long breath. "Maddie, I think we're talking about two different things here. And you've got it all wrong. I didn't tell anyone about last night. Amber was the only one who knew, and I told you she wouldn't say anything."

"Well, one of you is lying."

"It was Rhianna Dern."

"Rhianna? What does she have to do with anything?"

"Apparently she's Jassinda's cousin, and they were meeting up at the hotel. She saw us together and told her sister who told someone else, and I guess it just blew up from there."

Someone comes up to the front door. I run over and flip the OPEN sign to CLOSED. "Sorry," I say to the stranger. "Family emergency." I lock the door, then lean against the glass. "Why did you look so guilty when you walked into the shop, then? I'm sure you couldn't give a fig who knows about last night."

He steps forward, his hand jutting out like he wants to touch me. But he pulls it back when I slink away. For a second, I think I see disappointment on his face. Guess he's not used to girls evading his touch. *His touch.* I refuse to let the memories of it invade my mind again.

He shoves a hand into his pocket and pulls out a wad of cash. "I came here to give you this. Last night when I left, I wasn't thinking. I'd had some drinks and totally forgot I had charged everything to the room. I swear I didn't leave you with the bill intentionally. I didn't even remember it until my mom said something to me about the tennis clothes it was rumored I'd been wearing."

I sink to the floor. "Your *mother* knows? Oh, my god, Tag. Is there anyone in Calloway Creek who doesn't?"

He sits down next to me. "By now? Probably not."

I bury my head in my hands. "What am I going to do?"

"Tell me what you want me to say, and I'll say it."

"There's nothing you could say to make this better."

"No, I mean, when people ask me. Tell me what you want me to say to them, you know, to make this go away."

I lift my head. "Like make up a story?"

"Nobody has to know about After Dark. Or our little experiment in the bar. Or the bet."

The bet. Right. Him kissing me. It all makes sense now. I stand and dust myself off. "Oh, you're good. You're turning this around and making it seem like you're doing it for me when you're really doing it for yourself because you don't want people to think we were together. It's fine. I get it. But you know what, Tag? I'm not about to concoct a story that makes *you* come off better. People already look at me like I'm a freak, I've got nothing to lose."

"You think I'm embarrassed to have been seen with you?"

"Mommy, I'm hungry," Gigi says from across the room.

"Okay, baby. We're closing early today anyway. Mr. Calloway was just leaving. We'll go across the street for ice cream. How does that sound?"

She claps with delight.

I show Tag the door with my eyes.

"But we're not done here," he says.

"Yes, we are."

We're both aware that my daughter is watching us and that she no longer has the earbuds in.

He holds out the money. "At least take this."

"I don't need your guilt money. Now please leave before you cause a scene in front of my impressionable five-year-old."

"I need flowers first," he says loudly so Gigi can hear.

"Flowers," I say flatly. "Seriously?"

He scoots around me and peruses the selections in the cooler. He reaches in and pulls out the multi-colored rose bouquet I constructed earlier. "This one," he says.

I have half a mind to tell him he can't buy it. What the heck does he want with flowers anyway? He admitted last night he'd never given them to anyone before.

He walks them to the register where Gigi is sitting. "Pretty," she says. "Mommy's favorite."

Unlikely DATE

His brow arches. "Is that so?"

I stand by the door while Gigi rings up the sale. Helping him with anything is not something I intend to do today, even if he's now a paying customer. He hands over a fifty and she looks at me, waving the money in the air. "Give him back a five-dollar bill, a one-dollar bill, two quarters, one dime, one nickel, and one penny," I say, repeating it a few times until she gets it right.

She carefully counts out his change back to him. He counts it and chuckles. "$6.66? Seriously?"

I try not to laugh, because it's so apropos. He is kind of like the devil, after all.

Because he's so hot you melt into a ball of mushy goo when he's around?

I push away the thought and reply, "You're the one who chose the $39.99 bouquet."

"Thanks," he says to Gigi, picking up the flowers.

He holds my gaze as he makes his way to the door. His tongue swipes his lower lip, reminding me what it did to me just sixteen hours ago. I turn away, determined not to let his molten stare and misplaced charm get to me. I'm sure that's exactly what he wants—me pining over him.

I unlock the door and open it, a clear invitation that I want him out of my shop and my life.

"Bye, Maddie." He takes a few steps and turns. "Oh, I almost forgot. These are for you, Flower Girl." He holds the flowers out to me until I take them. Then he turns and walks away.

I stare after him, wondering what just happened.

Belatedly, I realize his breath didn't reek of cigarettes. It smelled like spearmint.

"Mommy, he gave you flowers! That was nice."

"Sure, baby," I say, my eyes still following the man whose kiss may have wrecked me for all other kisses.

He glances back and flashes a smile full of blatant male confidence. I duck into the shop, not wanting him to think I'm staring, and gaze at the roses. He's never given anyone flowers. My foolish heart does a flip.

I contemplate putting them back in the cooler. But a small part of me is reeling. I've only gotten flowers from men two times in my life. When Cody brought them to me after I gave birth, and when Patrick came to see me in the hospital after The Incident. Despite their good intentions, neither of them were men I'd ever dreamed of wanting flowers from. Not in the way girls get them from boys like in the fairy tales Gigi loves so much. Not in the way I've dreamed about getting them from *my* prince.

I laugh to myself. Tag Calloway is no prince. And even if he were, I'm not kidding myself into thinking I'd ever get a happily ever after with him.

"Come on. Let's take them upstairs and put them in water. Then we'll go get that ice cream."

She runs ahead excitedly.

Gran comes through the rear door before I'm up the stairs. "Knock, knock!" she sings, her right arm draped with a plastic grocery bag. "I was in the neighborhood. Thought I'd stop by."

I eye her suspiciously. "Gran, it's Calloway Creek. *Everyone* is always in the neighborhood. What's up?"

She holds up the bag. "Can't a woman come around to make cookies with her great-granddaughter?"

"Gran!" Gigi yells down the stairs.

I guess ice cream will have to wait.

In my apartment, I sift through the cabinets for a vase, realizing I don't have one (the irony) and settle on a glass pitcher instead.

"Excess inventory?" Gran asks, her brow raising suspiciously.

"Something like that."

When I unwrap the flowers, something falls out of them. $412 to be exact.

Chapter Fifteen

Tag

So the whole damn town knows. Fucking church ladies and their gossiping. They're worse than a group of teenage girls at a sleepover.

And you care because…?

I walk faster. It's only a mile back to my house, but I make it in record time. Then I put my running gear on and run to the gym, pounding the pavement along the way at a punishing pace that burns my smoker's lungs. I'm not sure what I'm trying to accomplish here—*run* her out of my head? Why the hell is she so far up in it anyway?

I have to run past the flower shop to get to the gym. Actually, that's not entirely true. I could have cut through the parking lot behind the movie theater, but the pavement back there is uneven. This way is better on my feet.

I slow my pace when I pass. The CLOSED sign is still up. I stop and read the times on her sign. It says seven o'clock. It's only six thirty. Was she really so upset that she closed early? I thought that was just a ploy to get rid of me. I'm not sure why she would stay open so late on Sundays, anyway. Maybe because her competition doesn't. All part of the game she doesn't think she's playing.

"Can I help you?" I turn to see Rose Gianogi, Maddie's grandmother, holding a cup of sugar. She lifts it up. "We're making cookies. Ran out of sugar. Borrowed some from the coffee shop."

"Borrowed? You're planning to give it back after you use it?"

"You're the Calloway boy with the smart mouth. What are you doing nosing through the window of my granddaughter's flower shop? You can read, can't you? The sign says closed." She eyes me up and down. "You don't seem the type to buy flowers."

"No, ma'am, I guess I'm not." I take one last peek inside. "I'll just be on my way."

"You best do that."

I don't have to glance back to know that Rose is staring at me as I jog away. I don't blame her. If I was Maddie's grandmother, I wouldn't want a guy like me hanging around either.

At the gym, I do leg presses, lat pulldowns, and bicep curls. I move to the row trainer and try to row the strawberry-blonde out of my head. When that doesn't work, I almost kill myself on the elliptical. Literally. I go so fast that my feet get tangled up, and I have to catch myself before face-planting into the dude on the machine next to me.

I grab a towel, run it over my face, and sit on the bench outside the locker room.

"Hey, stranger," a sultry voice says from behind.

Holland McQuaid takes the seat next to me, looking more than a little sexy in her sports bra and skin-tight leggings that leave no curve undetectable. She's Addy's age. In fact, I think they might be friends despite the fact that the rest of our families hate each other.

My eyes travel the length of her body, knowing she's exactly the type of girl I go for. She's hot. Supermodel hot. And even though I've been pushing myself to the breaking point for the last hour, I still have lots of pent-up energy. I could potentially kill two birds here. It would really piss off her brothers if they found out I fucked their little sister, which in my own sick-and-twisted way is amusing. And it would also get FlowerGirl529 out of my goddamn head once and for all.

Without even muttering a word to Holland, I grab her hand and pull her into the men's locker room. I find an empty bathroom stall, pick her up, and press her into the cold, hard wall. She giggles before I shut her up with my mouth, forcefully shoving my tongue past her plump lips and down her fuckable throat.

She reaches between us and grabs my cock, then pulls away. "Something wrong?"

It's now that I realize I'm as soft as a wet noodle. I nod to the door. "Just had a killer workout. Keep going. It'll come around."

Her lips find mine again, and it dawns on me that I don't like the taste. She's all coffee and chocolate. And her hair smells like sweat.

Suddenly, I'm craving peaches.

I peel her off me. "Fuck." I turn and punch the door, happy it has some give or I'd have broken my damn hand. "Fuck, fuck, fuck!"

"Aw, it's okay. Like you said, you had a hard workout." She opens the door. "I'm here every Sunday around six. Next time, we'll try this *before* you hit the floor. Bye, Tag."

I close the lid and sit on the toilet, knowing there won't be a next time.

Holland thinks I'm pissed that I can't get a goddamn woody.

If only. The reality of the situation is so much worse. Amber was right. For the first time in my life, I'm in uncharted territory. I like a fucking girl.

Chapter Sixteen

Maddie

Gran takes the cookies out of the oven. "Ran into someone interesting outside the shop earlier."

I put a hot plate on the counter. "Oh?"

"The oldest Calloway boy."

My eyes snap to hers. "Tag? He was still here?"

"Still?" She looks suspiciously at the pitcher of flowers before plopping onto a chair. "So the rumors are true?"

The humiliation just keeps on coming. "How did you…?" I sigh. "You go to the same church as Mrs. Gregory, don't you?"

"I was hoping it was just another blown-up story. You know how this town can be."

"It *is* another blown-up story, Gran."

Gigi skips over. "Mommy, are the cookies ready?"

I take one off the baking sheet and blow on it. "Only one. We still have to go get that ice cream."

Gran stares at me, waiting for more information. I love Gran like a mother. But, like a mother, she can be overbearing at times.

I nod to Gigi and whisper, "This is not the time to talk about it."

"Oh, dear. You like him. I can see it in your eyes."

"I don't want to," I whisper. "It just happened. I know I shouldn't. I know who he is. But—"

Her hand covers mine. "The heart wants what it wants."

Her declaration surprises me. Then, she does something else that surprises me. She drops it.

Now *I'm* the one wondering what's going on.

"Come on, Gigi," Gran says. "Let's all go get that ice cream." She takes Gigi's hand, and they walk to the door. She looks back at the flowers and chuckles silently.

Crossing the street to the ice cream place, I hear my name being shouted. It's Ava. She's holding the door to the coffee shop open with her foot.

"Wait!" She says something to someone inside and then removes her apron, balls it up, and throws it in. Then she runs after me.

"Slow night?" I ask.

She leans close. "Tag Calloway?"

My lips form a thin line. "I'm quite sure Patrick told you never to speak of it."

"That was before Regan told me she saw him leaving your shop earlier. Maddie, you *have* to spill. What's really going on?"

"I've got Gigi."

"Rose?" Ava says, calling ahead to Gran. "I'll bet Gigi would love to try out the new swings behind the ice cream shop."

"Swings?" Gigi asks gleefully, her face lighting up.

Ava looks proud of herself. I shake my head. "Fine, but there really isn't much to tell."

She pulls out her phone. "I'm texting Regan. She's going to want to hear this."

"You're making way too big a deal out of it."

"We'll be the judge of that."

We go into the ice cream shop, and I order Gigi's usual, a scoop of rainbow sherbet and a scoop of mint chocolate chip. A horrible combination if you ask me, but it's her favorite. And who am I to deny her anything?

Through the back door of the ice cream parlor, we exit into a courtyard that sits behind the strip of shops. There are picnic tables, shady trees, a jungle gym, and now, swings. Regan, Ava, and I meet here for coffee on a regular basis, and I often bring Gigi here for lunch. Not that we can regularly afford the sub shop, the Chinese takeout, or even the diner, that all back up to the courtyard. We bring sack lunches; tuna fish or cheese sandwiches along with apple slices and kettle chips.

Gigi races over to the swings, leaving her ice cream with me. Gran follows, shooting me a knowing smile.

Regan comes racing around the corner, clearly out of breath. "Did I miss anything?"

"Have you guys been stalking me all day just waiting to pounce?"

"Hurry," Ava says. "Before Gigi gets bored with the swings."

"I don't know what you want me to say. I'm sure Patrick gave you all the details."

"That was before I saw Tag go into your shop," Regan says. "And five minutes later, he came out with an armful of roses that he turned and gave to *you*."

Ava squeals and bounces in her seat.

"Seriously?" I shoot her a look. "Aren't you the president of the 'I Hate Tag Club'?"

"Co-president," she says, glancing at Regan. "But Maddie, the man gave you flowers. Turd or not, that has to mean something."

"You swear you didn't sleep with him?" Regan asks.

I cross my fingers over my heart.

She throws up her arms. "Of course. It makes total sense. Every other woman in this town, me included, gave it up quickly. He never had to work for it, which is why I personally figured I'd have to sleep with him to have any kind of chance. I thought he could get anyone he wanted, and if I didn't sleep with the man, he'd move to the next girl in line. We all stupidly thought we would be the one to break his cycle. That he'd find something in us he couldn't resist. And you've found it, Maddie. The man can't stand the fact that you didn't sleep with him."

"Were you really doing shots in your hotel room wearing robes?" Ava asks.

"Yes, but—"

"And he watched in the hotel bar as you flirted with other guys?"

"I suppose. However—"

"And he made a bet with you so you'd have to kiss him?"

The kiss. I hadn't thought about it since… Fine, who am I kidding? I never stopped thinking about it.

Regan points to my face. "This look says it all, my friend. You've got it, and you've got it bad."

I clear my head and my throat. "What exactly do I have?"

"Tag fever."

"Shut up."

"It's okay, Maddie," Ava says. "We've all had it at one time or another. I mean, I know I'm married and all, but a girl can look. Grumpzilla or not, he's some hellacious eye candy."

Regan holds up a hand. "Wait one goddamn minute. Kimberly Vasquez."

I look around the courtyard for Kimberly, a girl who went to school with Regan and Ava but moved away a few years ago.

"Kimberly didn't sleep with Tag," she says. "Don't you remember what a big deal she made about it? She devised a plan and everything. Said she was going to be the one to land him because she was going to do what no other woman had—resist him."

"Oh, right," Ava says. "She went to the gym for a month, lost fifteen pounds, got highlights, a fake tan, and lip injections. Even watched a bunch of sports and took *notes*."

"Her friend Krista Newman said Kimberly was devastated when he never called her after the night they went out. Said she only kissed him but wouldn't go any further. Claimed she wasn't *that* kind of girl. In fact, Krista said she was sure Tag's rejection had something to do with her leaving town."

I roll my eyes and take a bite of Gigi's melting ice cream, noting that the flavors do work surprisingly well together. "So this club you're in. Do you take notes and record meeting minutes and stuff? How do you guys know so much about him?"

"How do you *not*?" Ava asks. "Is there anything better to do in this sleepy town than keep tabs on all the hot men in it?"

"Charlotte," Regan blurts out.

"Oh, my god, yes," Ava says.

"Who?"

"Maddie, you really must keep up," Regan says. "Charlotte Brown, from CCU. She teaches physics or some brainy shit like that."

"You mean Charlie."

Ava laughs. "That poor woman's parents really did play a cruel joke on her. Anyway, the point is, she didn't sleep with him either. You know Sophie, Amber and Quinn's nanny? She's friends with Charlie. She's in my spin class. She said Charlie had a yeast infection when she went out with Tag. She wasn't going to tell him that, so she played hard to get. Just like you did. Just like Kimberly did. Yet he never called."

"I didn't play hard to get, Ava. I just didn't want to sleep with him."

"I'm calling bullshit," Regan says. "You went on an After Dark date, which in itself implies sex will be had. And it turned out to be Tag Calloway, which I get had to be a shock at first, but then you ate pizza and got rained on and toyed with unsuspecting men and got drunk and shared kisses. And you're telling me during all that time, you didn't want to do the deed?"

More than anything I've ever wanted in life. "No."

Ava steals a bite of Gigi's ice cream and spits it on the ground. "What is that shit?"

I smirk. Serves her right giving me the third degree.

"She didn't want him to see her naked," Regan says to Ava. She turns to me. "I'm right, aren't I? A random stranger was who you were prepared for, not the Adonis of Calloway Creek."

Gigi comes over. "Mommy, it's all melty."

I pull her up onto the bench next to me. "It'll still taste the same."

Her bottom lip juts out. "No, it won't."

I take a bite to show her. I am, after all, developing a taste for her unusual concoction. "See?" I rub my tummy. "Yummy."

She doesn't eat it. Yet my sweet girl won't ask for more. Even at five years old, she knows what a precious commodity money is.

Unlikely DATE

Especially ours. "I'm gonna go swing some more. Love you, Mommy," she says and morosely shuffles away.

"God, your kid is amazing," Ava says. "Every other kid I know would have thrown a tantrum." She stiffens. "Holy shit, Maddie, you have a kid."

Regan and I are confused by her sudden revelation. "You okay, Ava?" Regan asks. "She has had the same kid for five years now."

"I know that. And *Tag* knows that. But everyone knows Tag has a serious aversion toward children."

The two of them look at each other and then me. "What?"

"Tag hates kids, yet he showed up at your shop *and* bought you flowers."

"You have it all wrong. He was paying me back for stuff he charged to the room. He tucked the money into the flowers."

Ava stares me down. "There's a million other ways he could have paid you back. Mailed it. Had it couriered over. Stuck it through your mail slot. Hell, for that matter, why didn't he just pay it at the hotel? Face it, girl, he used it as an excuse to see you. The guy must want you bad."

I tug on my right sleeve. "Impossible."

Regan grabs my arm forcibly. She's frozen in place. I follow her gaze across the courtyard and into the parking lot behind the movie theater.

Tag stops running when he sees the three of us staring. I want to turn away but can't. He's even sexier in his running shorts than he was in the tennis shorts. And his shirt is drenched with sweat, reminding me of how he looked in his dress shirt last night after we got caught in the rain. Suddenly, every moment we made eye contact comes rushing back to me. Every feeling of the butterflies dancing in my stomach. Every touch we shared flashes through my head like a picture book ingrained in my memory.

He returns my stare and my heart thunders. For a second, I think he's going to come over. He hesitates as if unsure. And then the moment ends, and he runs off.

"Oh. My. Gawd," Regan gushes.

"Alert the fucking press," Ava says. "There's an imposter in town, and he's taken over the body of Tag Calloway."

Chapter Seventeen

Tag

The warm water of the shower runs over my shoulders as I stand here, dick in hand, fantasizing about her like I'm an adolescent boy in a girls' locker room.

Those eyes. Even fifty feet away, they burned into me. She didn't seem pissed to see me like she had earlier at her shop. She seemed surprised, almost pleased in some way.

And as the product of my fantasy swirls down the drain, it dawns on me that she's the first woman I've ever whacked off to. Sure, I tan the meat all the time. But I think about pussies and tits and tight little asses. Never faces.

Why her face?

Why *her*?

Because she's the only one you can't have.

Based on the look she gave me in the courtyard, I could probably have her if I tried hard enough. But could and should are two very different things. I shouldn't have Maddie Foster. Just ask Rose Gianogi. Hell, ask anyone.

I text Jaxon.

Me: Meet me for a drink at Donovan's?

Jaxon: Now? It's only eight o'clock. Since when do you go drinking so early?

Me: Since today. Are you going to meet me or what?

Jaxon: I can be there in thirty minutes.

I arrive in twenty. The pub is just around the corner from my neighborhood. It sits at the mouth of the street leading up to McQuaid Circle. Or as I call it, The Circle. Because anything with the name McQuaid in it makes me vomit in my mouth just a little.

Which is why my stomach turns when I spot Hawk McQuaid in the corner, playing darts and having a drink. Ignoring his lethal stare, I order some shots and am well on my way to ensuring tomorrow's hangover by the time my brother arrives.

Jaxon eyes the empties on the table. "I thought you reserved Sunday drinking for football season. It's June, dude."

Lissa brings me another, along with Jaxon's usual beer. Lissa's a few years younger than Jaxon. I guess you could say she's a 'nice' girl. Volunteers building houses for the homeless. Goes to church every Sunday. And she's had her eye on Jaxon since middle school. Worships him is more like it. In fact, the day of Jaxon's wedding, she hosted a wake. It was the death of her hope to ever be with him. By the look on her face, that hope has since been renewed with his impending single status.

"Thanks, hon," I say.

She turns her nose up at me and leaves.

"They have names, you know," Jaxon says. "All those women you call hon and sweetie."

"Yeah, but who can remember them all? They just blend together. And does it really matter anyway?"

"It matters to them, Tag."

"You tap that yet?"

"Lissa?"

"No—Charles Hutton, the old geezer passed out in the corner. Yes, Lissa."

"I told you. I'm sort of seeing someone."

"She hotter than Lissa?"

"Must everything come down to how attractive a woman is for you?"

"I'm just saying, your rebound girl needs to be hot."

"Calista is not my rebound girl."

"So you're saying it's serious? As in taking more vows? What's it been, two years? Are you going to be one of those old men with seven ex-wives? Dude, not wise on a teacher's salary."

"Technically, I'm still not divorced yet. I've been waiting on the papers to come through. With Nicky in Oklahoma and me here, it's been hard to nail things down." He looks pensive as he sips his beer. "I'll never get married again."

"Hallelujah to that, brother." I pull out my pack of smokes. "I'm just going to go out back for a second."

"Dude, you made me come out. Now I have to sit here and wait while you suck on a cancer stick?"

"I'll be quick."

On my way out, I pass Hawk. We give each other our normal death stare. But tonight, I'm especially irritable, so I grab one of his onion rings as I walk by.

"What the fuck, Calloway?" he says.

I take a bite, then toss it back into the basket. "Tastes like shit with your stench all over it."

Expletives follow me out the door.

Back in the booth after my smoke, something whizzes past my ear and hits the wall behind me. A dart. I pull it out, a half inch of plaster falling to the booth, and I stand defensively.

Hawk saunters over. "Got away from me." He holds out his hand. "Do you mind?"

I have the urge to stab his hand with it. Instead, I throw the dart forcefully to the floor, missing his toe by centimeters. "Shouldn't you be selling some poor unsuspecting sap the used car you were conceived in?"

He laughs off my insult. "You think I *sell* the cars? No, man, you got it all wrong. I sit back in my cushy corner office counting my millions. In fact, I may not even go to work tomorrow. Might play a round of golf instead. But you working folk wouldn't know about that, having to earn a living wage and all."

"First of all, you won't be playing golf in Cal Creek. I know for a fact you've been banned from the country club. And second, at least I take pride in my work, having built my business from the ground up."

"You mean the business that's got you in debt up to your eyeballs?"

"At least it's mine, and I don't just pretend to work in some fancy office paid for by my daddy."

"Says the guy whose pathetic father can't even afford the tuition for your sister's education," he spits.

I'm about to dick-punch him when we're interrupted by my uncle.

"Is there a problem here?" Jonah asks, his eyes pinballing between us.

Jonah, in addition to being my uncle, is Hawk's stepfather. Hawk hates him simply because he's a Calloway, but tolerates him because he's the father of Hawk's half-sister, Dani. And by tolerates, I mean he doesn't try to pierce his brain with darts when he sees him, but I'm quite sure there wouldn't be any tears shed if someone else did.

Hawk's parents divorced when he was a kid, then his mom married my uncle, whose wife passed some time ago. She went from being a McQuaid to a Calloway. It was a huge scandal that I'm sure had ancestors from both sides turning in their graves.

I chuckle. Then I goad him. Because, well, the dart. "Oh, look, it's your daddy."

"Fuck off," Hawk says.

"Listen, you two," Jonah says. "People are here to have a good time, not watch you go round and round again. Give it a rest, why don't you?"

He puts a hand on Hawk's shoulder, which Hawk promptly shrugs off. "We're not one of your assignments," he says. "Go keep the peace somewhere else."

Jonah laughs. "You say that like I'm a cop. I own a security business, son. Big difference."

"You know what else is a big difference?" Hawk says. "The fact that I'm not your damn son. I have a father, Jonah. You can drop the act and quit pretending like you need to be one to me."

"I'm not pretending, Hawk. You and your brothers and Holland are very important to me."

"Go tell it to someone who cares."

Hawk's friend shouts for him to return to their game. Before he leaves, he pulls the dart from the floorboard and stabs it on the table between Jaxon and me.

"You should have stabbed him in the heart with the dart," Jaxon says, watching Hawk walk away. "I'd love nothing more than to watch a McQuaid die a slow death by bar games."

I laugh. "You think I'd have gotten off on self-defense? He did practically spear my head with it."

"Quit fanning the flames," Jonah says. "One of these days, you'll all have to bury the hatchet. Heather and I were hoping Dani would be the catalyst to that, but it seems the lot of you are more stubborn than your great-grandfathers."

"The question is, why aren't you, Jonah?" Jaxon asks.

He smiles. "Got a woman I love, a business I'm passionate about, and a gaggle of healthy kids. What's there to be bitter about? The trouble with you kids is that you see this whole McQuaid-Calloway war as a game. But you know what normally happens during wars? Both sides suffer mass casualties. Now excuse me while I go finish my drink with the most beautiful woman in the world."

Jaxon and I follow him with our eyes as he returns to his table and slips in the booth next to Heather. They clasp hands on the tabletop.

I look across the table at my brother and then at the dart standing up between us. I raise my glass. "To winning the goddamn war," I say.

"I'll fucking drink to that."

I wave my empty glass at Lissa, then make a circle in the air with my finger, letting her know we want another round. Then I whistle at her and hold up two fingers. I have the feeling she wants to hold up a finger in response, but she doesn't. Because she's nice.

"Hey, Liss," Jaxon calls out to her. "Just one for me, please." She smiles back at him. "I do have to be up at seven in the morning to run summer football workouts, Tag. I'm not going to sit here and get wasted with you. Want to cut the shit and tell me why we're really here?"

I wait for my shots, knowing I need more alcohol in me if I'm going to get real with him. Lissa puts two on the table, along with one beer for Jaxon, even though he's barely nursing the one he's already got.

I throw one back. "There's something wrong with me."

His face turns stoic. "Are you sick?"

"No, no. Nothing like that," I say quickly, remembering the day we were told about Chaz. "I'm fine. Well, I'm not fine. I'm totally fucked."

"What is it?"

"I was at the gym about to get naked with Holland when she pointed out that my dick was as limp as a rag doll even though her hand was all over it."

"Holland?" His eyes flicker over to Hawk. "You fucked his sister?"

"No, I didn't. I couldn't. That's the point, Jax. I couldn't get a woody to save my goddamn life."

He doesn't even try holding in his laughter. "Well, you are approaching thirty. Guess the good days are gone, brother."

"Fuck off with the age jokes. You're like ten seconds behind me. I'm being serious here."

He leans back in the booth, eyes narrowing. "Are you trying to tell me this has *never* happened to you?"

I shake my head.

"No way."

More head shaking.

"Not even whiskey dick? Stage-fright dick? Recently-slapped-the-monkey dick?"

He stares at me in awe. Part of me feels a hundred feet tall. My cock's ability to stand up to any occasion has always been one of my best qualities.

Until now.

"Maybe I *am* sick."

"You're not sick. Could be it was the girl. I mean, Holland McQuaid? Your subconscious probably knew that Hawk, Hunter, and Hudson would come after you, tie you to a fucking tree, tar and feather you, and slice off pieces of your dick to display as trophies on their mantles."

"Yeah. That must be it."

His head cocks sideways as he studies me. "This doesn't have anything to do with the rumors Mom told us about, does it?"

"That's ridiculous."

Or entirely fucking true.

"You really had a blind date who turned out to be Maddie Foster?"

I dig my teeth into my lower lip, searching for something to say.

"Oh, shit, brother. You have a thing for her."

"A *thing*?"

"Yeah, you know, a boner. You want to bone the flower shop owner. Therefore, you couldn't close the deal with Holland—which, I have to say is a blessing in disguise because I've already buried one brother."

"Maybe that's all this is, though. She wouldn't sleep with me. My dick is not happy about it and wants revenge."

"And that explains why you couldn't have sex with Holland?"

I shrug.

He laughs and drinks his beer, suddenly interested in staying for another. "Welcome to the world of grown-ups, Tag."

"What's that supposed to mean?"

"Feelings. Responsibilities. Relationships."

"I don't do relationships."

"You might want to tell that to your dick."

"For the sake of argument, let's say I did have a *thing*. What would that feel like exactly?"

"Let's see. If I remember correctly: fast heartbeat, sweaty palms, feeling like an idiot, feeling inadequate, need I go on?"

"If you remember? That's not what you feel with Calista?"

"It's what I'm trying to feel with her."

"Jesus. You're not still pining for that bitch of an ex-wife who cheated on you?"

"Not my ex yet," he says, staring into his beer. "Hey, we're analyzing you here, not me."

"She hasn't been with anyone since she got hurt in the fire."

"I've heard that."

"You did? How come *I* didn't know?"

"Because you don't give a shit about anyone but yourself, Tag. Especially when it comes to women. Why is that?"

"*You're* asking me that? The guy who got eaten alive and spit out by one."

He grits his teeth. "Not. About. Me."

"I'm tired of talking about this. I'm going to disprove your theory." I pull out my phone and page through the endless names of women in my contacts, trying to remember which ones would ride me until I saw stars.

"You mean you're going to try to fuck her out of your head. Yeah, you go ahead and do that. Just enjoy the feeling you'll have when you're lying there alone the next morning and you realize what a piece of shit you are, because instead of going after the girl you really wanted, you settled for a cheap substitute." He throws a ten on the table. "Then again, I'm not sure my big brother has ever felt guilty about a goddamn thing in his life."

He says goodbye to Jonah and Heather, then looks back at me before walking out the door. It's the first time I've ever seen this particular emotion cross Jaxon's face. Disappointment.

Then I realize something else. That, just like Amber, my younger brother could be right.

I stumble home, catching myself on something as I trip through my front door. And I find myself on the ground, draped in my bomber jacket. The jacket that still smells like peaches.

I hold it to my face and inhale.

Chapter Eighteen

Maddie

"Read another one, Mommy."

I put the book in my lap. "It's late. Mommy's tired."

It's been a long day. The longest one I can remember. And the most emotionally taxing since The Incident.

"Please, Mommy? Pretty please?"

My beautiful little girl could sell ice to an Eskimo. I pick up another book and open it to page one. "Once upon a time, there lived a young prince in a beautiful castle. Although he had everything his heart desired, the prince was spoiled and selfish."

"But he wasn't," she says. "He became good and kind, and he loved her. And he was only ugly on the outside until she loved him too. Right, Mommy?"

"Are you going to tell the story, or do you want me to read it?"

She points to the page and shuts up, snuggling next to me.

Gigi falls asleep before I finish. I'm not sure why I lie next to her and page through the rest of the book. Princes. Princesses. Happily ever afters. They aren't real. It's all a bunch of made-up stuff to promote commercialism. Greeting cards. Candy makers. Even my own flower shop. We all exist for the sole purpose of the fantasy that is being sold to every poor shmuck who reads these books.

And I'm indoctrinating my own daughter into this world. She actually thinks these stories are real. Her two favorites: *Beauty and the Beast* and *Shrek*.

It occurs to me that both are tales of having to look beyond one's appearance. My little optimist may be smarter than I give her credit for.

I stare at the last page of the book, tracing my fingers across the now-handsome prince as he and Belle dance at the ball. Then I run my thumb across the scar up my arm. That's the difference—in the end, Beast became handsome. Would Belle have stayed with him if he hadn't? She fell in love with the beast, but after that new-love feeling wore off, and she was left with him in all his hairy glory, would she have stayed? I mean just how bright can inner beauty shine?

The doorbell rings; the residence one, not the one for the shop. It's after nine. Everyone I know knows that's past Gigi's bedtime. I tuck a blanket around her and head for the stairs. At the bottom of the stairs are two doors. One leads to the shop, and the other to the back alley. That's where the doorbell is. I peek through the hole and then back away quickly, pressing myself against the wall as if the man on the other side can see me.

Nervous flutters dance inside me. It's Tag.

I glance down at my clothes—an old T-shirt and a pair of pajama shorts. I tug at the hem on the arm, knowing it won't even begin to cover my scars.

I crack the door. "What are you doing here?"

"Honestly? I have no idea."

"Are you having second thoughts about the money? You want it back?"

"The money is yours, Flower Girl."

Something about the way he calls me that… It's sexy. Intimate. And not a common endearment like babe, honey, or sweetheart. I know it was my After Dark name, but still, when he says it, it feels like it's a name he uses only for me.

I'm glad it's dark out; otherwise, he'd see me staring at his lips. For more than twenty-four hours, I've been on a roller coaster. And it's going up now—the chains underneath have taken hold, and it's clinking and clunking its way higher as my heart pounds faster and louder. I've been on this ride since he walked into the restaurant yesterday evening. I hated him, then I endured him, then I worshiped him, then this morning, I hated him again. Then he had to go and do the whole apology thing and the flower thing and the money thing. And now…

I'm being silly. Why would Tag Calloway use an endearment if it wasn't purely derogatory?

Why would Tag Calloway ring your bell after hours?

"What do you want, Tag?"

"Can I come in?"

So many answers to that question scroll though my head. *Yes! Yes! Yes!* is the one that's flashing like a giant illuminated billboard.

"Gigi is sleeping."

"Then we'll be quiet." His arms cross, and muscles bunch against his tight shirt.

I can hardly breathe. Because now I'm thinking of all the things we can do quietly.

"I suppose I could make coffee." I open the door in a way that keeps my arm covered. "Go on up."

At the top of the stairs, I run to the kitchen and quickly put on a lightweight cardigan.

"You don't need to do that," he says, eyeing my arm. "I've seen it before."

"Habit," I say, but I keep it on. I busy myself making coffee, wondering why he's standing in my living room.

When I turn, he's taking in the shabby surroundings. My outdated appliances, discolored carpet, Gran's afghan on the couch, which is thankfully covering the punch stain. The exposed plumbing from when I had a leak fixed but couldn't afford the drywall repairs.

I refuse to be embarrassed. I am, after all, a single mother trying to make ends meet. "Not what you were expecting?"

"I wasn't expecting anything."

"Well, good. Because I happen to like it here."

"I can see why. It's a great space. It has good bones. I'll bet with a little renovation this place could be very urban chic."

"I didn't realize you were in the home-reno business."

"I'm not. Not officially, anyway. I did renovate my house almost single-handedly, though. You know, I have a ton of leftover materials in my shed. Maybe you could use them."

"Tag, I don't even own a toolbox. I keep a hammer and a wrench in a drawer in the kitchen. What would I do with construction materials? Listen, I'm pretty sure you didn't come here to talk about my apartment."

He spins and tumbles toward me, catching himself on the end of the couch.

"Are you drunk?"

"It's a distinct possibility."

Unlikely DATE

I go back to the kitchen counter and pour him a cup of coffee. He sits at the table, and I put it in front of him, not bothering to ask if he wants anything in it.

"Thanks." He blows on it and takes a sip. "I was thinking. The whole town thinks we're sleeping together, so we might as well be."

My jaw slackens and a succession of exasperated huffs exit my lungs. I get that I just read two fairy tales, and maybe I had unrealistic expectations of him transforming into some sort of prince after that look in the courtyard, but never did I think he'd come here and proposition me simply because people think we had a clandestine hookup last night.

I reach into my cabinet and get a Styrofoam cup and pour his coffee into it. "This is now coffee to go." I hand it to him, then go to the door at the top of the stairs and hold it open.

He doesn't move. He takes a sip from his cup, very much looking like the cocky jerk that he is. "I'm drunk. Might fall down the stairs. Then I'd have to sue you, and all you have is the shop. And since I don't know shit about flowers, you can see it only makes sense that I stay put until I can walk without swerving."

Although he's being an ass, he may have a point. He almost fell over his own feet. Even if I helped him down the stairs, there's no way I could keep him from falling if he started to take a tumble. I shut the door and go lean against the counter. "When this pot of coffee is gone, so are you."

"Fair enough." He inhales sharply. "What's that heavenly smell?"

"Cookies. Gran and Gigi made them earlier."

He stares at me, waiting.

I roll my eyes and then pick one off the top. "Fine, here," I say, walking it over to him.

He captures my wrist and pulls me down onto him. "I'd rather eat you."

At this point, I'm not sure if I should hit him or straddle him. I stuff the cookie into his mouth and hoist myself off his lap.

"You're no fun," he says, spitting cookie crumbs with the last word.

"I'm not sleeping with you just because everyone in Calloway Creek thinks we're doing it."

"That's not the reason."

"What is?"

"Curiosity."

"You really are a prick. This is all a game to you. I don't know why I ever thought anything different. You want to see me naked. Judge for yourself how freakish the girl with the burns is."

"News flash, Flower Girl. I've already seen your scars." He nods to my torso.

I pull my cardigan tightly around my middle.

"That's right. You passed out at the hotel last night."

"You sicko," I say, louder than I meant to. "You looked under my robe?"

"Easy there, slugger. It fell open. When I came out of the bathroom, you were passed out on the bed and I saw you."

My skin crawls as I think of him looking at me when I was so vulnerable. How much did he see? What did he think? How disgusted was he? I point to the door. "Get out."

"I haven't even had my second cup."

"Fall down the stairs for all I care. Sue me. You won't get much, I promise you. Just get out."

He finishes his coffee and stands, walking slowly to the door. Then suddenly, he spins, pulls me into his arms, and looks down at me.

I try to push him away. Or I tell myself I am. I'm not. I'm doing the opposite of pushing him away. Apparently, because I have some magical uncanny ability to attract a man who is completely and horribly wrong for me and who will undoubtedly trample all over my internal organs on his way to his next sacrificial meal.

His heated stare is unwavering, and his eyes snare mine, holding them against their will. My heart is at war, excitement and fear battling to the death while my brain tries to decide which side it's on. Blood pumps through me, echoing in my ears as his mouth inches closer to mine. I curse myself when my tongue swipes my lower lip, an invitation I didn't mean to extend. Yet I can't pull away.

His hand cups the back of my neck, a familiar touch that parts of my body remember from last night. The feeling of his warm breath, although terrifying, is somehow inviting.

I watch his Adam's apple bob when he swallows, his eyes glued to my lips, and his breath becoming as unsteady as my beating heart. His other hand clasps the side of my face, his pinky caressing the hollow of my neck. Time stops. The flutters inside me intensify. I'm willing myself to pull away. I'm daring myself not to.

Finally, a rush of helplessness washes over me, and my lips part for him. His hungry mouth comes in for the kill, claiming mine in a forbidden kiss so intense my knees give way. He holds me up, pulls me against him, and deepens the kiss. All my senses unfurl at the taste of him. Any thoughts in my head are silenced, because all I want is more. Of this. Of him.

Simultaneous shivers of pleasure and panic shoot through me as blood rushes to every part of my body. I fist the front of his shirt as our mouths mold together and our tongues play symphonies. My body can't get enough. It aches for more. I want to breathe him. Eat him. Drink him. I'm drowning in him, and I don't even want to come up for air.

He pushes me against the wall, steadies me, then pulls away. He takes a step back. "Thanks. I'm sober now."

Wait. What?

I straighten my shirt in a failed attempt not to seem as completely wrecked as I truly am. "You shouldn't have kissed me without permission."

"You think you didn't give me permission? Go look at yourself in the mirror, Flower Girl. Your cheeks are flushed, your eyes are lidded. And I'm willing to bet your heart is racing. I'll tell you a secret." He touches his chest. "So's mine."

He starts down the stairs. I walk to the top step. "You didn't taste like cigarettes."

Shoving a hand into his pocket, he comes out with a pack of gum, tossing it up in the air before catching it.

Gum. He bought gum.

For me?

"See you tomorrow, Flower Girl." He's down the steps before I can say another word.

I shuffle over to the couch and plop down, pulling a pillow onto my lap and wondering what just happened. He kissed me. Again. I didn't lose a bet. He didn't try for more. He just kissed me.

I touch my lips, still plump and tingling, and gaze at the door, only being sure of one thing in my life, that my heart is a ticking time bomb.

Chapter Nineteen

Tag

I've never been less helpful at work than I have been today. Sitting through meetings and conference calls, all I can think about is *her*. I even called a client by the wrong name, something that never happens. I'm always right on point. Meticulous. The best sports marketer in the tri-state area. (Based on a poll of myself.)

Why in the hell has Maddie Foster taken up residence in my head?

My assistant places a stack of letters on the corner of my desk. "Your mail, Mr. Calloway."

"Thanks, Nora."

She hesitates in the doorway before leaving.

"Is there something else?"

"No. It's just… you seem different today. You're never in a good mood. Did a McQuaid die or go to jail or something?"

I laugh—also something I never do at work—and get a second strange look from her.

"Not that I'm aware of. And Nora, I may be taking off a little early today."

Her eyebrows shoot up, but she knows better than to question me. "Is there anything you need me to do? Reschedule your five o'clock maybe?"

"I already emailed John Dyson. Put him on my calendar for Wednesday at four, please."

"*You* emailed him?"

"Is that a problem?"

"Of course not. I'll get it on your schedule right away."

She leaves, but not without giving me another look.

~ ~ ~

I back the Range up to my shed and load what I think I'll need. I'm missing a few items, so I drive to the hardware store, pick up some materials, and am pulling up behind Gigi's Flower Shop right around the time she'll be closing up for the day.

As if on cue, the back door opens, and Maddie comes through carrying two large trash bags. She stops when she spots me. I can't be sure, but I believe I see her chest heave before she speaks. "What are you doing here?"

I hop out and take the bags from her. "Helping you." I walk them to the garbage bin and toss them in.

She looks confused. "You came here to take my trash out?"

I open the back of my SUV. "I came here to fix the hole in your wall."

"Why?"

"Because nobody should have to live with a hole in their wall, and because in the winter, it will let in cold air. And like I told you yesterday, I have extra materials."

Mostly.

"And *you're* going to fix it," she says. "*You.* The sports guy."

"I remodeled my house." I pull a piece of Sheetrock out of the back. "Or maybe you forgot because your brain went to mush after that kiss."

Her face turns an adorable shade of pink that has me stirring below the belt.

"I... I just don't get why you would want to do this."

"Maddie, you could call a handyman and pay him five hundred dollars, or you could let me do it for free."

"Free?" Her suspicious eyes question me. "In my experience, nothing is free."

"You think I have ulterior motives?"

"Yes."

"You think I want to sleep with you."

"Or something."

If she only knew how I fantasized about all the *or somethings* last night.

"My desire to sleep with you and my wanting to fix your wall are mutually exclusive."

"So you go around fixing holes in walls often? I hear Mrs. Chen needs some work done on a leak in her ceiling. Are you going across the street to help her next?"

"Okay, you got me there. I suppose I am helping you because I want to sleep with you, but what I meant is that one does not have to lead to the other. And you'll owe me nothing."

"Nothing?"

I step closer and stroke her earlobe. "Are you hard of hearing, Flower Girl? That's what I said. Nothing. No matter how much I want to peel you out of those clothes, push you against the wall, put my tongue in every crevice of your body, and make you shout my name, I promise to be a complete gentleman."

I get my tools, sling my bag of supplies over my shoulder, and pick up the piece of drywall. Then me and my stiff cock walk through her back door.

I go limp when Maddie's little girl runs over.

Why do I keep forgetting about the horrid little creature?

"Hi, Mr. Smokey the Bear."

Maddie comes in behind me. I turn to her. "Why did your kid just call me that?"

"She saw you light up yesterday when you left the shop."

"You're big, like a bear," her daughter says. "And you did a no-no. Mommy says smoking is bad. How come you do bad things?"

If she only knew.

"Yes, how come?" Maddie says.

"That's a loaded question I'm not sure I want to answer without a lawyer present."

She laughs. "Gigi, Mr. Calloway is here to fix the hole in the wall."

Her hazel eyes, that are a smaller version of her mother's, peer up at me. And it's now that I realize she's a carbon copy of Maddie. Right down to her reddish-blonde hair and light smattering of freckles across her nose and cheeks. "Can I help?" she asks excitedly.

I don't do kids. I've never even talked to one. When Brody, one of my reps, brings his brat to the office—which is almost never because, and I repeat, *I hate kids*—I make Nora speak to him on my behalf.

I look to Maddie. She takes her daughter's hand. "Come on, let's let Smokey work. You can help me make dinner."

"Macaroni and cheese?" she asks.

Maddie looks embarrassed. "Sure, baby."

Baby. How come when she says that word, my dick thinks she's talking to him?

They bound upstairs ahead of me, and I follow. I quickly get to work, spreading out my supplies before moving the couch away from the hole. I see a roach trap and use my shoe to push it back under the couch, knowing Maddie would be ashamed by it.

She thinks I'm rich. A lot of people do. They assume because I live in my own house, own a business, and drive a Range Rover that I must be rolling in dough. What most of them don't know, with the exception of Hawk McQuaid apparently, is that I'm in debt up to my eyeballs. I put everything I have into Calloway Sports Marketing, and every dime I make goes back into the business.

Another thing she doesn't know is that I grew up in a place not much nicer than this apartment. My dad is a plumber. And although he's the best one in town, supporting a wife and five kids was never easy. It wasn't until most of us had gotten through college and moved out that they were able to enjoy some extra money. Addy still lives with them while finishing her degree at Calloway Creek University, but with all the scholarships she receives because of her disability, she's not a burden.

I use a Sheetrock knife to carve around the hole and make it a perfect square, then I cut a piece of drywall to fit. When I go to match it up, the little girl runs over. "Wait!"

She runs into the back and comes out with an armload of things.

"Put these in."

I look at Maddie for help deciphering the child's demand.

"Like in the book?" Maddie says to Gigi.

"Yes!" Gigi squeals.

"We read a book the other day about kids who put some of their possessions in a time capsule and sealed it behind a wall." She turns to Gigi. "Let's see what you have."

Gigi holds out a plastic doll, a drawing, and a piece of bubble gum.

"Are you sure, baby? Once you put them in there, we won't be able to get them back."

"But maybe some other little girl who lives here a thousand years from now will find them and play with them. Maybe she won't have toys. She'll want a Barbie. And she'll know it was me because this picture is of me and you. And I know she'll love my favorite gum. This one blows bubbles. But maybe she'll be hungry. Should we put food in there?"

Maddie snickers. "No, we shouldn't put food in there. I'm sure she won't be hungry." She goes to the kitchen and comes back with a piece of paper, a pen, and a plastic bag. "Why don't you write a note to her, and then we'll seal everything in this bag."

I watch impatiently as Maddie coaches her daughter to write a few words.

"Sorry," she says, sensing my impatience. "She's just learning how to write."

"In school?"

"She doesn't go to school. Technically, she'll start kindergarten in August, but I'm going to homeschool her."

"She's never been to school? Aren't kids supposed to go to nursery school or something?"

"It's called preschool. And no, she doesn't go. I teach her myself."

"Tori and Kara go to school," Gigi says.

"Her friends from McQuaid Circle," Maddie tells me, as if I'd be the least bit interested. "We have playdates sometimes."

"Look, Mommy, I wrote my name. Is it good?"

"It's very good."

"Did *you* go to school?" miniature-Maddie asks.

I realize Gigi is looking at me. "Who, me? Yeah. Double majored in marketing and sports management."

Gigi stares blankly.

"She's five," Maddie says. "A simple yes will do."

"Okay, whatever. Yes, I went to school."

"I wish I could go," the girl says sadly. "Tori got new clothes. She has a pretty yellow dress she's going to wear to meet her teacher. I want to wear a pretty yellow dress. If I go, I could be a double manager."

"Why doesn't she go?" I ask Maddie, because as it turns out, I might be a little interested. "There's a school right around the corner."

"Schools aren't safe," she whispers to me. She opens the ziplock bag for Gigi. "Put everything in here and we'll put it behind the wall."

Gigi kisses her Barbie, folds her note, drops in the gum, and carefully places her picture in the bag. She hands it to me, and I stuff it through the hole. I hear it drop down the other side and wonder if the kid will get mad that I wasn't more careful. But she's happily skipping away.

"Anything else you want to put in there before I seal it up?" I ask Maddie. "Diary? Family photo? Letter to your future self?"

"I'm good. Thanks."

I line up the drywall and grab a handful of screws, dropping a few. Gigi runs over and gathers them up. She plops down next to me. "I can be your helper. Mommy says I'm a good assistant. Don't you, Mommy?"

"You're a great helper, baby."

I roll my eyes at the wall. "Fine. Hand me a screw."

She holds one out in her tiny palm. I take it. She hands me another. When I'm done securing the piece, she asks, "What now?"

"Now I need the compound," I tell her. She gets a blank look on her face. "The mud?"

"Five, Tag, not fifteen," Maddie calls from the stove.

"You put mud on the walls? Yuck," Gigi says.

"It's not like mud from outside. It fills the gaps between the Sheetrock so the wall is smooth." I reach back and get it, along with my joint tool for spreading the drywall compound. I put the mud in the crevices and smooth it down. Then I put joint tape over it and stand back.

"That doesn't look fixed," the girl says. "Are you sure you're a fixer man, Smokey the Bear?"

"It's not done," I tell her. "It has to set for twenty minutes, and then I'll need to add more mud."

She giggles at the word. A timer in the kitchen goes off, and she runs over to her mom and asks to stir in the milk and cheese. I sit on the couch and set my phone timer.

"Twenty minutes, huh?" Maddie says, looking from me to the gooey macaroni. "I, uh… It's stupid, I know it's only mac and cheese, but if you want some, you're welcome to it. It's the least I can do."

Macaroni and cheese? What am I, ten? She holds up a plate, waiting for my answer.

"Throw in a glass of wine and you have a deal. Or maybe some Patrón?" I wink.

"Tequila with macaroni and cheese?" She cringes.

"Tequila goes with everything, doesn't it? It mixes particularly well with late-night bets."

Unlikely DATE

She pinks. "Sorry, I don't stock a full bar here." Her gaze falls to the floor. "And you wouldn't want my wine."

"Whatever you have will be fine."

"You may regret saying that." She pulls two glasses from her creaky, peeling, hanging-off-the-hinges cabinet. Then she gets a bottle of Pinot from the fridge. I recognize it from one of the endcaps in the grocery store. I think it was $5.99 a bottle.

She pours the wine and sets our meals on the table.

"We need the good napkins, Mommy," Gigi says. "I'll get the pretty ones we use for guests." She opens the pantry and pulls out some white paper napkins embossed with seashells.

Maddie looks like she wants the chair to swallow her. "I'm sorry. It's not like we wipe our mouths on our sleeves when we eat alone. It's just… nice napkins are expensive."

"You have nothing to be ashamed about."

"Says the CEO who drives the Range Rover." Her head shakes back and forth. "I can't believe I'm serving you cheap wine and macaroni from a box. I don't think I've ever been so embarrassed in my life."

"Maddie, I'm serious. It's fine."

"I'm calling NDA on this one. Please don't tell anyone."

"Why would I tell anyone?"

"Right. Yeah, you wouldn't. Why would you?"

We eat in virtual silence unless Gigi asks a question. Which she does. A lot. *Why do they call it mud if it's not mud? Who do you think will find the bag in the wall? Do you think they will be aliens? Why do you smoke? The man where Mommy fixes her car smokes, and he has black hands. Will your hands turn black? Aren't the flowers pretty? Which is your favorite? You gave Mommy flowers; does that mean you're her prince?*

It's the last question that has wine spurting from Maddie's mouth. "Hasn't it been about twenty minutes?"

"Close enough," I say, standing and taking my plate to the sink. "I'll just go put another coat on."

"Why are you putting a coat on?" Gigi asks. "Are you leaving? Is it cold out?"

"Coat of mud," I say. "It means I have to apply another layer. Put more on."

I don't miss Maddie's smile. She's amused that I'm explaining things to Gigi.

I slather the compound onto the tape and smooth it out as Gigi watches. It occurs to me that I don't hear the rattle of dishes. When I look over my shoulder, I see why. Maddie is sitting at the table, nursing another glass of wine. And she's staring at me too. Only not the same way Gigi is. Not with innocent curiosity. No, Maddie's stare is anything but innocent. Her eyes smolder. Her lower lip is caught between her teeth. Her finger traces the base of her wine glass like I wish it were tracing the base of my cock. Is she thinking about our kiss? And if so, which one? Or maybe she's thinking about more.

She stands and goes to the sink when she realizes I've caught her ogling. I try to compose myself as well. Having a stiffy with a five-year-old three feet away is just goddamn wrong.

I slough off the excess mud and clean up my supplies. "This will need to dry completely before I can sand and paint it."

Dishes are now being washed. Maddie is busying herself so I don't catch her staring. Daydreaming. Fantasizing. "Did you say something?"

"I'll come back tomorrow to sand and paint it. Do you have paint that matches?"

"Ha! I seriously doubt fresh paint has touched these walls in fifty years. Gran doesn't have the best eyesight, so she never really cared much about how it looked. And me, I just figured I'd get around to it someday."

"Well, that day is tomorrow. Since you don't have matching paint, we'll have to do the whole thing. The entire room."

"*We?*"

"It's a big job, Maddie."

"You know, it's fine. The hole is patched. We can just leave it like this for now."

"I have paint. Gallons of it. And drop cloths and brushes, too."

Lie. Lie. And another lie.

"You're okay with a cream color, right?" I ask.

"I can't let you do this."

"The paint will just go bad if it doesn't get used. After work, then?"

She looks at the wall. At Gigi. At me. I can see the battle going on in her head. Not about the wall. I'm sure she couldn't care less about it. The battle is about me. Letting me back into her house. Because she knows every time she lets me in, her resolve crumbles a little more. Every time she sees me, her body hums, her blood pumps, and her panties moisten.

And even though I know I shouldn't play this game, not with *her*, I can't stop. I can't stop until I have her. The question is, what will I do after?

What you always do.

But even knowing I'll most likely burn the girl who's already been on fire, I press on. "So? What's it going to be?"

"After *your* work," she says. "The shop is closed on Tuesdays. It's my one day off."

I gather my supplies and tuck them in a corner. Might need them tomorrow. "Great. See you then. I'll bring food."

I'll bring food? Since when do I ever bring food?

"You don't have to do that. I can make sandwiches or something."

"Sandwiches and six-dollar wine. I can't wait." I was being sarcastic, but when she frowns, I feel guilty. *Wait, guilty?* "I was kidding, Flower Girl. Sandwiches are one of my favorite food groups."

I start down the stairs. "Bye, Smokey the Bear," Gigi calls after me.

Right, I didn't even acknowledge the kid before leaving. "Uh, bye."

I reach the bottom and call up. "Maddie, I might need my toolbox. Can you bring it down?"

She comes down the stairs and hands it to me. "Thanks for what you did today. I really appreciate it."

I put the tools down. "Yeah, I don't really need these."

"What? Then why?"

I take her into my arms, once again, not asking permission. And once again, she doesn't move to pull away. My mouth covers hers. I run my tongue across her lower lip, then I kiss the upper one. Then I press my closed lips fully to hers. It's not like the kiss from last night or even the night before. It's more of a see-you-later kiss. Not that I know what that even is. I've never given one before. But if I were to, this would be it.

"Bye, Flower Girl," I say, stepping away.

If I had eyes in the back of my head, I'm fairly sure I'd see her slumped against the doorway. Wanting more. Needing more. But I don't look back. Because I know a guy like me can't fulfill both. I can give her what she wants. But I'm fooling myself to think I could ever be what she needs.

Chapter Twenty

Maddie

I pull into the retirement community for our weekly trip to see Gran. She loves it here. Even more so lately. I guess it took her a few years to really establish friendships outside of those she had along McQuaid Circle. I drive around the central lake with a fountain in it. There are VIP homes that back up to the lake, some bigger than Blake Montana's parents' house. Gran, however, lives in the more modest apartments along the back woods. She's still very self-sufficient, barring the arthritis that came from fifty years of trimming flowers, and the mild COPD that was the result of years of smoking.

Smoking.

Don't think about Tag. Don't think about Tag.

We park in the lot and take the elevator to the second floor. Gigi loves elevators. The only time I'll let her inside of one is when we visit Gran. I despise them, avoiding them whenever possible. They're death traps if you ask me. But since we're only going one floor, I surmise it's not that great a risk.

Gran doesn't answer the door. She knows we're coming. We've been coming at the same time every Tuesday for three years. "Gran!" I yell, getting worried.

A neighboring door opens. "She's not home," the older woman says. "Mind keeping it down? Some of us still got our hearing."

She's new. I know all Gran's neighbors. I want to ask what happened to Mrs. Garfunkel, but I'm afraid of the answer. She either died or had to be moved to the assisted-living building. Neither is something I want to think about.

"I'm sorry. I was looking for my grandmother."

"Ahh, so you're Maddie. And this must be Rose's namesake."

Most people think I named my daughter after the flower shop, but the shop was named after Gran. Rose Gianogi grew up with the nickname Gigi. Gigi was named after *her*. Rose just seemed too old fashioned and *'Titanic.'*

"So you know my grandmother. And you are?"

"Delilah Duncan. My husband, George, lives here too. He's asleep on the couch. All that old man does is sleep on the couch."

"I'm happy to meet you, Mrs. Duncan. Do you happen to know where my grandmother is? It's unusual for her to miss one of our weekly visits."

"She said she was going out for lunch. Reckon she just let time get away from her." She opens the drawer of a table inside her front door and sorts through it. "I have a key. I could let you inside."

"You've only just moved in, and Gran gave you a key? She must really like you. *I* don't even have a key."

"This is an old folks' community, dear. People drop like flies around here. Everybody has a key to their neighbor's apartment, because you never know." She motions to the door across the hall.

Unlikely DATE

"Except for him. That old geezer is meaner than a skunk. Smells like one too. And he's still alive." She chuckles. "Rose tells me nobody likes him, and he doesn't like anyone. It's just my luck to live across the hall from a dud. Anyway, let's get you inside, and you and this precious little girl can get yourselves a glass of water while you wait."

She opens the door for us, then goes back to her apartment.

Gigi runs to the recliner near the large picture window. She loves how it raises you up and lowers you down. Gran doesn't need such a fancy contraption yet, but all the units come furnished with one. Gigi is playing with the chair when she squeals, "Gran!" She hops off the recliner and knocks on the window. "Gran!"

I go over to see Gran strolling with a man along the walking path. She doesn't look up. She can't possibly hear the knocking from where she is. She doesn't look anywhere but at him. She's smiling and laughing and leaning and... completely smitten.

Oh, my gosh. *Gran has a boyfriend?*

"Who's that man?" Gigi asks.

"I'm not sure." I squint for a closer look. I blink twice, certain my eyes have betrayed me. Because if I'm not mistaken, the man who just kissed Gran on the cheek is one of the richest people in Calloway Creek. And he's also a legendary player.

I'm stunned. No wonder Gran didn't roast me when I told her about Tag. She's dating someone who is exactly like him, only fifty years older. The Casanova of their generation.

They part ways, him walking toward the VIP homes and her coming around the side of the building. I sit on the couch, crossing my arms, waiting for her to arrive.

She swings the door open, humming a showtune. She stops when she sees us. "You're here. Wonderful. I take it you met the Duncans, then?"

"Tucker McQuaid, Gran?"

She blushes. I'm quite sure I've never seen my grandmother blush. She goes to her kitchenette and fills a kettle.

"Tucker McQuaid?" I say again, more forcefully this time.

"Shush now, you'll scare Gigi."

"Gran, do you have any idea what you're doing?"

She puts the kettle on the stove and looks me in the eye. "Do *you?*"

~ ~ ~

Patrick picks his jaw up off the floor. "Tucker McQuaid? As in the eighty-four-year-old billionaire who owns a dozen car dealerships?"

"I saw them with my own eyes. He kissed her cheek, Patrick. And she looked like a schoolgirl in love."

"I heard that he moved into the retirement community after his wife died a few years ago."

"And I heard he paid to expand the largest VIP home into something fit for a king. The King of Calloway Creek, so to speak."

"He had four mistresses," he says. "*At the same time.* No wonder his wife died prematurely. She was probably sick and tired of him to the point that death was more appealing than dealing with all his indiscretions. Rumor has it that after his wife died, he paid off his mistresses and never saw them again." He shakes his head. "Rose and Tucker. That's such an unlikely pair."

I stretch my neck and make sure Gigi is busy playing on Patrick's Xbox. "They're not the only ones."

"No." He inches closer. "Girl, have you been holding out on me? You've seen him again?"

I hold three fingers up then hide my face in my hands. "Three times actually."

"Three? But it's Tuesday morning. I saw you on Sunday."

I explain how Tag came to the shop, paid me back (inside flowers), stumbled over drunk later that night, and then showed up yesterday to fix the wall.

"You mean the hole you wouldn't let *me* fix? And he kissed you again?"

I glance at Gigi. "Patrick, you do too much for me as it is. And yes, he kissed me again. Twice."

He blows out a low whistle, and his body shivers. "This is as exciting as when the firehouse found out Captain Crawford had two wives. No, strike that, this is more exciting. I mean, this is you and Tag Calloway."

"It's ridiculous to even think it, Patrick. What could he possibly want with me other than to add me to his list of conquests?"

"I'd happily be added to that list."

I swat his leg. "Shut up." I sit back and close my eyes. "What if he just wants to see me—all of me—out of morbid curiosity?"

"He told you he saw the scars already. He knows what's under your robe, so to speak, and he didn't go running for cover like you think every man will. I'm not sure I get your point, Maddie. You were willing to be some random guy's one-night stand three days ago. Why not his? You could do way worse. And the man is right. The whole town thinks you're shagging already."

"What if I changed my mind? What if I don't want a one-night stand?"

"So this crush you said you'd be over by lunchtime…?"

I shake my head. "Not just a crush, apparently."

"Can I give you a bit of advice?"

"That's your job, isn't it?"

"He doesn't want a one-night stand either," he says. I go to speak, but he shushes me. "Maddie, the guy is seriously working for it. The flowers, the stare in the courtyard, the hole in the wall, the *'I'll be back tomorrow, and we'll paint it together.'* Do you not understand that Tag Calloway could stand in McQuaid Circle, snap his fingers, and a dozen women in heat would come running? Without him so much as lifting a finger?"

"I thought you said he snapped."

He laughs. "The man ate macaroni and cheese—from a *box*—with you and your daughter. He wants more than in your pants."

"But why?"

"You're looking at this the wrong way." He stands and then pulls me up. He forces me toward his front door. "Instead of asking yourself why, you need to ask why not." He shoves me through and closes it behind me. "Now go home and shave!" he shouts through the door.

I don't tell him that I shaved my legs in the bath last night. The bath I took after Tag left. The bath where I worked out all my pent-up frustrations.

I didn't even get to say goodbye to Gigi. I know they had this whole day planned together, but still. I knock on the window and get Gigi's attention. I blow her a kiss. She blows one back, and I plant it on my lips like always.

It's a short drive home. Normally, I wouldn't even drive to Patrick's, as he lives down one of the closest residential streets, but since we were already in the car coming from Gran's, it was easier. I love living in a town where you can walk everywhere. Sure, the newer part of Calloway Creek isn't walkable like McQuaid Circle is, but I rarely go to that part of town. Who needs Target, Home Depot, and McDonald's when you have a convenience store, a hardware shop, and five small-business eating establishments all within an area the size of a football field? Not to mention the train station, bank, pub, movie theater, bowling alley, and gym. McQuaid Circle is a town within a town. And I love my little town.

And now, how convenient that Tag's house is just a short walk around the corner.

Tag. I stop well short of my usual parking place behind the shop when I see a familiar car, or should I say SUV, parked in the spare spot.

My heart thunders. It's barely noon. He said he would come after work. I'm not ready. There are things to be done. Floors to be cleaned. Toys to put away. And damn it, Patrick was right—things to be shaved. Well, more things anyway. I did all the usual places last night. But this afternoon, with Gigi out of the apartment, I'd planned on googling ways to trim *down there*. You know, just in case.

Warmth floods through me as I think about all the just-in-case scenarios. Just in case he feels you up. Just in case he feels you *down*. Just in case you get naked together.

It's the last just in case that has me terrified. I don't care what Tag said about seeing some of my scars peeking out from under my robe. Until you've seen me naked—fully naked—no one can understand the totality of it. Some days I can barely look at myself in the mirror. As soon as I moved into the main bedroom after Gran moved out, I took down the full-length mirror on the back of the door. The small vanity mirror in the bathroom is all that's left, and often I feel even that is too much.

Tag doesn't see me. He's perched on the back bumper of his car. And he's smoking. I observe for a minute. He's casual. Confident. He doesn't look around like I do when I'm in public, always wondering who could be watching. He regards his cigarette, then looks up at my bedroom window. *Does he know it's mine?* Then he stomps out his smoke before he's even halfway finished and pops a piece of gum into his mouth.

I pull into the space next to him and get out. "I thought you were coming after work."

"I got to thinking what a big job it is, and I had a pretty light afternoon. We can probably finish by dinnertime if we work fast."

He's missing work for this? Or maybe he just didn't want to risk having to be here for Hamburger Helper night.

He holds out a bag for me. "Do you mind?"

I take it and walk for the door, wondering if he's watching me. Wondering why I'm so darn nervous when I'm around him.

"Aren't you missing something?" he asks.

I turn and wait, wondering if he wants me to carry more.

"The small human you're normally attached to. Where is she?"

"Gigi is with Patrick today. They're going to the park."

"You didn't want to go with them?"

"It's nice for her to spend a little time without me. We're together twenty-four seven."

He threads three plastic bags containing supplies over his forearm, picks up two cans of paint, and follows me. "Surely she goes to friends' houses and your grandmother's."

"Not without me."

"I've seen you out with friends, though. You must have a babysitter."

"I do. It's Patrick."

"What about day care? Has she ever gone?"

"No."

"Why is that, exactly?"

I shrug.

Once in my apartment, I put the bag on the floor and quickly clean up the breakfast dishes.

"Are you telling me Patrick is the only person who you let her spend time with alone?"

"I guess so."

"What if he's not available?"

"What is this, twenty questions?"

"No. I guess I just find it odd. Amber and Quinn have a nanny for Josie."

"I've met Sophie. She's nice. And that's wonderful for them, but not everyone can afford that, Tag."

He studies me. "So you're saying you'd have a nanny if you could afford one?"

"Why would I need a nanny? Gigi loves being at the flower shop. And with me teaching her, she's way smarter than her cohorts. You saw her write the letter last night. Most five-year-olds can barely write their names. Why the sudden interest in my daughter? Don't you hate kids?"

He turns pensive for a moment and then snorts. "Yeah, I do."

"So how do we do this?" I ask, perusing the pile of paint and supplies. "Start at one end and go around the room?"

"You've never painted before?"

I shake my head.

"First, we'll move the furniture away from the walls and put drop cloths on the floors to protect them from drips and spatters."

I eye the carpet that's unraveling at the seams and has more stains than I can count. "Because as you can see, my floors really need protection."

"We'll deal with that later."

We will?

"Then we'll cut in the paint around the windows and doorways. I'm pretty good at it, so we can forgo the tape to save time. Then we'll use the rollers to do the rest." He runs his fingers along the wall.

Suddenly, I wish I was the wall and his fingers were lightly touching me, running up my leg, tickling my inner thigh, and pushing inside me.

"Two coats ought to do it," he says, completely oblivious to my inner thoughts.

I'm not sure how I'm going to spend all afternoon with him without saying or doing something stupid. As in staring at him like a lovesick idiot. Or tripping over myself and going face-first into a can of paint. "Seems like you have this all under control. I should just leave you to it."

"Oh, no you don't. I supplied the materials, but you're putting in the sweat equity."

"Sweat sounds about right. It's supposed to hit eighty degrees today, and all I have is a small window air conditioner."

"Then you'd better dress appropriately. And wear something you don't mind being spattered with paint." His gaze travels the length of my body. "Better yet, wear nothing at all," he says with a wink.

I swallow. Naked painting with Tag Calloway. A normal girl might take him up on the offer. It sounds messy. Fun. Hot. But this is me we're talking about. My eyes meet the floor, knowing I'm anything but normal. I thumb to my room. "I'll, uh, just go change."

He chuckles under his breath. He knows he's toying with me. And damn it, I'm foolish enough to let him.

I rummage through my drawers. Why is picking clothes to paint in harder than choosing a dress for the prom? I bypass all the

T-shirts that I only wear when it's just Gigi and me. And I don't want to ruin any of the clothes I wear for work. Defeated by the task, I sit amidst the pile of clothes on the bed.

Then I remember something in the bottom drawer among all the sexy bras and underwear that I haven't worn in four years, not even on the blind date. I tug on the knob. It comes off in my hand, so I pry the drawer open with my fingers and find what I'm looking for. One of Patrick's button-down shirts he left here a few months ago when Gigi spilled pasta sauce on it. I never could get out the stain. Gigi uses it as a smock when she finger paints.

When I pull it out, one of the bra clasps catches on a button, and the white lacy bra comes out with it. I run my hand over the lace. "Oh, what the heck." I dig further down in the drawer, find the matching panties, and put them on. I'm thinner now than I was back then, having lost a lot of weight after The Incident, but they still fit.

I wrap Patrick's shirt around me. It fits me better than it fits Gigi. It drowns her and touches the floor when she wears it, which makes it perfect for protecting her clothes. On me, it looks like a mini dress. I leave the bottom buttons undone and tie the two ends together, making sure nothing more than the sliver of skin around my belly button shows. Then I roll the sleeves up to just the right point on my arms. Finally, I pull on a pair of black exercise shorts—my favorite pair that fit me like a glove. They might get ruined with paint, but it'll be worth it. If I have to stand there and watch Tag in his tight shirt and well-fitting jeans, I'll be damned if I won't fight fire with fire.

Lastly, I gather up my long locks and tie my hair into a messy bun. "Done," I say, wishing I had a mirror in the bedroom after all, because I have no idea what I look like.

Out in the living room, Tag has moved the furniture, spread the drop cloths, and opened the paint. The floor creaks, alerting him to my return. He's crouched down, stirring the paint. "Thought you fell asleep back there," he says without looking up.

I walk closer. He stops what he's doing. His eyes lock on to my legs and slowly work their way up my body. I can feel them on my knees, my thighs, the sliver of skin on my stomach. Every part of me tingles. Instantly, I feel my panties dampen, and I wonder if he's close enough to smell what he's capable of doing to me with just his eyes.

I tug on the shirt, making sure it's covering the right side of my abs.

"Don't do that," he says. He takes in the long sleeves that are rolled to below the elbow. "You'll be hot."

"It's the only shirt I have for painting."

He laughs, taking in the many stains and splatters. "I can see that. I thought you said you've never painted before."

"Gigi uses it for finger paints."

He stands and closes the gap between us. I swear to God, the air crackles, and electricity shoots between us. He fingers a button on the shirt, and my breath hitches. I stare at him, knowing I'm putty in his hands, wanting him to shape me, mold me, work me into someone I desire to be. At the same time, I'm terrified of him. Of his reputation. His crassness. His ability to make me do things I've never dreamed of. To make me think things I've never imagined.

I've never wanted and not wanted something so badly in my life.

"At least let some air in," he says, unbuttoning the second button as his finger lightly brushes against my left breast.

Then, as quickly as they came, his fingers are gone, and he kneels down and stirs the paint as if he didn't just leave me a hot mess of mushy hormones. Does he have any idea what he does to me?

I step over to my window unit and click it on. He chuckles under his breath.

Oh, he knows. He knows all right.

I let the cool air run over me as I ponder just how long I'm willing to play his game.

Chapter Twenty-one

Tag

If I keep this up much longer, I'll stir the damn color right out of this paint. But until my raging boner goes back into hiding, I can't stand up.

Her shorts reveal every luscious curve of her hips and showcase her toned thighs. Her legs are creamy white. There's a soft sprinkling of freckles on the inside of one of her knees, and damn, I want to connect the fucking dots with my tongue.

Not helping. Stir. Stir. Stir.

If she were anyone else, I'd have her face down on the couch, pile-driving her gorgeous ass. But she's not anyone else. She's so far from anyone else that she's in another stratosphere. What the hell is it about her? She's all wrong for me. If you take away the rocking body and schoolgirl shyness, she's the opposite of what I look for in a woman. She's an introvert to the nth degree. She has zero self-confidence. She's got a kid, for Christ's sake. That alone should make her off-limits and put her at the top of my list entitled: *Women Tag Calloway should never, under any circumstances, sleep with.*

I study the patch job on the wall, remembering what's behind it, and shake my head, wondering how the goddamn mini-her somehow makes Maddie sexier.

It's the thrill of the chase. The game. That's got to be it. I should just feed the beast. I know she'll let me if I try hard enough. Everyone does.

Do it, get her out of your head, and move on with your life.

Because in the past forty-eight hours, I've gotten exactly squat done at CSM, and it's her fault. I'm starting to regret ever following FlowerGirl529 three days ago. I should have turned around, taken the train home, and jerked the fucking monkey.

"Are you okay?"

I look up to see her questioning eyes.

"You're mumbling about a monkey? Is everything all right with the paint?"

"The paint." I stop stirring. "Yeah. Let's get to it." I pull two brushes out of the bag and hand her one. I dip mine into the paint and swipe it along the edge of the can to get rid of the excess, then I run it along the side of the window frame. "Here's how you cut in. Make a stripe a few inches wide. Just enough to make it easier when we roll on the paint. Start with the underside of the windows, or over the top if you have a stepstool. That way if you mess up, nobody will see it."

"I have a steady hand," she says. "I can do it here."

She dips her brush into the can, then swashes paint right below where I had.

"Easy strokes," I say. "Otherwise, you'll get paint all over." I put my hand on top of hers and show her how to do it. The skin along her arm pebbles at my touch. I'm standing over her shoulder, and the scent of her hair invades me, reminding me of the jacket I haven't worn since that night.

I tell myself it's because of the heat wave.

I'm really good at lying, so I might even believe it.

I step away. "I think you've got it. You finish this window. I'll do those over there."

We paint in silence, which might be even worse, because I can't get rid of the thoughts in my head. She starts humming a popular tune—one my dick decides he wants to dance to. I can't stop stealing glances at her. That ridiculously oversized shirt stained with every color of the rainbow. The massive reddish bun on top of her head that flops from side to side as she moves. Those shorts. Oh, those goddamn shorts.

She stops humming when she sees me watching her. "Something wrong?"

"You have incredible calves. I was just wondering how you got them."

"I run the stairs every morning."

"At the CCU arena?"

"No." She nods to her door. "Here."

"You get those calves by running up and down one flight of stairs?"

"I do it fifty times. It's great cardio."

I stand here stunned, thinking how strong they would be wrapped around me while I fuck her. "I'll bet."

She goes back to painting. A chunk of curls falls out of her hair tie. She reaches up to fix it and streaks paint in her hair.

"You got paint on you."

"I did?" She looks down at her clothes, her legs, her sexy-as-all-get-out bare feet. "Where?"

I go over and use a finger to get some of it out of her hair before it spreads. I show her my finger. "Most women pay a lot of money to streak their hair."

She giggles and touches the top of her head, getting it on *her* hand now.

"Personally, I think it would look better here." I smear my finger underneath each of her eyes. "War paint."

Her mouth falls open. "You did not just do that."

"Looks like I did," I say in my usual arrogant fashion.

She struts to the paint can, dips her brush in, and paints something on the front of my T-shirt. *Game fucking on.* I take the shirt off and hold it out so I can see it. A laugh rumbles deep in my chest. She painted a circle with a diagonal line through it—the universal *'no'* sign.

Before I come back with a cocky comment, I notice her eyes trained on my nip piercings. Her inspection of them seems to last for hours, though it must be only seconds. She chews on her bottom lip, mesmerized by the dangling platinum rings. My cock is most happy with her perusal. It wants her to look at *him* that way. With eyes so hungry that, like Medusa, they will turn him into stone.

Her gaze travels twelve inches north, to my lips. It's intense. Everything about her is potent. She has all the power here, and she doesn't even know it.

Brush still in hand, I lean forward and run a stripe of paint down her cleavage with such force, it takes out two of her buttons. The shirt falls open, revealing a sexy bra with lace patterns in the shape of flowers. Subconsciously (or not), her right hand keeps the shirt from gaping open too far in that direction. She makes no such attempt to keep it from opening the other way, so I make no attempt to hide my blatant stare of the creamy, supple, perfect breast fleshing out from the lacy cup.

As if gravity pulls us closer, we both step forward at the same time, our bodies and lips mashing together softly at first, then with more urgency. She sighs against my lips, muttering my name like it's a prayer. I drop the brush and free her hair from the tie. It cascades down her back in waves. As I kiss her harder, the heat from her mouth has all my nerve endings on fire. She touches my cheek softly, first with one hand, then another, holding me in place so I won't pull away.

Not a goddamn chance.

"I'm going to touch you." It's not a question. It's a declaration. Still, the warning gives her an out if she wants it.

She doesn't.

I let out my breath and touch her waist, just above her shorts, working my way up to her left breast. I cup it over the bra. It's not enough. I need more. "I'm going to take it off."

Her eyes go heavy. It's not a yes. Not a no either. I undo the front clasp. She holds the right side of her shirt closed as I push the bra out of the way, clearing a path for me to feel her fleshy softness. My dick throbs against my fly, wanting his pound of flesh—or rather two pounds of it, one on either side of him.

"I'm going to taste you."

A gush of air escapes her. *Definitely not a no.* I duck my head and pull her nipple into my mouth. I flick it with my tongue, just the way I like women to flick mine. Her breast tastes like her hair smells. Peaches just became my favorite flavor. Her chest heaves and her back arches, causing her hair to dangle further down and tickle my hand on her waist.

I.

Need.

More.

"Take off your shirt, Flower Girl."

"No."

Aaaaand, ego deflated. Once again, she has all the power.

"Maddie, I want to see you."

She holds the right side of the shirt firmly against her body. "You see plenty."

Her voice is missing the sultry edge it had moments ago. She's about to stop. So I capitulate. I lean in and let my words flow against her ear. "Keep it on. Draw me a damn road map for where I can and can't touch you, for all I care. As long as I can keep touching."

I nip on the rim of her lobe. She cranes her neck, allowing me more access. I suck on her neck like I was sucking on her tit. She moans and the sound zaps me to the core.

"I want to taste you," I say, licking down and across her throbbing pulse. "I want to taste *all* of you."

"I want to taste you too."

I stand back and raise a brow.

Redness spreads down her face and across her chest. She looks at my nip rings. "I mean, there."

If my dick could speak, he just uttered ten curse words.

I hold my arms wide out. "What's stopping you?"

"Here?"

Scanning the room, my eyes settle on the sofa. I urge her over and sweep the toys onto the floor. I sit. "Climb on."

A debonaire man would have said something more eloquent. But I'm a leopard. Kind of hard to change my spots.

Her thumb taps against her outer leg. I reach out and trap her hand, then pull her down until she straddles me. Her eyes fall to my chest, and I put her hands on my pecs. She fiddles with my nip rings. I can't help but thrust up into her. My cock is greedy; he doesn't like the denim between us. But I realize I'm on shaky ground here, not knowing how far I can take this.

Unlikely DATE

When she presses down onto me and rocks herself over my lap, I pass fucking go and hope to collect my two hundred dollars. "Might be more comfortable if I take these off."

Her response is delayed as she meets my gaze. She's definitely not a talker. Maybe over time, that will change.

Over time?

Her hand trembles slightly. I capture it under mine. "Skivvies on, okay?"

All rational thought leaves my head when she nods her answer. I lift her off me, toe my shoes off, push down my jeans, and pull her back onto me before she has ten seconds to change her mind. The friction between us when she gyrates on top of me is almost enough to get me off, especially when her tongue finds my nip.

"Jesus," I mutter. Then I feel her smile against me.

Power. She knows she has it.

She's the only one who ever has.

Never has a woman paid so much attention to my pecs. They like the bling, but they want my cock more. Maddie has me reeling. I'm a blind man with a cup on the corner, begging for it to be filled.

She tugs on one of my piercings with her teeth. I stiffen. "Oh, fuck, stop."

She pulls away. "I'm sorry. Did that hurt?"

I stand, her in my arms, and deposit her on the couch. I open her legs and insert myself between them, leaning in close. "In all the best ways, Flower Girl." I hook my thumbs over the top of her shorts. "I'm going to take these off now."

Her eyes flutter. She moistens her lips, and her ass squirms.

That's a yes, another yes, and a yes, please.

I peel off her skin-tight shorts, her lacy panties coming off with them. I throw her shorts aside and open her legs again, marveling at her glistening pussy. *Fuuuuuuck me.*

I tug her to the edge of the couch and put my head between her legs. I don't touch her in the place she craves. Not yet. I'm going to make her come. I'm going to make her come so hard she'll be seeing stars into next week. First, I nuzzle her, the rough hair along my jaw scraping her thighs as I nudge them wider. Then I go south, my tongue moving from freckle to freckle, connecting those dots on the inside of her knee.

She slinks further toward me, wanting my tongue where it counts; begging me with her throaty mewls. I sit back on my haunches and hold her stare as I glide a finger inside her. Her tight walls close around me, reminding me no man has been here in half a decade. Part of me wants to gloat, shout cocky expletives about going where few men have gone before. But I don't. And I won't. I already know I won't utter a goddamn word. This, what's happening here, won't ever be a topic for guys' night. Quinn and my brothers will never hear a drunken play-by-play like they have countless times before. I add a second finger, and her head leans back into the couch. I smile. Because Maddie Foster's pussy belongs to me.

I remove my fingers, and my tongue plunges into her. She grabs a fistful of my hair, her fingers gliding through it, securing me in place. I work my thumb in circles on her slippery clit as she strains her body against me. My tongue and my fingers trade places, my fingers searching for the holy grail inside her as my mouth assaults her stiff nub.

She fists the couch on either side of her, and she rocks violently against my mouth as she climaxes. Hot expletives I've never heard from her echo on the walls and float in the air long after she's said them. My fingers stay inside her, tickling the same place over and over until she goes limp.

I rise to my knees, marveling at the masterpiece I've created: her post-orgasmic glow. I've never seen another one like it. Her shirt is still knotted at her waist, her right side still covered. Her pussy red and engorged. She's the fucking Mona Lisa.

And I know I'd spend every last penny I have to see it over and over.

My dick is popping out of the waistband of my shorts, wanting what he thinks should be his. Maddie stares at the exposed tip. "Do you have a condom?"

"Is the sky blue?"

She hasn't even recovered, and she's asking for more. She traps her bottom lip between her teeth. It's fucking sexy.

I put my hand on the knot of her shirt. She puts hers on top. "Nuh-uh."

"After what you just let me do? Come on, Maddie. I want to see you."

She rises on her elbows. "I'm giving you permission to go all the way here, Tag. It's what you wanted all along. What does it matter if you see me?"

Yeah, Tag. What does it matter?

"It matters," I say. "I'm not sleeping with you unless I can see you."

"Then I guess you won't be needing that condom."

I frown. "Seriously?"

She slinks away from me and pulls on her panties. I stand and make my way to the bathroom, wrestling the eel until I come, and not even trying to be quiet about it. Then I return to the living room, dress, and pick up the paint brush. "Are we doing this or what?"

She huffs out an incredulous sigh and dips her brush.

Chapter Twenty-two

Maddie

Gigi happily plays on the jungle gym with her friend Kara after eating ice cream—her usual Tuesday night treat. Regan and Ava sit across from me at the picnic table—our regular Tuesday night meeting place—gaping in disbelief.

"He didn't sleep with you?" Regan asks for the second time. "Really?"

Ava's brows draw down in confusion. "Tag Calloway had you half-naked, tongue plowed you into oblivion, but he wouldn't close the deal?"

I shake my head.

"You're sure it was Tag and not Jaxon? You could be confusing the two."

"You saw the way they eye-fucked each other right here in this courtyard the other night," Regan says. "It's him."

I pick at the table. "He said he wouldn't do it unless I took my shirt off."

"You could have turned off the lights."

"It was one o'clock in the afternoon, Regan. Plus, darkness doesn't matter." I tug down my sleeve. "He would still be able to feel them."

She scolds me with her eyes. "Your vagina's not broken. You have a great rack. Half the women in this town would kill for your hair. Face it, you're hot. Believe me, that's all he would be thinking about."

My lips fold thoughtfully. "He said something to that effect on Saturday."

"Four days," Ava points out. "He's been after you for four days. That's got to be some kind of record. I heard when Jennifer Kidman played hard to get last week that he was out the door before she could beg him to reconsider."

"I'm *not* playing hard to get." My head slumps and I shamefully cover my face with my hands. "I all but begged him to go all the way. He'll probably never have anything to do with me again."

"You mean to tell me the man standing outside the pub over there, staring at you like he just discovered the ninth planet, wants nothing to do with you?"

I stiffen. "He's *here*?"

The courtyard behind the strip of shops is adjacent to the outdoor patio of Donovan's Pub around the corner. My back is turned away from the pub. I'm glued to my seat. If I turn, he'll know we're talking about him. If I don't, I might combust.

"He's leaning against the wall, smoking a cigarette, looking all James Deanish," Ava says. "I swear, Maddie, if I weren't with Trev, *I'd* be pining away for him. He may be an ass, but the guy is hot. Greek god hot."

"Ryan Reynolds and Harry Styles hot," Regan adds.

"Chris Hemsworth from *Thor* hot."

"Bradley Cooper in *A Star is Born* hot."

I roll my eyes. "Will you guys stop? You're supposed to hate him. *We're* supposed to hate him."

"He went back inside," Ava says.

I'm not sure why that makes me sad. I should be relieved. Except that I'm not. He left my apartment five hours ago, and all I've been able to do is think about him. His thumb scraping lightly across my nipple. His strong, competent hands exploring my body. And now my apartment smells like paint, and I know every time I smell paint, I'll think about him smearing it down my chest. Peeling off my shorts. Licking me into unconsciousness.

I turn. Tag is staring at me from thirty yards away. He takes a drag off his cigarette, then stuffs it out in a bucket next to a table. He never breaks eye contact.

I quickly spin back around. "You said he was gone."

Regan and Ava can't hold in their laughter.

"You bitches."

"Oh, come on, Maddie," Ava says. "Nothing this exciting has happened around here in months."

"We should leave," Regan says. "Give them a minute."

Ava settles into place. "Screw that. We're front and center."

His throat clears behind me. My skin prickles and my arm hairs stand on end. "Hi, Flower Girl," he says softly in my ear, his minty breath swirling around me like a plume of smoke.

"Hi." I turn slightly. "What brings you here?"

I want this bench to swallow me. Could I be any more awkward?

"You do."

Even in my periphery, I can tell Regan and Ava are grinning from ear to ear.

"How's your day going so far?" he asks, followed by a smile that holds a gallon of smugness.

It's a loaded question I'm not sure I know how to answer. I shrug. "Just like any other day, I guess."

His low, throaty laughter dances between us. "Is that so?"

"Now that I think about it, it just hasn't been a very fulfilling day."

"Fulfilling?" He raises a brow.

"You know, satisfying. Rewarding. Gratifying. To one's liking."

"I know what the word means, Maddie."

"And you? How's your day?"

"Lunch was fantastic," he says, a note of triumph lacing his words.

Heat crosses my face. We never ordered food. Frustrated and hungry for him, I cross my legs and squeeze my thighs. The pressure does nothing to squelch my desire.

Gigi runs over and latches onto Tag's leg. "Smokey the Bear!"

She's never done that to any man but Patrick. Then again, Tag did eat macaroni and cheese with her and seal her time capsule in the wall.

I half expect him to shake her off like a bug on his shoe.

"Come here, baby." I pull her over next to me. "I'm sure Mr. Calloway needs to get back to his friends."

"*Mr. Calloway* would like to take Ms. Foster to dinner tomorrow," he says.

Regan, or maybe Ava, lets out a gasp.

I replay the words in my head to make sure I heard them correctly. *Say yes.* I shake my head. "I have work."

"You close at seven."

I glance at my daughter. "I have Gigi."

"Get a sitter."

"Patrick's on shift tomorrow."

He looks at Regan and Ava as if he wants to ask why they can't watch her. Instead, he says, "Thursday then. We'll go to Lloyd's."

"*Lloyd's?*" I say an octave too high. "You mean the steakhouse owned by the McQuaids? You eat there?"

"Technically, no. But it's the best in town. And it's right around the corner, so you'd be close to home. What do you say?"

People will see us. They'll talk even more than they are now. It's a terrible idea.

Say yes.

"I, uh..." I start. Regan kicks me under the table as I search my head for a plausible excuse.

"Mommy, you always wanted to go there," Gigi says excitedly. "You said only princesses get to go. You have to go, you *have* to. You'll be a princess."

"Kinda hard to say no to that, isn't it?" he says.

"I supposed if Patrick says—"

"You know he'll do it," Ava says. She turns to Tag. "That's a yes. She'll be there. Eight o'clock?"

"Eight it is. I'll swing by on the way and pick you up."

"I can walk."

His strong mouth presses into a smirk. "I've seen you walk in heels, Flower Girl. I'll pick you up."

"Fine. I guess... I guess I'll meet you out front."

His smile. I'm not sure I've ever seen one like it. It's charming. Unpredictable. Dangerous. "See you then, Maddie." He pats Gigi on the head and walks away.

Gigi claps. "It's just like *Beauty and the Beast*, Mommy."

In my mind, I'm wondering which one of us is Beauty and which is the Beast. "It is?"

"He's Smokey the Bear. That's kind of like the Beast. And you are Belle, hidden away in your castle."

Damn. Her words. They hit me hard. She's five now. She picks up on things. Things like: I never go out. Things like: I *do* hide.

"If you say you love him, you can live happily ever after. Right, Mommy?"

"Fairy tales are fun to read, baby. But they aren't real." I nod to the swings. "Look, Kara is calling you over."

She runs off. I pick at the table again, refusing to make eye contact with my friends. I know what's about to happen.

"Holy shit, Maddie," Regan says. "You have a date with Tag. A date. At a restaurant. With food. We're in uncharted territory here. When should we plan the wedding?"

"Will you shut up? It's just dinner." I shrug as though it doesn't matter, but on the inside, I'm trembling so badly I question my ability to stand.

"Face it, girl. It's a date," Ava says. "With the man who never dates. This is like winning the lottery. How will you do your hair? What will you wear? Should we come over and help you get ready?"

"It's not the prom, guys. It's one meal. Would you quit making such a big deal?"

I dare to peek over my shoulder in the direction of the pub. I curse myself when he sees me looking. Then again, in order for him to catch me, he had to turn and look too. I take a deep breath.

"Sister, you just sighed," Ava says. "Oh, boy."

"What?"

She laughs. "I remember doing a lot of sighing when Trevor and I first got together."

"You think this is anything like you and Trev? We're messing around, Ava."

"The man fixed your wall, painted your living room, skipped work for you, and is taking you to Lloyd's. The guy's in love, Maddie."

I choke on my coffee. "Love? You two should know better than anyone that Tag isn't capable of love. I'm his plaything. His distraction. Maybe he's going through a mid-life crisis."

"He's twenty-nine," Regan says.

"Whatever."

"Maybe he found God," Ava adds.

The three of us look at each other and burst out in laughter. On the inside, though, I'm a scared little girl about to dive headfirst into the deep end. I just hope I have the good sense to come up for air.

Chapter Twenty-three

Tag

After lunch, I sit at my desk, wondering about her.

Why does she never let anyone watch her kid but Patrick? Is he secretly Gigi's father? Does he have special powers? What makes a gay man more qualified than her friends or her grandmother? I open my laptop. I google *Calloway Creek fire Maddie Foster*.

The first picture I see is the house they lived in—or what used to be a house. It's unrecognizable. The only thing left standing is a charred water heater, a chimney, and a washing machine. The rest is the gutted remains of sooty-black siding and roof beams. I zoom in and see a melted bed frame. Jesus, was that her bed? I scroll down and see another picture of the house engulfed in flames, a flickering orange glow beyond a smoky haze. Fire trucks and police cars are in the foreground, an ambulance off to one side. A plume of fire pierces one side of the roof. She was in there with Gigi. My heart pounds as I imagine what she must have been doing to try to get to her.

A third picture shows a younger Maddie, happy and seemingly carefree, holding her baby daughter next to Cody Jamison. I didn't know Cody. He was a lot younger than me. Closer to Cooper's age. He was a mechanic like his dad. They moved to town when his father bought the Goodyear place over by the school for the deaf and blind. Ah, man; it's not far from Maddie's shop. A half mile at best. It makes me wonder why she's never mentioned them. And when I say never, I'm referring to the four times I've seen her since Saturday.

I study the picture, but it's not her I'm scrutinizing; it's him. For a mechanic, he was pretty clean cut. Tall, dark, clean-shaven, decently built. And he's looking at them like they're his world.

Fuck. I close the lid to my laptop, realizing I'm jealous of a dead man.

Nora taps on my doorframe. "Mr. Calloway, we're all set for the photo shoot with Joaquin Villanova next Wednesday."

"Where is it?"

"In the city. Calloway Creek University reserved the tennis courts in the park for the afternoon."

"The city, huh?"

Where you were with her *on Saturday.*

"Did they hire my recommended photographer?"

"They did."

"Good. Is my two o'clock here?"

"In the meeting room."

"Thanks, Nora."

She doesn't move from my doorway.

"Is there anything else?"

"No. It's just that you're different this week."

"Different good or different bad?"

"Let's just say I haven't dreaded coming into work."

I offer up a disbelieving snort. "Nora, I know I'm particular and want the things I want, but it can't be that bad."

"Have you ever thought to wonder why you went through six assistants before me?"

I shrug. "Because I slept with all of them?"

My forty-two-year-old assistant, which Jaxon hired on my behalf one day last year when I was drunk, rolls her eyes, looking like my mother. "Because before this week, you never said thank you. You never smiled. You never gave anyone an afternoon off, including yourself, and you walked around like everyone owed you something."

"Fuck. Really?"

"And you curse a lot."

"I'm not sure that's ever going to change, Nora."

"But something has."

I pick up my leather-bound notepad. "I have a meeting to get to."

"Sure thing, Mr. Calloway."

I turn back after I'm out the door. "You should call me Tag."

"Whatever you say, Tag."

My meeting lasts far too long, and I'm way too distracted. The pictures of the fire linger in my mind. Thankfully, Brody is here to pick up my slack and does a great job of schmoozing our potential client, an indoor football arena team from New Jersey that is pinning their last hopes on our ability to pack their stands in the upcoming season and save them from bankruptcy.

This year has been stellar for CSM. In fact, it's been the most lucrative we've had since I started the company four years ago after interning and then working for a major sports marketing firm in New York City for three years. It was a risk I took with money I didn't have. But it's starting to pay off. Those debts Hawk

McQuaid holds over my head will be paid off by the time I'm forty. Earlier, if things keep going as they have been.

A publicity plan is created. A timeline set. A contract is signed. All in all, a productive afternoon.

Back at my desk, I regard the laptop. I set down the files in my hand and open the lid. The pictures appear. I scroll down and read the article.

Man dies protecting child, woman severely injured in Calloway Creek house fire.

A 22-year-old man died, and a woman and child were rescued from a house fire on Marigold Lane in Calloway Creek.

Calloway Creek police and Calloway Creek Fire and Rescue responded to the fire around 10:45 p.m. CCFD Chief Keith Armstrong said firefighter Patrick Kelsey ran into the back bedroom, pulling the one-year-old child from the arms of her deceased father, who had died protecting her. Family members identified the man as Cody Jamison, mechanic and son of Evan and Ellen Jamison, owners of Goodyear Auto on Third Avenue.

The child, identified as Gigi Jamison Foster, daughter of Cody Jamison and live-in girlfriend, Maddie Foster, suffered only minor smoke inhalation due to the sacrifice of Jamison, who covered the toddler and shielded her with his body, and the quick actions of firefighter Patrick Kelsey.

Foster, 23, is reported to be in Memorial Hospital on a ventilator with second- and third-degree burns covering ten percent of her body. The woman's grandmother told our reporter that doctors believe she will survive, but it's not going to be an easy recovery for her.

The fire is still under investigation and the Jamisons plan to announce the funeral plans for their son in the coming days.

The guy was a goddamn hero. He died protecting his daughter. And Patrick—it makes sense now—he saved Gigi. She would have died right along with Cody had it not been for him. He's the only one Maddie trusts. Does she think it will happen again?

I eye the pack of cigarettes on the corner of my desk. No wonder she hates them so much. I push them over the edge, and they fall into my trash can. Then I pop a stick of gum into my mouth.

I should look up who owned the house. Probably some slumlord who didn't bother fixing the faulty wiring. I'm about to do a search when I notice what I hadn't before. The article is dated four years ago, just days before I opened the doors at CSM. I do a double-take at the date. May twenty-ninth. 529. FlowerGirl529. The date that changed her life forever.

FlowerGirl529 and SportsFan601. The significance of our numbers couldn't be more opposite. While my life was just beginning, hers almost came to an end.

No wonder I never heard much about the fire. As always, I was too wrapped up in my own life to care what was going on around me.

I force open my file drawer, stripping the knob right off the screw, and shove some folders inside. I study the knob for a moment before I set it on the corner of my desk and tell Nora I'm heading out.

~ ~ ~

7:05 p.m. My hands are full of take-out food and my arms are lined with plastic bags of supplies. I ring the bell. After a minute or two, I ring it again. Then Maddie appears in the doorway.

"What are you doing here?"

A frown snaps between my brows. "Are you going to ask that question *every* time you see me?"

"When you show up unannounced—yes."

"Can I come in?"

"That depends on how you answer my previous question."

I hold up the bags. "I'm going to fix your cabinets. And I brought dinner."

"Dinner? But dinner is tomorrow. And Gigi's here. Why do you want to fix my cabinets?"

"Because half of them are missing knobs, and the others are barely on the hinges. And I know Gigi's here. She's always here. That's why I brought macaroni and cheese from Goodwin's."

"You stopped at the diner?"

"You do like mac and cheese, no?"

"Goodwin's mac and cheese is Gigi's favorite. They make it with bacon bits and real cheese."

"It's everyone's favorite. Are you going to let me up, Flower Girl?"

She holds the door open and lets me pass. We go up the stairs. Gigi immediately runs to the Goodwin's bag, recognizing the logo. She bounces. "Is this for me, Smokey the Bear?"

"It's for all of us," I say. "If it's okay that I eat with you. I brought broccoli, too. I hope you like it."

"Yummy!"

"Gigi, go wash up," Maddie says. She takes the food from me and puts it on the table, then she hides the bags of Ramen and the pack of hot dogs that were on the counter. "How did you even know we'd be home?"

"You're *always* home."

"That's not true."

"You're right. You're always home except for Tuesdays, when you take Gigi to your grandmother's and Patrick's and then out for ice cream; and Saturdays when the two of you go to the park; and sometimes on Fridays when I see you and your friends at Donovan's."

She takes a step back. "Are you stalking me?"

"Don't flatter yourself. You told me about Tuesdays. Everyone goes to Donovan's on Fridays, and I hike the Cal Creek trails every weekend and see you and Gigi over at the park. You're predictable, Maddie. And you need to get out a lot more often."

"We do just fine."

"I almost hit on you on St. Patrick's Day at the pub. Do you remember the party?"

"It was huge. I think I peed green for days."

"We all did. Donny must have used a gallon of food coloring in everything we ate and drank that night."

She scoops the meal onto plates. "Why didn't you? Were you embarrassed?"

"Fuck, Maddie. I wish you'd quit saying shit like that. No, I wasn't embarrassed. I guess I didn't want to be the dick who screwed innocent Maddie Foster."

"You mean *poor* Maddie Foster."

"You're the only one who thinks that about yourself. You think people talk about you, and they do, the same way they talk about old Joe Henson, the hermit who never leaves his one-room cabin at the mouth of the creek. If you're a freak, it's because you never go out. Not because of your scars. Do you know how many people commented on you being at that party? It was like a bear coming out of hibernation. Or a Phoenix rising from the ashes. Other than you sitting outside the pub with Regan and Ava on the occasional Friday, and drinking coffee in the courtyard, it was the first time any Cal Creek resident had actually seen you having fun. You were the talk of the town that night."

"I had no idea that's why people were looking at me." She sits heavily on the chair. "It was a dare. Just like the After Dark dare. My friends wanted to get me out there."

Gigi comes racing out and starts devouring her dinner. Maddie spoons broccoli onto her plate. "Veggies, too, little lady."

"Yes, Mommy."

The three of us sit and eat at her small round table that rocks back and forth as we put our weight on it. Maddie and Gigi tell me about some interesting customers they had today. About the late supply delivery that put off all their deliveries by two hours. About the woman who booked her as the florist for her daughter's small wedding later this month. It's so weirdly normal. So oddly pedestrian. So unexpectedly fascinating.

Unlikely DATE

When Maddie clears the table, I turn it upside down, then fish through my supplies until I find something that works. I secure a felt pad to one of the legs, put it upright again, and test it. "There, no more wobbly table."

"I was going to get to that," she says.

"You don't have to defend the fact that you have zero free time because you work your ass off, Maddie. You put in ten-hour days, get one day off a week, and are raising a kid by yourself."

"I don't get *any* days off from that." She watches Gigi step up on a stool in front of the sink and wash her plate. "Good thing she's so amazing."

Maddie dries the dishes and puts them into one of the cabinets with a broken hinge. She laughs. "I guess I do need a handyman. I just don't understand why you want to be it."

I shrug. "I'm done fixing up my house. I don't do well with boredom. Needed another project."

"Is that what I am to you? A project?"

"You?" I allow my eyes to travel from her head to her toes, taking in her wavy hair, clipped in back to keep it off her face; her sheer blue blouse, which brings out the aqua specs in her eyes; her tan skirt, which shows her shapely calves; and those bare feet that make me want to become some fetish toe sucker. "Believe me, there is nothing about you that needs to be fixed." I wave my hand around her apartment. "This place, however, needs a complete overhaul. Look at the walls. They're already breathing life back into the room. Just think what hardwood floors, new lighting, and updated appliances would do."

"I'm quite sure you don't have all that in your shed. I won't be anyone's charity case. You want to fix some broken hinges or replace light bulbs, be my guest. But you're not going to buy me anything new. That's where I draw the line."

213

"But if it comes from my shed, it's okay?"

She shrugs. "I suppose. If that's what floats your boat, who am I to say no?"

I smile. She doesn't have to know that in the last two seconds, I've planned a trip to a nice secondhand shop outside of town. She doesn't have to know I'm going to stock up on flooring, lights, and whatever else I can find to spruce this place up. She doesn't have to know I'll get off on a technicality if she finds out. She did, after all, say I can't buy her anything *new*. And it *will* all come from my shed—once I put it in there.

She also doesn't need to know that this completely foreign feeling I'm experiencing, the one that has me hearing the rush of my heartbeat in my ears at the sight of her, is totally messing with my goddamn head.

I dump out my supplies. "Let me fix those cabinets, then."

Chapter Twenty-four

Maddie

"What about this one?" I ask Patrick, turning around so he can see the dress from all angles.

"It looks just like one of the others."

"No, it doesn't. This one is cream. The other was white."

"But with the blue cardigan, they all look the same."

I sigh and finger the buttons on the summery sweater. "Can I help it that all Regan and Ava have are sleeveless dresses? The only nice dress I have that I can wear without this, he's seen."

"They're all beautiful, Maddie."

"You look like an angel," Gigi says. "Twirl around, Mommy."

I do and the skirt of the dress floats up. She giggles.

"Are you all packed, kiddo?" Patrick asks her.

"Even my toothbrush. Mommy didn't have to remind me this time."

"You don't have to take her for the night," I say. "It's only dinner."

"Are you kidding?" He flips her onto his shoulders and prances around the living room. "We have plans. We're building a fort around the dining room table and are going to sleep inside it. Aren't we, squirt?"

Gigi squeals in delight. "Can I bring my pillow?"

"You bet." He puts her down, and she runs to her room. His hands land on my shoulders, his head ducking down to eye level, and he talks to me like the father I never had. "Stop worrying. Like you said, it's only dinner. Whatever happens, happens. But without us here, you have options."

Gigi drags her pillow behind her and tugs on Patrick's hand. "Let's go."

I kiss them both on the cheek and watch them descend the stairs. Then I go to the bathroom and look in the mirror. I take off the cardigan and study my arm, wishing I could afford the kinds of makeup they use in movies. I've tried all kinds over the years to conceal my scars. The best ones rub off on my clothes. The others cake in my elbow crease. I slip the sweater back on, knowing it's the simplest way to achieve my goal.

I lift my dress, taking one last peek at my brand-new underwear. I had Lincoln watch the store for an hour during lunch while Gigi and I ran to Target, where I bought the sexiest bra and panty set I could afford. Because… options.

For years, I've been too busy and pre-occupied to even think about being with a man. I've buried my dreams, built and fortified walls around me, surrendered any chance of a happy ending. But now, thoughts of last night swirl in my head. The way he brushed against me accidentally on purpose every time he walked near me. The way his stare held mine across the room while he fixed my faulty cabinets. The way his lips felt on mine when he stole a kiss before leaving. Even the way he said goodnight to Gigi. The man who hates kids hugged my daughter back when she clung to him before going to bed. I really should warn her against falling for bad boys.

That's exactly what Tag Calloway is—bad. For her. For me. For anyone who thinks they're stupid enough to change him.

I glance away before my reflection calls me an idiot.

The bell rings and my heart pounds. I'm going on a date. An actual date. With Tag Calloway. In public. Before my negative thoughts have me bailing on the whole thing, I grab my purse and carefully navigate the stairs.

When I open the door, I'm stunned. Everyone is used to seeing him in his regular CEO attire—the crisp button-down shirts and linen slacks. I didn't expect him to be wearing a tie that matches his striking golden chestnut eyes. And his beard has been trimmed and thinned out more than it was when he had his head between my legs the other day. I shift my weight from heel to heel. Even his hair seems tamer. It occurs to me that he's spent at least as much time getting ready as I have. And the thought of it makes my stomach do cartwheels.

But the most shocking thing about the man standing before me is what he's holding: flowers. The man who never gives flowers to women has now given them to me twice. The first one didn't really count, however; they were *my* flowers from *my* shop, and he only used them as a means to pay me back. These, though, are the actual, bona fide thing.

"Don't worry," he says, handing them over. "I didn't use your competition. My mom has rose bushes."

"They're beautiful. Your mom obviously has a green thumb. Thank you." I don't tell him that I wouldn't have cared if he bought them from Tito's over on Seventh Avenue, or even the grocery store flower shop. The fact that he brought them at all is unbelievable. That he took the time to cut them and bundle them himself is downright amazing. I put my nose in the bouquet and inhale their scent. "Let me just put these in water in the back room."

I almost trip over myself walking through the shop. Why am I so freaking nervous? This isn't any different from Saturday. Except that it totally is. Everything about this night is intentional. It's not a mistake; not a random selection from some algorithm.

"Everything okay?" he asks, walking up behind me.

"Fine." I arrange the flowers in a vase and leave them on the counter for later. "There, all set."

"Let's go then. We don't want to miss our reservation." He leans in. "You look beautiful, by the way."

I smile. "Thank you."

He toys with a button on my open cardigan. "You'd look even more amazing without this."

"I—"

His fingers go to my lips, shushing me. "You'd look amazing without *all* of it."

My eyes close as I remember what his tongue did to me. I resolve to stay upright when my knees try to buckle.

He nips at my earlobe. "I'm going to see you naked, Flower Girl." The tone of his voice is low and purring.

I let out an indecisive sigh.

He pulls back. "Maybe not today, maybe not tomorrow, but someday."

Someday. If my heart were hooked up to one of those machines, it would be beeping incessantly. He's planning on having a *someday* with me. Part of me wants to shed the sweater, show him I can be the woman he wants. Then again, why should I have to change myself for any man?

Unlikely DATE

His hand guides me by the small of my back as we go out the door to his waiting SUV. He unlocks the passenger door.

"Lloyd's is three blocks away, Tag. I can walk. My feet aren't broken."

Unlike other parts of me.

"Just get in, Maddie."

He holds out his hand for support. I take it and step up on the running board before sliding into the seat. I'm surrounded by buttery leather, and the new car smell mixed with stale smoke permeates my nostrils. I've never been in a luxury car before. I feel like a queen on her throne.

It takes us exactly one minute to drive to the restaurant. He parks in the back, in the parking lot that is practically connected to the alley behind my shop.

The tie. The hair. The flowers. The ride. *Is he trying to impress me?*

I keep my head down, ignoring the stares as we enter the restaurant. Everyone is wondering why we're together. Why Tag Calloway is taking Maddie Foster to dinner. At one of the nicest places in town, no less.

He takes my elbow. "Stop it."

"Stop what?"

"The thing you do with your thumb."

I trap it inside a fist. "Everyone is looking at me."

"They aren't looking at you. They're looking at me."

I snort. "Cocky much?"

"They're wondering what a Calloway is doing in a McQuaid restaurant."

We're led to a booth in the corner. I slide in and he sits across from me. "What *are* you doing in a McQuaid restaurant?"

"Truth? They have killer steaks. Don't tell anyone, but I order takeout from here once a month. Have an Uber driver deliver it to me." I follow his gaze as he looks around the place. Mahogany booths padded with more expensive leather. Pressed white tablecloths. An array of forks—several of which, I have no idea their purpose. "The interior could really use updating."

I look at him sideways. "What are you talking about? It's amazing."

"I'm a Calloway, Maddie. It's ingrained in me to find a fault in everything that family does."

"Fair enough." I pick up the empty crystal water glass and inspect it. "Look here, there's a fingerprint on the base. The nerve. Are you sure you even want to dine here? Who knows, there could be rats in the kitchen."

He laughs. "That's the spirit."

A waitress appears, handing us leather-bound menus. "Would you like sparkling water or tap?"

Tag looks at me. *She* doesn't. "Uh, tap would be fine," I say.

"Would you like to order drinks?" she asks, still staring at my date's lips.

She's exactly the kind of girl Tag goes for. Huge boobs. Tiny waist. Legs up to there. Eyes that scream 'Take me to bed.' And perfect, flawless skin.

"Maddie?"

I realize he's waiting for me.

"Yes. A drink. Wine would be nice."

"White or red?" he asks.

"Whichever you prefer. I'm easy." The waitress snorts. *Did I really just say I'm easy?* "I mean, I'm up for anything." *Oh, my gosh, stop now.* "Go ahead and order whatever you'd normally get."

He orders something I've never heard of—a bottle of it.

The curvy waitress leaves, and I wonder just how hard it is for him not to watch her walk away.

"Sorry," I say. "I don't get out much."

He chuckles. "You're adorable."

"Adorable isn't what I was going for. Sophisticated, perhaps. I'd even settle for adultlike."

"Well, I happen to like adorable. It's a refreshing change."

Change from what—slutty, pretentious, vain? I open the menu and start perusing. It's the only thing I can do to keep from looking around at all the people who are surely watching us. My eyes settle on an entrée that sounds scrumptious, a petite filet with grilled scallops. Then I notice something. "Tag, the menus don't have any prices."

He leans over the table and peeks at mine. "I guess they're old school here. Mine does."

"Yours has prices and mine doesn't?" The muscles in my jaw tense. "That's so sexist. What if we were splitting the bill? What if I was paying? How do I know what to order?"

"Yes, it is sexist. If you want to submit a comment card via their website, I'm sure they'll hand it right to Lloyd himself," he says. I roll my eyes because Lloyd is dead. "And you're supposed to order what looks good."

"What looks good?"

He lounges back in his seat, realization crossing his face. "You always order based on the price, don't you?"

I shrug. "Yeah, well, when you live on a budget..."

"You're not on one tonight."

"It's not fair to you. What if the entrée I get is the most expensive one?"

"What do you want?"

"I was thinking the petite filet with the scallops."

He scans the menu. "I assure you, it's not. And even if you ordered the Chateaubriand, it would still be okay."

"I don't even know what that is."

So much for sophisticated.

The waitress brings our bottle of wine, opens it, pours a tiny bit in a glass, and leans into him as she hands it over, her deep cleavage clearly an invitation for him to accept. Ignoring her, Tag swirls the wine in his glass, sniffs it, tastes it, and nods. "Good," he says, and then she fills it along with mine.

I try to savor my glass, guessing it costs more than I make on a good day at the shop.

Another waiter walks by, with a tray of desserts. A whiff of chocolate lingers. "Gigi's friend Kara says Lloyd's has the best dessert she's ever had. I think she called it a chocolate mudslide cake."

"We'll get one for her, then."

I shake my head. "I didn't say that so you'd get one, Tag. I was just making conversation."

"You don't need to try so hard, Maddie. I'm not judging you. I'm not keeping score here."

I look around. People *are* staring. "I guess I'm just nervous. I'm not used to this."

"Having dinner?"

"You know what I mean."

The waitress returns. Tag orders for us. Including dessert—one for us to share and one to go.

The moment she leaves, I give him a nasty look. "Caveman much? I changed my mind; I *was* going to get the Chateaubriand." Without hesitation, he goes to call the waitress back, but I stop him. "I'm kidding."

He looks relieved. "Okay, good. I mean, it's fine if you would have ordered it, but dang, that is one overpriced piece of cow."

I'm surprised to hear him say it.

He takes a drink. "You think I'm well off."

"You are."

"My huge mortgage, sky-high car loan, and CSM business debt beg to differ."

"But—"

"Appearances, Maddie. I told you before, it's all about appearances."

I pull down the sleeve of my cardigan.

"I'm not talking about looks. I run a business. People need to think I'm the powerful CEO they can trust with their marketing."

"You aren't?"

"I'm good at my job. They're wise to trust me. But building a business isn't easy or cheap. Someday I'll be wealthy. Just not today."

I look around the expensive restaurant, feeling guilty.

"Stop it. I wanted to bring you here."

"For appearances?"

"I don't know. Maybe. Cut me a break here. I've never had to work at this before."

I bite my lip to suppress a smile. So he *is* trying to impress me. "Tag, do you know how uncomfortable I feel here? I'm so out of my element. If you want to do something nice for me, take me to a picnic in the park. Or buy me an ice-cream cone. I don't need all this. The truth is—I don't *want* all this."

He stares at me. Then he calls our waitress over. "We'd like everything to go. Including some utensils."

"You're leaving?" she asks, then finally looks at me like I'm an afterthought. She smirks as if this is a date gone bad; one she's happy to be witnessing. She probably thinks she can slip him her number, and he'll come back for her later. *Tramp.*

"Are you sure we need forks, babe?" I say, surprising myself at my feigned confidence. "I thought we were just going to hand-feed each other naked by your fire pit."

The waitress scurries away, leaving Tag belly laughing. "There she is."

"There who is?"

"The girl who called my bluff at the pizza joint the other night and fed bullshit back to me on a platter."

My face heats up.

"And how do you know I have a fire pit?"

"Lucky guess."

His eyes are ablaze with heat as he stares me down.

"Fat chance, buddy."

"I guess we'll have to settle for a picnic in the park, then."

This time, I don't hold in my smile.

The waitress brings a large bag with all our food, and the check. After Tag pays and we leave, he hands me the bag. "Wait here."

He runs around the corner, returning a minute later with a blanket—from his car, I presume. "Shall we?" he says, motioning to the park on the other side of McQuaid Circle.

This date is shaping up to be better than expected.

Chapter Twenty-five

Tag

Crossing to the park, I see the Jamisons' Goodyear shop down the street, catty-corner to where we're walking. "Do you see Cody's parents often?"

"No."

"But don't they want to see their granddaughter?"

"I'd rather not talk about his parents."

I lead us to a spot of grass between two trees. "This okay?" I eye her short dress. "Or do you want to find a bench?"

She takes the blanket and spreads it. "This is perfect." She removes her shoes and sits.

I try not to think about how her bare feet are even sexier without the heels on. I sit too, placing the bag of food between us. "Will you tell me about him?"

"There's not much to tell, really. I met him shortly after moving to Calloway Creek. I was twenty and he was nineteen. I think he liked that I wasn't from here. He wasn't either. I suppose that made us both outsiders or something."

I hand her a take-out container, and she attempts to balance it on her lap and cut the steak. Luckily, the serrated plastic knife seems to cut through it like butter. I can practically see her mouth water, and it makes me wonder when the last time was that she had a meal like this.

"You dated for a long time," I say, having a slightly harder time slicing into my ribeye.

"About eighteen months before I got pregnant."

She pops a scallop into her mouth as I silently wait for more.

"It was an accident. The condom broke. And it was a huge dose of reality."

"How so?"

"Suddenly, I couldn't see myself with him long term. He was fun, and we were young, both apprentices to our family businesses, but something was missing."

"What?"

She swallows another bite as I watch her eyes trace a path up the side hem of my pants. She turns away and shrugs. "Passion."

"You didn't love him?"

"I liked him a lot. I tried to love him. But I always knew there should be more. I was stupidly staying with him until something better came along. I guess I deserved to get pregnant, stringing him along like that. Ending the pregnancy was never an option for me. And I couldn't much hide it from my grandmother, who I shared an apartment with. Gran is very old fashioned. She wanted us to get married. And even though I felt trapped having a baby with a man I wasn't in love with, I knew marrying him would put me into a box I didn't want to be in."

"But you decided to move in with him."

"To appease Gran. Even though she was old fashioned, I think she believed if we lived together, we'd eventually get married.

I suppose in her book it was the lesser of two evils; the greater one being not having a man to help care for my child."

"But you never got married."

She shakes her head. "We never even slept together again. I had a lot of morning sickness throughout the pregnancy, then after Gigi was born, I was exhausted. I used those as excuses. I'm not even sure why he put up with it for so long."

"Maybe he was in love with you."

She swallows, looking guilty. "I think he was. Like Gran, he thought I would come around. We lived like roommates sharing a bed. I never disliked him throughout any of it. He was a good friend, in fact. Just not the man I wanted to spend my life with."

"Do you think you'd have eventually moved out?"

"Honestly? I don't know. Gigi loved having him around, and he was great with her."

"Staying together for the kid. How noble of you." I'm well aware of the bitterness in my voice.

"You say that like it comes from experience."

I nod to her food. "How's your steak?"

"Best one I've ever had."

"Next time I get takeout, I'll have you over."

Her eyes snap to mine. "To your *house*?"

"Maddie, I'm not sure what you think we're doing here, but a lot of people would call it dating."

She chokes. "Dating? Tag, you don't date."

"What would you call this?"

"Another attempt to get in my pants."

I allow my eyes to blaze a trail from her sexy feet all the way up to the hem of her short dress. "You're not wearing any. Besides, if that's all I wanted, I could have been deep in your so-called pants the other night. If you recall, I was the one who said no."

"It's not going to happen, you know. You seeing me naked."

"Oh, it'll happen, Flower Girl." I close the lid on my meal, do the same to hers, put them aside, and scoot to her feet. I pick one up and put it in my lap. I rub the arch with my thumbs.

"You like feet?" She tries to pull it away. "Gross."

I trap it. "I've wanted to touch these since our paint fight the other day. Believe me, there's nothing gross about them. About *any* of you."

She relaxes and lets me massage her. She lies back on the blanket, her hair framing either side of her, her eyes salaciously closed. Her lips part and air escapes in a satisfied sigh. She's fucking gorgeous.

I move her foot to the left and rest it against my erection. Her eyes fly open to find me smiling. "Relax, Maddie. Just enjoy."

She closes her eyes again. Her toes wiggle against me, making me harder. Shit. We're having a picnic, and all I can think about is having *her*.

I look around, assessing the area. We're between two trees, which offers us a little privacy. There's a family across the pond at the playground. A few couples walking along the path about twenty yards away. I lie next to her, keeping myself propped on an elbow, blocking her from the prying eyes of innocent children on swings. Then I wait for a break in the meanderers. I lean toward her and whisper against her soft, silky hair, "I'm going to make you come."

She stiffens and her eyes dart around. "Are you crazy?"

"A little bit, yes. But I'm doing it anyway."

When she sees we're practically alone, she throws an arm over her head and lies back. She's going to let me do this.

I remove her arm. "I want to see your face when you come."

Her face turns a deep scarlet, redder than her hair. "There are people over there."

"I'll be quick. And just so you know, you being embarrassed just makes me harder."

I put her hand on my crotch. She bites her lip and lets it rest there. She closes her eyes, giving me all the control, though I know better. She's the one driving this train. And suddenly, I know she has the power to derail it at any time. And the thought hits me square in the chest.

Her body shudders as I move my hand from her knee up under her dress, keeping the material in place in case an unsuspecting pedestrian should wander by. I haven't even touched her pussy, yet this is already one of the hottest things I've ever done. When my fingers reach her panties, I find them drenched.

I glance up. The people are getting bigger in the distance. I know I don't have much time.

I push the wet scrap aside and plunge a finger inside her. She moans silently, just enough to drive a man wild. "You are so wet," I whisper. "And so goddamn tight. Do you know what I would give to push my cock inside you right now?" I find *the spot*. The one I found the other night. Its location is burned into my mind—chronicled along with the memory of her falling apart in front of me.

My thumb rubs circles on her clit. Her hand presses harder against my dick, rubbing me on top of my pants. I'm painfully hard as I add a second finger inside her. She arches her back.

"That's right, you're so close. I'm so fucking hard for you."

Her eyes flash open. She spots the people down the way. "Tag, they're coming." Her thighs tighten around me and her hips buck.

"So are you, baby. So are you."

Her eyes close, and her neck arches against the ground as her walls pulsate against my fingers. A squealing sound escapes her throat, and I know she's holding in a scream.

When she relaxes, I withdraw my fingers. Her eyes open and she stares at me. I stare at her. And then I see it.

Passion.

I lean down and kiss her cheek. Then I move her panties into place and bring my fingers to my mouth to lick them. Looking embarrassed once again, she sits up and scoots away, glancing at the couple coming closer who are oblivious to what just happened.

"Why, Ms. Foster. I do believe you get off on exhibitionism."

A defiant lower lip juts out. "I do not."

I laugh. "I'm calling bullshit. You opened your eyes. You saw them getting closer. And it made you hot. The thrill that someone might see me fingering your pussy made you come all over my hand."

"That's not fair. I was too close to stop it."

Her pout is fucking adorable. "I'm kidding, Maddie. But you have to admit, knowing we could get caught made it hotter, right? Dangerous."

"You're what's dangerous," she says.

It's like a spear to my gut. My thumb strokes her cheekbone. "I'm not. Not to you. That's a promise."

"You shouldn't make promises you can't keep."

"I'm not. Not this time."

"Do you, um, want to go back to my apartment? Gigi is spending the night at Patrick's."

"That depends. Do I get to see all of you?"

"I…" Her eyes stray from mine. "I'm not ready."

"Then, no, I won't be going there. Not unless it's to renovate."

There's the pout again. I hold in my laugh.

She looks at my crotch. Even sitting, it's obvious I have a raging hard-on. "But don't you have needs?"

"I can take care of my needs. Like I did the other night in your bathroom." Her face pinks. "That's right. And I plan on doing a lot more of that."

"Let me get this straight. Not only won't you sleep with me but you're holding your body hostage from me until I get naked? I can't touch you?"

I lie back and cross my ankles, well aware of my conspicuously tented pants. "That's right, Flower Girl. You want to do the mattress dance, you gotta shed the costume."

"Maddie?"

I sit up and turn around. Then I look back at Maddie, who appears horrified. This isn't the couple on the path; they came from somewhere else.

She stands. "Uh, hi, Evan and Ellen. Tag, do you know Mr. and Mrs. Jamison?"

I get up, deflated enough not to make a spectacle of myself. I hold out my hand to Evan. "You've worked on my dad's Nissan a few times."

He doesn't shake. He doesn't even acknowledge me. He's looking at Maddie. He's looking at her like she's the devil reincarnate.

Ellen turns to me. "You better watch yourself, Mr. Calloway. This one's a black widow. She draws you into her web and then goes for the kill."

Maddie's eyes flood with tears.

I step between them as a barrier, refusing to let anyone speak to her that way. "Hold on there. Aren't you Gigi's grandparents? What are you talking about?"

Evan shoots me a warning look that's impossible to miss. "She hasn't told you, has she? Typical black widow. Watch yourself." He takes his wife's hand and leads her away.

Ellen turns around. "How convenient for you that you get to move on with your life while my son rots in his grave."

Maddie is visibly rattled. I pull her to me. "Are you okay?"

Her body shakes.

"What the hell was that all about?"

"You don't know?"

I cup her face in my hands. "No. I don't."

"I killed Cody," she says, her tears overflowing her lashes.

I sit down on the blanket, pulling her between my legs. "Shhh. I'm sure that's not true."

"It is true. The night of… The Incident… Cody was working late. Gigi had finally gone to bed, and I got into a quick shower. She was almost a year old, and I still felt like a frumpy new mom. So I decided to make myself feel better about my appearance and straighten my hair. The problem was, Gigi started fussing so I threw my hair in a bun and went to her."

I think I see where this is going, so I pull her tightly against me.

"I forgot I left the straightener on and went to bed. There was a box of tissues next to it. And towels hanging on the wall." Her voice cracks with painful emotion. "It went up so fast, and there wasn't time to do anything. I couldn't get to her. He…" Her body shakes with sobs. "He climbed through her window and saved her. She would have died if it weren't for him. And he died because of me."

I blow out a long breath. "And they never let you forget it."

She cries quietly, and I let her. I don't want to push her anymore. We sit this way for minutes, her back molding to my chest.

"Gigi stayed with them for months after, while I was in the hospital. They filed for custody. Called me an unfit parent."

"Jesus."

"I was scared to death. It *was* my fault, after all. I thought they were going to take her away. But the judge ruled in my favor. Said it was an accident."

"It was."

"An accident that was my fault."

"You can't keep blaming yourself, Maddie. Accidents happen. My brother Cooper tries to take all the blame for Chaz's death, did you know that?"

"But I read about it in the news. That *was* an accident."

"One he feels responsible for."

"Maybe we should start a club."

I laugh. Because what the hell else can I do? I turn her around so she's facing me. "It's not your fault."

She ignores my comment and points to the Jamisons, who are mere shadows now. "Even though they tried to take her from me, I still let them see her. I let them see her even though it scared me. Even though Patrick wouldn't be there to protect her if anything went wrong."

"I feel a *but* coming."

"But one day last year, when Gigi was four, she came home and asked me why I burned Daddy. It's then I knew they were still trying to take her from me, and they'd do it emotionally if they couldn't do it physically. I know they hate me even more for keeping her from them, but I had to do it. For her."

"Of course you did. What they did is unforgivable, trying to turn your daughter against you."

She wipes mascara from under her eyes. "I apologize. I went and ruined a perfectly good evening."

"You didn't ruin anything. But if you insist, I'll let you make it up to me. Sunday night? If Patrick is available, of course."

She sniffs away her tears with the smallest curve of her lips. "I think that could be arranged."

"And if he's not available, I'll bring the mac and cheese."

An hour later, after we drive around town and do nothing but talk, I pull up behind her shop and walk her to the back door. I want to go in with her. I want it more than anything. But I'm afraid if I do, I'll cave. She thinks I won't sleep with her unless she shows me her body.

It's a lie I've been telling her. Hell, it's one I've been telling myself.

Standing here looking at her, I know the real reason. I won't sleep with her because I'm afraid if I do, there'll be no turning back. If I do, my resolve will crumble, and I'll become just like every other schmuck ruled by the fairer sex. I'll be like all the other men who fall under some spell and into some kind of trap just to please another human because she has a pussy between her legs.

I'll become the very person I've sworn never to become since the day I found out my mother cheated on him. I'll become my father.

Not even the woman standing in front of me is worth all that. So I kiss her on the cheek.

Then I walk away like a goddamn dog with his tail between his legs.

Chapter Twenty-six

Maddie

He left. He promised he wasn't dangerous, and then he left. I saw it in his eyes as we stood out back. Something changed. Something shifted inside him. I saw the moment he decided he didn't want me. I knew it would happen eventually.

I just didn't know it would hurt this bad.

Yes, you did.

I sit in the middle of my living room, the odor of fresh paint still lingering, reminding me of nights I will never experience again.

He's been in my life for five days. Five days of my every thought being of him. Five days of longing, needing, and wanting.

Five days of being in love with him.

Stupid, stupid girl. How did you let this happen?

I change into a T-shirt, toss myself on my bed, and cry myself to sleep.

~ ~ ~

I jolt awake, terrified. "Gigi!" I yell, racing into her room as the smoke detector beeps over and over. Something's wrong. She's not here. Where's the smoke?

The noise starts again. Only it's not coming from the ceiling. There's no fire. I slump against the wall and catch my breath. It's the doorbell. At two in the morning. Someone is ringing my doorbell repeatedly. I pad down the stairs and crack the back door.

Tag is pacing outside. He looks up, sees me, bolts through the door, and pushes me against the wall so hard it hurts. His lips capture mine. It's a desperate kiss, like he's clinging to life, and I'm his last breath. Surrendering to him without a second thought, my fingers drive into his lush, dark hair, grabbing fistfuls as his mouth continues to crush against mine.

"I tried to stay away, but I couldn't," he says between kisses. He thrusts into me, his erection pressing against my stomach. "I drove around all night." His tongue devours my neck, licking the remnants of salty tears that settled there earlier. "I'm sorry I left." He lifts my shirt and runs a hand under it, latching onto my breast as I unabashedly moan into his mouth. "I want you so fucking bad."

He picks me up and carries me upstairs. So many things are going through my head right now. Why did he come back? What does he really want? What do *I* really want?

I only have the answer to the last question. I want him. I want all of him. And even though he's still dangerous, even though he could burn me far more than I've already been burned, even though he could walk back out that door at any second, I know if I don't do this right here, right now, I might regret it for the rest of my life.

"Put me down," I say at the top of the stairs.

He doesn't let me go. "Maddie, I want you." He glances at the oversized CCFD shirt I've slept in since the day Patrick brought it to me after my release from the hospital. It doesn't quite cover the scars on my arm. He takes them in. "Keep it on. Take it off. I don't care. I want you any way I can have you. And I need you to fucking touch me. I need you to touch all of me."

My heart pounds. I've never heard him say anything so raw and defenseless. He's ripping himself open for me, looking at me like a wounded animal that needs rescuing.

"Tag, put me down."

Reluctantly, he does. It's dim in the living room, but not dark. The light from the stairwell and from Gigi's bedroom filters in softly. I swallow. It's now or never. I take a few steps back, putting needed distance between us. I close my eyes and lift the hem of the shirt, taking it up and over my head, looking away as I drop it next to me on the floor, leaving me in nothing but my underwear.

His eyes are on me. I can feel them. I need him to say something, but he doesn't. I force myself to look at him. He's staring at my right side, at the patchwork of discolored skin down my ribs. Seconds pass like hours, his tortuous stare assaulting the most vulnerable parts of me. I resist the urge to pick up the shirt. I fight the intense need to cover myself with my arms. Tears prickle the backs of my eyes. My throat stings. In my entire life, I've never felt more utterly exposed.

He clears his throat like a viscous knot has taken hold. "Maddie, fuck."

I bend to pick up the shirt. He reaches it before I do and throws it across the room.

"Listen to me," he says. "I have something I need to say, and you have to hear me." He cradles my chin, forcing me to look up at him as he gazes into my watery eyes. "You look at your scars and see death and destruction. You see flaws and imperfections. I look at them and see a road map of your life. I see everything you had to go through to become the person you are today. The single mom who busts her ass to provide for her kid. The woman who is kind and selfless and humble. These scars are part of who you are. Without them, you have no story." Not tearing his eyes from mine, he touches the sensitive skin on my ribs, skimming a thumb across one of the leathery, uneven scars.

I inhale sharply and pull away, not ready to be touched there.

"You think they're ugly," he says, eyeing the ragged skin of my flesh. "I think they're part of what makes you beautiful."

Tears stream down my face. He catches them with his thumb. He steps back and removes all his clothes, then he kneels and slides my panties to the floor. We stare at each other in our nakedness. His penis is erect. It twitches when I gawk at it. And it occurs to me that he's seeing me, *all* of me, and he's still hard.

He stands. "So, Flower Girl, can I pick you up now and make all kinds of fucking love to you?" There is desperation in his voice, an ache that is so inherently honest.

Gratitude chokes me, rendering me incapable of answering with words. I jump into his arms. He catches me and our mouths collide. I've never felt so exposed yet so safe at the same time. He carries me to my bedroom, lays me down on the bed, and hovers over me, staring one last time before his tongue connects with the skin between my breasts. I arch my back, pressing myself into him as he takes his time with each nipple. Licking. Fondling. Biting.

I reach between us and wrap my hand around his penis.

"Jesus, Maddie."

His penis is long, thick, and solid; a steel rod encased in velvety smooth skin that is warm satin beneath my stroking fingers. I run my hand up and down, prompting his nips on my neck and chest to become even more deadly. He groans into my shoulder and then, unexpectedly, his penis jerks, and hot cum projects all over my blue cotton sheets.

He looks at the sticky mess and shakes his head. "Well, shit, that didn't take long." He chuckles. "And now that we've gotten that out of the way, I can take my sweet time with you."

I try to calculate in my head how long I was touching him. Ten seconds? Twenty? It's a heady feeling knowing I can have that effect on a man who has been with countless women before me.

I stiffen when his lips travel near my right side. "Relax," he says, holding me captive under the weight of him. "I told you I want all of you."

He plants soft kisses down my belly, careful not to make contact with the tender flesh of my scars. But he gets close, and my body tenses under his touch.

"You're perfect," he says, as if he knows what I'm thinking.

Perfect. It's not a word I would ever use to describe myself, not even before The Incident. How can he be so blind to my reality?

"Do you hear me?" he says, raising his head to capture my gaze. "You're fucking perfect."

My heart dances. My body melts. My insides flutter. "So are you."

He buries his head between my legs. "Not even close," he says before plunging his tongue inside me.

The smell of paint permeates me. I know it's all in my head. I also know I'm not sure I'll ever be able to experience what he's doing to me right now without smelling it. The thought makes me giggle.

"Something funny?" he asks, stopping his assault of my clit momentarily.

I'm embarrassed to tell him something so silly, so I lie. "I was just thinking how funny it was that you got off so quickly."

He raises a brow. "Baby, you have no idea how I love a challenge. Start counting."

"Huh?"

"You know, one, two, three. Start counting. By the time you reach thirty, I promise I'll have you screaming my name."

I'm silent, not falling prey to his game.

He pushes a finger inside me. "One," he says. Then he adds another. "Two." Then he licks my clit. "Three."

When he sucks my clit into his mouth and can no longer speak, I cry, "Four."

By the time I get to eight, I realize I like his game. I also realize he's going to win when my body throbs in places I didn't know it could throb, and the number ten morphs into a garbled version of his name being shouted to the heavens.

When he climbs up my body, gloating, his hardness presses into me. But the moment his gaze connects with mine, the smirk disappears and there's nothing left but passion. This is it. This is the piece that was always missing. I don't know how it's possible after only five days, but I swear to God, I see the future in his eyes.

His erection rubs against me. His penis is hungry, and I'm all too willing to feed it.

"I want to feel all of you," he says. "With nothing between us. Are you on the pill?"

I swallow and nod.

"I have a condom. I'll use it if you want me to. But I promise I've never gone without one."

I reach down and put him at my entrance.

"Are you sure?"

I throw his words back at him. "Are you?"

"More than I ever have been in my whole fucking life."

Then he sinks inside me.

I gasp at the feeling. He stills, letting me get used to him. He knows as well as I do that nobody has been there in a very long time.

"Are you okay?" he asks, his voice shaking with strain.

"I'm good."

I'm more than good. I'm great. I'm… I'm… perfect.

He moves inside me, gently at first, then when I wrap my arms around him and pull him hard against me, he thrusts harder. I massage the globes of his ass along with the rhythm of his movements. He grunts into my shoulder, saying something unintelligible. I think I make out the word *wait*.

He's as close as I am. Our bodies are perfectly in sync. Our breathing precisely in tune. He twists a bit and hits the spot inside me that has me reeling. I squeeze his ass hard, and he does it again. And again. And when he works a hand between us and rubs my clit, I explode, bucking my hips and fisting the sheets, riding wave after wave, pulse after pulse of the never-ending orgasm.

"Unnnnnng!" he grunts, finding his climax seconds after mine. Then he collapses on top of me, both of us breathing, sweating, laughing.

"Holy shit, Maddie."

"You can say that again."

He lifts his head. "Yes, we *should* do that again."

I swat his ass.

"I'm serious. We should never stop doing that."

He rolls off me, and I snuggle into him, wondering what happens now. "What changed?"

"Well, I moved about five centimeters to the right and found your G-spot."

I giggle quietly. "Not that. What changed after you left earlier?"

"Oh, that. Serious talk, huh?"

I pull up the covers, which are heavy with the rich scent of lust and sex. "You don't have to."

He takes the sheet from me and draws it down again. He tugs my head back into the crook of his shoulder. "You know how you told me earlier that when you got pregnant, reality struck, and you couldn't see yourself with him for the rest of your life?"

I nod silently.

"It was like that for me, only the opposite. When I was driving around, I kept looking at the empty passenger seat, and I realized the only person I wanted in it was you. All the time, you."

My heart leaps for joy, but then my head knocks it down a notch. I steel myself up to say what I know could be a deal breaker. What he seems to always forget about when it comes to me. "I have a child. We're a package deal, Tag."

He thinks on it. I stop breathing. He takes my hand. "The Range does have a back seat."

Is this really happening?

"There's something I need to know. Why did you leave earlier? I thought I saw something in your eyes. Like a light switched off. You changed right in front of me. What happened?"

"It's hard to explain. I saw my future. I thought I was becoming my dad, my brother. Both were cheated on by the women they loved."

For a second, I have to forget about those last few words. We can come back to that later. "Oh, no. I knew about Jaxon, the whole town did, but your mom and dad?"

"I found out when I was fourteen. Before that, I thought they were this perfect couple. The hardworking father. The doting stay-at-home mom. But what pissed me off even more than her cheating was him staying. I knew I could never deal with that. I hated him for being a doormat. I hated her for making him one. And I swore it would never happen to me."

"And that's why you've always slept with women for sport?"

He chuckles. "That's an interesting way to put it." He climbs on top of me, gazing down into my eyes. "This time, it's not a game."

"I thought you liked games."

"Not with you. Not about this."

I'm afraid to ask, but I do anyway. *"This?"*

"Us."

"There's an us?"

"If you want there to be. As long as you promise never to make a fool out of me."

I'm bewildered. "You're afraid I'll cheat on you? *Me*, Maddie Foster, cheat on *you*, Tag Calloway."

"It's fucked up, I know. But there you have it. I'm just an insecure little boy who doesn't want to get hurt."

"You think you're the only one who stands to get hurt here?"

"I'm not going to hurt you, Maddie."

"You can't promise that."

"I suppose neither of us can. All we can do is promise to try."

"And Gigi? What about her?"

"I've never been good with kids, so I might need a lot of guidance."

"She likes you."

"Yeah, well, what's not to like?" He leans in and nibbles my ear. "And as far as kids go, I guess she's pretty cool."

"Pretty cool, huh?"

He shrugs. "Whatever."

It's hard for me to hide my smile. So I don't.

"You don't have to gloat, Flower Girl." He kisses my neck. "Mmm, my girl tastes good."

His girl? My eyes snap open. I replay the words in my head.

He laughs at my reaction. "Sounds fucking strange to hear myself say it."

"Are we really doing this?"

He settles next to me, yawning. "We really are."

I lay my head on his chest. My hand goes to rest on his bicep when I feel a bandage that I hadn't noticed before. "Are you injured?"

"It's a patch."

"For quitting smoking? When did you decide to quit?"

"Yesterday."

"Is it working?"

"Haven't had one all day. Don't think I wasn't tempted on my drive." Then he rips it off and throws it on the floor. "Not sure I need it." He sweeps a piece of hair off my forehead. "I seem to have a pretty good incentive."

He's quitting smoking. *For me.* And I'm his… *girlfriend?*

As much as I'd like to lie here and bask in the glory, my bladder is screaming. "Bathroom," I say, scooting away from him and sliding on my robe.

By the time I return, less than five minutes later, Tag is sleeping soundly, looking far more innocent than the man I know he is. I stand in the doorway and stare. How did my life transform so spectacularly over the course of the last hour?

I shed the robe, smile at the small yet oh-so-large gesture, and gently get into bed next to him. But I'm afraid to go to sleep. Because if this is a dream, I never want to wake up.

Chapter Twenty-seven

Tag

I turn over and stretch, my back sore from sleeping on the old, soft mattress. Maddie is awake. And she's pensively watching me, her eyes full of unasked questions.

I offer a roguish grin. "If we're going to be doing this often, we're getting you a new mattress."

An emotion crosses her face. *Relief?*

I pull her to me. "You didn't think this was a one-time thing, did you? We made promises, remember?"

"People say a lot of things in the heat of the moment."

"If I recall, the promises were made *after* my dick made its way inside you, not before."

"So you remember that?" She plays with one of my nip rings. It gets me hard.

"The promises or my dick being inside you?"

"Very funny."

I arch my back. "I'm serious about the mattress. How old is this thing?"

"Well, it was Gran's before it was mine. And she never buys anything new so…"

I shiver. "Stop. I don't want to know what I've been sleeping on all night. I'll bring the one from my spare bedroom."

"You can't sleep over again. Gigi always comes in here at seven. Always. Every morning. Like clockwork."

I kiss her and get out of bed, not wanting to be late for my morning meetings. "Then I'll leave by six thirty."

I hit the bathroom, then retrieve my clothes from where I dropped them last night. When I go back to Maddie's room, she's sitting up, the covers drawn around her.

"This is strange," she says, watching me dress.

"No shit, it's strange." I pull on my skivvies and pants and then sit on the edge of the bed to put on my shoes. "I've never slept over at a woman's house before."

"Never?"

"Never had one sleep at mine either."

Her lips turn upward.

"That pleases you?" I ask.

"I suppose it is kind of nice to go where no woman has gone before."

I laugh. Then it occurs to me just how right she is. She has no fucking idea just where she's gone. Where she's going.

"So, uh…" She picks at the sheet. "What happens now?"

"Now I have to go home and shower. I have meetings this morning."

"Of course." She pulls the sheet with her when she goes for her robe. "I have to get ready for work and go pick up Gigi."

She doesn't drop the sheet until the robe is on.

"You don't have to cover up in front of me, Maddie."

"Habit."

I step over and wrap her in my arms. "You don't have to cover up for anyone."

"You better go," she says. "You don't want to be late."

I kiss her on the nose and head for the stairs. I stop in her doorway and turn. "What happens now, Flower Girl, is that we go out to dinner, or on picnics, or whatever. We go to movies. Bowling. All the crap that couples do." I glance at the bed. "And we do a whole lot of what we did last night. Okay?"

"I suck at bowling," she says, her grin wide.

"I'll teach you."

Heat from her eyes penetrates me. "Why do I get the feeling you can teach me a *lot* of things?"

Dick, meet hard.

"If I don't leave right now, I'm going to take a sick day and fuck you all over that old, filthy mattress."

She giggles, slides her way around me, and shakes her scrumptious ass on the way to the bathroom. "See you later, Calloway."

~ ~ ~

Pulling up to my house, I see a familiar van parked out front. I pull the Range into the garage then pound on the side door of the van.

It slides open and the smell of marijuana wafts out. I wave it away. He's still self-medicating, I see. "Jesus, Coop, it's eight o'clock in the fucking morning."

"Nothing else to do while I waited on your sorry ass." He holds out the pipe. "Want some?"

"I quit smoking."

"Weed isn't smoking."

"That may be the stupidest thing I've ever heard you say. That shit has killed way too many brain cells."

"You know what I mean." He cocks his head. "And you quit? When?"

"Tuesday. When did you get here?"

"A few hours ago. Where the hell were you?"

"You wouldn't believe me if I told you." I walk toward the house. "Coffee?"

He jumps out of his van and follows. "Sounds good. Hey, you wouldn't mind if I crashed here for a while, would you?"

"Nope. But you'll have to sleep on the pullout."

"What happened to your guest room?"

"Nothing yet. But I need to take the mattress somewhere."

"So I'll buy you a new one."

"You live in a van, Cooper. I hardly think you can afford to buy me a mattress."

"I live in a van, bro. I have practically zero expenses and all kinds of money coming in from sponsors. I can afford anything I want. Have you seen how many followers I have?"

It blows my mind how my daredevil brother has people paying for him to do crazy shit. A few years ago, he did a base jump off the Cliffs of Moher in Ireland, something highly illegal. He put the whole thing on YouTube. Some rich philanthropist bailed him out of jail and funded more of his hairbrained excursions. It just blew up from there.

I put my wallet and phone on the counter, throw the coffee filters at him, and head to my room. "Make yourself at home. I have to get ready."

Twenty minutes later, when I return to the kitchen, Cooper has my phone in his hand. He holds it up. "Who's FlowerGirl?"

I swipe it from him. "None of your fucking business."

I read the text on the screen. It's from Maddie. She's never texted me before, and damn it if it doesn't stir something up inside me.

FlowerGirl: Thanks for last night. I'll never look at my mattress the same way again. Enjoy your shower. I know I'll enjoy mine. ☺

Fuck.

"Dude, your face just lit up like a goddamn Christmas tree. Who the hell is FlowerGirl?"

There's no point in not telling him. All he has to do is walk down the street and he'll hear the rumors about me and Maddie. Rumors that are now truths.

"It's Maddie Foster."

He stops drinking mid-sip. "The girl from the fire?"

"How about we call her *the girl from the flower shop?*"

His eyebrows touch his hairline. "You're fucking her?"

I toss him a wicked look. "I'm"—I can't believe I'm going to say it—"dating her."

He laughs. He thinks I'm joking. I give him a hard stare.

"Wait, what? Seriously?"

"I know. I can't believe it myself."

"When did this happen?"

"Last night. Today. Well, Saturday. I don't know."

"You spent the night at her place? Whoa. But doesn't she have a kid?" He sets down his cup so hard that coffee sloshes out. "Tag, you despise kids. What gives?"

I pour myself a to-go cup. "Honestly, I'm not sure. She's different."

"Than the other two hundred girls you've been with?"

"If I can't figure it out myself, I sure as hell can't explain it to you. Listen, if you want a real bed, you could always sleep at Mom and Dad's. And speaking of them, you know they'll be mad that you didn't show for your birthday and then roll into town five days later."

"They were pissed, huh?"

"Disappointed is more like it. We all get it, Coop. But it's still your birthday. Throw them a bone once in a while."

"It's just a day like any other." He walks over to the couch, the one that pulls out into a bed. "And this will do just fine. Or I'll buy a mattress for the guest room if I stay for more than a few days. I'm not sleeping in my old room. Ever."

"Then sleep in mine and Jaxon's."

"Still no."

"You're not even going to go to the house? Come on, man."

He shrugs. "Haven't decided yet. I don't much like it there. Besides, they can come here."

"If you'll still be in town tomorrow, you can see them at Amber's. She's having an afternoon barbeque. They put in a pool. You should see it. Cost a damn fortune."

"And why do they still live there? Doesn't Quinn have like fifteen million bucks?"

"It's her childhood home. And maybe he did it for her."

He studies me. "You've changed. I hope it's not something in the water around here."

"I have a meeting to get to. Get some sleep. And don't smoke that shit in my house."

He salutes me.

My middle finger salutes him back.

Unlikely DATE

~ ~ ~

Ten hours later, I'm ringing Maddie's doorbell like a stupid love-sick schmuck who can't go a whole day without seeing his lady.

She opens the door and smiles at the bags in my hand. "Mac and cheese from Goodwin's?"

"Gigi's favorite." I lift up the other bag. "And some washers to fix your leaky bathroom faucet." I nod to the Range. "And I brought the mattress. No way am I sleeping on that other one again."

"Again?" Her teeth trap her lower lip as she holds the door open and lets me through.

I almost tell her that I never plan to leave. That I plan to wake up every day looking at her face. That I plan to sneak out every morning and return every night.

That I think I'm fucking in love with her.

Chapter Twenty-eight

Maddie

I sit in the front seat of Tag's SUV, staring at Amber's house, afraid to open the door.

"It's going to be fine," he says. "Regan and Ava will be here, too. Nobody's going to team up on you."

I feel like I'm walking into the firing squad. Tag's friends and family will be here. It's the first time we're going anywhere as an official couple. And after this, if something happens—if we break up—I'll go back to being poor Maddie Foster. Only then, I'll also be the gullible girl who stupidly fell for the bad boy.

"Why are we sitting here, Mommy?" Gigi taps Tag on the shoulder. "Smokey the Bear, are we still going to the party?"

"We're going, baby," I say. "And we talked about this. You have to stop calling him that. He doesn't smoke anymore."

She unstraps herself from her booster and pokes her head between us. "What should I call him, Mommy?"

"Yeah, Mommy," Tag says. "What should she call me?"

My heart skips a beat. I'm not sure why him calling me Mommy affects me so much. Maybe it's because it means he's more accepting of Gigi. Over the past few days, they've spent a lot of time together. Dinner on Monday and Wednesday. Ice cream and board games last night. And now this, a family outing of sorts. Part of me thinks he's not even Tag Calloway anymore. That his body has been invaded by aliens. Nice aliens, who like kids, whisper sweet nothings to me when Gigi isn't listening, and know their way around a woman's body. Oh, does he know his way around it.

"Maddie?"

They're both waiting for an answer. "I'm not sure. I've raised her to be respectful, but Mr. Calloway just seems so formal considering..."

"I'm your boyfriend?"

I'm shocked he said it in front of Gigi. I'm shocked he'd say it in front of *anyone*.

"He's your boyfriend?" she asks excitedly.

"I guess he is."

She claps.

"Gigi," he says. "How about you just call me Tag?"

She smiles a toothy grin, minus her two lower incisors. "Tag." She tries out the name. "I like it better than Smokey the Bear anyway. It's shorter. And easier to yell."

"It is." Tag chuckles. "Just ask your mom."

My cheeks flame. "Okay, you two. Let's go."

Gigi runs ahead and impatiently waits for us to join her at the door.

Amber greets us. "I'm so glad you could come. Who's manning the shop, Maddie?"

"My grandmother still helps out from time to time."

"That's nice. I hope you brought your bathing suits. It's a hot one today."

Gigi holds up her backpack. "I brought mine. But Mommy doesn't go swimming. She never takes her sweaters off."

I want to sink into the doormat.

"Well," Amber says, "if my sweaters were as pretty as hers, I wouldn't take them off either."

I smile my thanks. Amber and I have never really been friends. I'm not sure why. She's friends with Regan and Ava. They all went to school together at Calloway Creek High. Regan and Ava became my friends by proximity, what with Ava's coffee shop on the corner, and Regan's bookstore down the street. But the four of us have never hung out together. It's always been either the three of us or the three of them.

Gigi runs to the back door and looks through the sliders. I go to her side and admire the back yard. "Wow," I say. "I don't know what this looked like before, but it's amazing. It's a tropical paradise out there."

"You should see it at night," Amber says. "Tiki torches line the pathway to the pool, and the waterfall lights up from underneath. Quinn kind of went overboard. He even put in a waterslide, though Josie won't be able to use it for a few years."

Gigi jumps in place. "A waterslide? Mommy, can I go on the slide? Please, please?"

"Yes. Why don't you ask Mrs. Thompson where you can change?"

"Come with me, Gigi," Amber says. "I'll show you the way."

"She knows how to swim?" Tag asks when they leave. "But Gigi said you never go swimming."

"Patrick taught her. He's a firefighter. He's seen more than a few drownings. He had her swimming laps by the time she was three."

Tag opens the door, we step onto the deck, and all activity stops. Heads turn our way. Two dozen people are staring at me, mouths gaping. I tug on my sleeve.

"They're not looking at you," Tag says. "They're looking at me. I've never brought a girl to a party. I've never brought a girl anywhere."

I shore myself up and paste on a smile.

"Maddie," Tag's mom says, being the first to greet me. "It's wonderful you two could make it. Where's that gorgeous daughter of yours? She's always so helpful when I come to the flower shop."

"Nice to see you, Mrs. Calloway. Gigi will be out in a minute."

"Call me Libby."

I'm greeted by Tag's father, brothers, sister, his aunt, uncle, and cousins, and a few more of Amber's friends that I'm quite confident have been in bed with my date.

"Maddie!" Regan calls from her place by the pool. "Come sit here."

"Go," Tag says. "I'll scope out the drinks."

Looking around the deck and back yard, it's clear one thing doesn't belong here: me. Regan, Ava, and the other women are tanning in their tiny bikinis. All Tag's cousins are in bathing suits and are currently having a cannonball competition to see who can make the biggest splash. Even Tag's sister, Addison, is brave enough to sun herself on the deck in an attractive suit that would have any man looking at her boobs instead of her disability.

I'm what's out of place—the only one wearing a sweater on a ninety-degree day.

Gigi comes racing out of the house. "Tag, Tag, watch me jump!"

She jumps in the deep end and expertly swims to the ladder. "Can I go down the slide now, Mommy?"

"Sure, baby. Just make sure someone is close by."

Gigi gets out of the pool, grabs Tag's hand, and pulls him. "Come in with me."

He takes his shirt off and tosses it on the grass.

Gigi stares at his pecs, as do all the other females in the vicinity. "You have jewelry."

He laughs. "I sure do. Now go ahead. I'll sit on the side in case you need me."

"Watch me, Mommy!"

"I'm watching."

She carefully climbs the stairs, sits at the top of the slide, and jettisons herself down, squealing all the way. She swims over and splashes Tag. He slips into the water. "Oh, you're going to get it now."

His powerful arms ripple with movement when he picks her up and gently throws her a few feet in the air. She falls under the water and comes up laughing. Then she holds onto him because she can't touch the bottom, and he lets her. Tag is standing in the pool holding my daughter.

"Holy shit," Ava whispers between the three of us. "I'm sitting here watching it with my own eyes, and I still can't believe it."

"Did you drug him or something?" Regan asks. "Put some kind of spell on him? Because I need some of whatever you're feeding that man."

"I know what you told us at lunch yesterday," Ava says. "But I kind of thought you were embellishing."

Ava's husband, Trevor, walks over. "And what are we talking about?"

"*We're* talking about none of your business," Regan says.

"It's him," he says, nodding to Tag. "It's the nipple rings, isn't it? What do you think, babe, should I get one?"

Ava hops off her lounger and pushes Trevor into the pool. They have such a sweet relationship. Like a lot of residents of this town, they were high school sweethearts.

"Hey, Maddie. Regan." Jaxon sits next to us.

"Hi, Jaxon," Regan says, shifting in his direction. "Long time no see."

"Didn't I see you at Donovan's the other night?"

"But it's been a while since we've had an actual conversation."

"Yeah, like high school."

"Well, maybe we should."

Is she coming on to him?

Cooper takes the chair next to his brother. "Hey."

Regan tugs on her bikini, making sure it shows plenty of her voluptuous curves. "Hiya, Cooper. I saw your latest YouTube video. Were you scared jumping out of that plane?"

"No."

"I follow you, you know."

He looks uninterested. "Thanks."

"So what does one have to do to jump from a plane? Do you do those tandem jumps where you're secured to another person? That sounds like fun."

"I can refer you to a jump school if you're interested. There's a really good one not too far from here."

"Yeah, sure. Whatever." She stands and beckons me to follow. "Let's go get some food, Maddie."

"Were you flirting with them?" I ask as we walk to the buffet.

"They're both single and fair game in my book, even if Jaxon isn't technically divorced yet. And I figure if Tag can do to you whatever the hell he's doing, maybe it runs in the family."

"I doubt it. Tag and I talked a lot the other night. He told me about his brothers. Jaxon hasn't been in a serious relationship since Nicky cheated on him and disappeared to Oklahoma. And Cooper—well, he's just broken. When Chaz died, Tag says a part of Cooper died along with him. Believe me, he's not relationship material. Tag is worried he's going to daredevil himself to death one of these days."

"I believe it. I really do follow him online. Some of the things he does are wicked scary." She pops a cherry tomato into her mouth. "So, this thing with you and Tag…"

I look over to see Tag and Gigi hanging out on the side of the pool. "I still can't believe it. I'm pinching myself, Regan. It's only been a week since the After Dark debacle, but somehow it feels like we've been together forever. He's so easy to be with. He's fun and charming, and—" I stop talking and sigh heavily.

"And what?"

"I don't know. I guess I'm just waiting for the other shoe to drop."

"There doesn't always have to be another shoe, Maddie."

"There always has been for me. The whole thing with my mom and dad. Then the condom breaking, not that I'd take that back in a million years. And then, you know, The Incident. Not to mention Gigi's grandparents think I'm a murderer. FYI, I ran into them in the park on Thursday, about two minutes after Tag gave me a very public orgasm."

Her mouth falls open. She fans herself. "You're due, then."

"For what?"

"Happiness. A whole lot of it wrapped up into one massive ball of testosterone and decorated in nipple rings."

Arms come around my waist, and minty breath flows over my ear. "Didn't mean to ignore you."

Regan's eyes are laser focused on his arms surrounding me. I'm well aware Tag Calloway has never shown any public displays of affection. I'm sure everyone here is thinking the exact same thing: who am I, and what have I done to him?

"Did you have fun in the pool?" I ask.

"It feels great. It's so damn hot today."

I know. I'm sweating my ass off.

He reaches around me and pours us each a shot of tequila. We toss them back, then he puts a lime in my mouth and quickly kisses it out. *Oh, wow.*

"You should sit on the edge, dip your legs in," he says casually like he didn't just make me swoon.

"Sounds good. Want to come, Regan?"

"You go ahead. I'm going to sit back and watch the show."

"The show?" Tag asks.

"Ignore her," I say. "She's drunk."

Regan giggles as we walk away.

We sit on the edge of the pool. He's right, it feels heavenly. I want so badly to be able to shed my clothing and jump in like a normal person. Tag hasn't said anything. He's not pushing me to go in. But our relationship is new. What if he gets tired of me not going in the pool? The pool being a metaphor for anything in my life that requires exposing my body. Will it be enough that I shed my clothes in private?

"What are you thinking about?" he asks. "You're staring at the water. Can you not swim?"

"I can swim."

"It's okay that you don't want to go in. I mean, it would be nice if someday you did, but I'm not going to push."

Yet.

I glance around at the women in the back yard. "Is it weird that you've slept with like half the women here?"

"You're not jealous, are you? Because if anyone should be jealous here, it's them."

"Them?"

"Because you landed Cal Creek's most eligible bachelor."

"It's a good thing you haven't completely changed. You're still the cocky guy I know and love." I stiffen at my unfortunate choice of words. "Um… I, uh, I always thought you were *in*eligible. Eligible assumes you're available, but you made it clear to everyone that you weren't."

He snickers. "I suppose you're right." He puts his arm around my waist, and I feel the wetness of his swim trunks dampen my shorts. "You have, you know."

"I've what?"

"Landed me."

For the umpteenth time this week, my heart flips over. How can this be happening to me? It still feels like a dream. For two nights now, he's slept over and crept out before dawn. He's made love to me in ways I never dreamed of. He's wormed his way into my life. Into Gigi's.

Three little words tickle the back of my throat. Words I want to say but can't. Words I feel to the very core of my soul; ones you only read about in Gigi's books.

He gazes into my eyes. Does he have any idea what I'm thinking? If he did, he'd run. He'd run away faster than his legs could carry him. Because if he knew my thoughts, he'd find out that in less than a week, he's become the only man I never want to live without.

"Mommy, Tag, watch this!" Gigi yells from the other side of the pool. "I can swim all the way to you."

I clear my head and look at my daughter. "Let's see."

She jumps in and kicks her little legs, making it all the way to us with only two breaths.

Tag tousles her wet hair. "Fantastic. You're a fish. Can you swim back now?"

She pushes off the wall and does what he asks. When she reaches the stairs, she climbs out and takes a bow. People cheer.

I clap proudly. "God, I love that girl."

"Yeah," he says. It's just a simple word. When he says it, however, he's looking right at *me*.

Chapter Twenty-nine

Tag

Food is placed on the table.

"Thanks, Lissa," Jaxon says, eyeing his double bacon burger.

For as long as I can remember, Cooper, Jaxon, and I have met for lunch at Donovan's Pub every Saturday Cooper is in town. Sometimes Addy joins us, but she's usually got weekend plans that don't include her protective older brothers.

Lissa glances at Jaxon over her shoulder as she walks away.

"Is she ever going to give up on you?" Cooper asks. "I'm pretty sure if you haven't asked her out in the past two years, it probably won't happen."

"She's nice enough," he says. "Just not my type."

"Your type being…"

I pinch a fry off Jaxon's plate. "Tall, brunette, green eyes, rack that stops traffic."

Cooper draws his brows. "Seems like you just described his ex."

"Bingo," I say.

"She's not my ex yet," Jaxon says.

I cock my head. "Funny how you never fail to remind us of that."

"You still into Nicky?" Cooper asks.

"I'm dating Calista," Jaxon says.

"That's not what I asked."

"She cheated on you, bro," I say.

Jaxon scrubs a hand across his jaw. "There are two sides to every story."

"I'm not sure what your point is. She cheated. And even if she hadn't, we all know she was married to her job. It was always more important to her than you. It was never going to work out."

He pushes his barely touched food away. "Whatever."

Cooper devours what's left of Jaxon's burger after finishing his own. He turns to me. "So this thing with you and Maddie Foster... It's serious? I mean, you haven't slept in your own bed in weeks."

"Says the guy who's crashing at my place because he's homeless."

Coop shoots me a look. "I'm not fucking homeless just because my pad is on wheels."

"Since when do you side with Mom and Dad on this?" Jaxon asks me.

I shrug. "I just think it's a rootless existence. And what's the point?"

Jaxon lets out a low whistle. "What the hell have you done with our older brother?"

"I'm telling you," Cooper says to him, "he's fucking whipped. He sneaks home at six thirty every morning."

I put my empty beer glass down. "Maybe you should have something better to do than keep tabs on me. Like get a real fucking job."

Unlikely DATE

The three of us go on and on, ribbing each other like we always do. It may not seem like it on the surface, but you'd be hard-pressed to find other brothers as close as we are. I just wish Coop would move back to town for good. At this point, though, I think it would take an act of God to make it happen.

A long, manicured fingernail runs down my left arm. I turn to see Laney Bennett salivating over me like I'm a finely cooked filet mignon with a side of peppercorn sauce.

She scoots in next to me, making me slide over in the booth.

"If it isn't my favorite brothers."

On the inside, I guarantee all three of us are rolling our eyes. Laney is a year older than me and is twice divorced. She's always looking for her next meal ticket. I believe she's made it her point in life to collect alimony. Which is why she's at the wrong table.

"What's up, Laney?" Jaxon says, always being the polite one. "How are things?"

"Things are boring," she says. "This sleepy town needs some excitement."

I bite into my bratwurst, not bothering to chew or swallow. "I hear Jugs is hiring. That's exciting."

Cooper chokes on his drink.

Laney lets my comment roll right off her. She leans close. "I only do private performances."

Laney Bennett is only one of a handful of women in this town I won't touch with a ten-foot pole. Okay, so I did her once in high school. Because, come on, she's hot. But I soon came to realize she had the personality of a box of rocks that not even her rockin' body could make up for.

"Sorry," I say. "My dance card is full."

She studies me. "So the rumors are true? You're actually dating that girl from the fire?"

"Maddie. Her name is Maddie. And yes."

She cringes. "Have you *seen* her burns? They must be hideous. And I heard they're all over, like even on her lady parts. How can you put your hands on that? Wait, I get it, you must be pity-fucking her. Is this one of those arrangements where she's paying you to make her look good or something? What could you possibly be getting out of it? It's not like you need the money." She squeezes my thigh. "You do own a business."

The more she talks, the more I want to rip her plastic head right off her store-bought body. I remove her hand from my leg. "Laney, get the fuck off my seat."

"Is that any way to talk to a lady?"

"If I see any ladies around here, I'll let you know. And if I hear you say anything bad about Maddie or spread more false rumors, I'll make sure everyone in Cal Creek knows your pussy tastes like spoiled mayonnaise."

Her jaw hits the table. She picks up my plate and dumps what's left of my brat and chips into my lap, then walks away.

Cooper can't contain his laughter. "That was epic. Although I would have gone with rotten fish."

Jaxon shakes his head. "I guess dating Maddie hasn't quite turned you into a gentleman. You're still the same old asshole."

I pick up my lunch and brush the crumbs off my lap. "That was totally worth the stains." I stand. "I have to get going. I promised Maddie I'd start on her floors today."

Jaxon asks, "What do you think she's going to say when she finds out you've secretly been buying all the materials for her renovations?"

"She's not going to find out. Besides, I only buy the on-sale stuff." I glance at Cooper. "It's not like I have one-point-six-million followers and a half dozen sponsors. Some of us have to make our own damn money."

Cooper shrugs. He has no shame.

Jaxon shakes his head. "Secrets. They're a bad idea. They always come out one way or another."

He's talking about Nicky. I get the idea there *is* another side to the story that he's keeping from us, but I let it slide. I know he hates it when we talk about her.

I leave a twenty on the table. "Catch you guys later."

I swing back home, change my clothes, and stack the last of the laminate hardwood in the Range, then head over to her place.

"Tag!" Gigi runs across the shop and into my arms when she sees me. Three weeks ago, I might have moved away and let the little girl face-plant into the floor. Now, however, as strange as it is, I feel protective of her.

The shop is bustling with activity. Blake and Lincoln are here—at the same time. It's a situation I find amusing considering their aversion to each other is only slightly less than mine and the McQuaids. Rose is here too. I guess it's all hands on deck.

"Maybe you should do this another day," Maddie says. "There is no way I can help. My wholesale delivery was late, and I have a hundred arrangements to put together and deliver by four o'clock."

"I don't need your help," I say, putting Gigi down.

There are scissors, knives, and all kinds of dangerous implements all over the counter and floor. Not the place for a curious five-year-old, even if she is used to being in the shop.

"In fact, I think Gigi should be *my* helper today."

Gigi's eyes light up. "Yes! I want to be Tag's helper."

"Sorry, baby. I need you to help *me*."

Gigi silently pouts.

I stare Maddie down. She doesn't need her daughter's help. In fact, I'm quite sure she could get her job done a lot faster without Gigi underfoot. I pull Maddie aside. "You have to trust me with her sooner or later."

Her face twists with indecision. "I don't know."

"We'll be right upstairs. If she so much as gets a paper cut, I promise to come get you."

Gigi sits on the stool behind the counter, staring at us. She knows what we're discussing. She's very intuitive. "Please, Mommy. I want to help him. Our floor will be so pretty."

I lean in and say quietly, "Think of all the days, months, and years she's spent here in the shop with you. She's five. She must be bored. She needs other people, other experiences. This could just be a baby step toward giving those to her."

Maddie's eyes rake over the tables of flowers. She can't deny how busy her day will be. "This *is* one of the largest weddings I've ever done. I suppose it would be nice if she weren't underfoot. Okay, fine. But with my proceeds from this contract, I'm going to pay you back for some of the renovation materials."

I draw my brows. "But—"

"Oh, come on," she says. "You didn't really think I'd believe you had all that in your shed, did you? But I figured I'd pick my battles because things are going so well."

I step closer and touch her hand. "Things *are* going well, which is why it's time for you to trust me."

She calls Gigi over. "Be a good girl. Don't get in his way. No hammers or nails or doing anything that could cut off a finger or toe. If Tag says you were good, we'll get ice cream later."

"Great. Let's go, squirt," I say and give her mom a quick kiss.

Gigi looks up. "Paddy calls me squirt."

"Hmm. Then I need to come up with another name for you." I lead her to the stairs. "Tell you what, you can pick."

"You can help."

"Let's see. There's knucklehead, smarty-pants, little nugget."

She giggles. "Those are silly names."

"Then how about, cutie pie, pumpkin, princess—"

"Princess!" she shouts, her face lighting up.

"Princess it is. Okay, princess, we need to move everything out of the kitchen, and we'll start there. I'll carry the table, and you carry the chairs. Then when I move the refrigerator, you can be my spotter."

"Spotter. What's that?"

"You tell me if I'm going to run into something or trip over anything."

"I can be a good spotter."

Three hours later, the small kitchen is done, and I'm ready to move on to the living room. I would have been done faster, but we had to stop for snack time. *Twice.*

I check my supplies. "Houston, we have a problem."

"Houston? That's another silly name. You said you would call me princess."

"That's just a thing you say when something is wrong. When astronauts are in space and radio back to Earth, they talk to people in Houston, which is a city in Texas."

"Texas. That's where Josie is from. She's so cute. And her nanny is really nice. Do you think someday I might have a nanny?"

"I'm not sure. The great thing about the flower shop is that you can work there with your mom, so you don't need anyone else to help take care of you."

"I guess that's nice. What's the problem you would tell Houston?"

"I'm running out of floor tack. It's the glue that holds down the boards."

"Does the Mazon place have it? Mommy says it has everything."

I chuckle. "You know they probably do, but I need it right now. Come on, let's go down and tell your mom."

Downstairs, the shop is quiet. Blake is manning the register.

"Where is everyone?"

"Went to make the delivery."

Without telling me? Without freaking out that Gigi would be here without her? "Huh."

"Maddie's friend Patrick showed up right before they left. He went next door to get coffee for everyone for when they get back. It's been a long day."

So she did call in the cavalry. She trusts me, just not as much as she trusts him.

"Do you know when she'll be back? I have to run to Home Depot."

He shrugs and goes back to his phone.

I get my phone out and dial Maddie. She picks up right before it rolls to voicemail. She sounds out of breath. "Is everything okay?"

There's so much noise in the background that I can barely hear her.

"It's fine. She's fine. But I need to go get some tack. I was thinking maybe Gigi could come."

"Snacks? Tag, I can't hear you. The band is practicing, and we're trying to get everything set up."

At least that's what I think she said.

"I need to run and get tack. I can wait for Patrick if you want, or I could take Gigi with me."

"Patrick's at the shop. You're good. Wait!" she screams, but not at me. "No, don't put that there! Tag? I have to go. She'll be fine. I'm sure you're doing a great job."

Wow, okay. I guess she trusts me after all. I turn to Gigi. "I guess we're going to Home Depot."

She jumps up and down. "Yay! Do they have cookies there like the grocery store?"

"I don't think so. Anyway, you already had two snacks. Don't tell your mom, or she won't let you be my helper anymore."

Gigi talks my ear off on the way. It's not a long drive. Nothing in Cal Creek is too far from anything else. When we get there, I look at the large carts, not knowing what the protocol is. "Do you want to sit in the cart?"

"That's for babies. I'm not a baby."

"No, I guess you're not. This won't take long. I just need to figure out where the tack is."

A woman with a service dog walks by. "Look at the doggie," Gigi says, starting toward it.

"I don't think you're supposed to touch her, Gigi."

"It's okay," the woman tells her. "You can pet her. She's my therapy animal. Her name is Princess."

Gigi's smile is a mile wide as she looks up at me. "Princess. Did you hear that, Tag?" She kneels down to pet it. "You're a pretty girl, aren't you, Princess?"

"Looks like you made a friend," the woman says. "She really likes you."

"Mommy says we can get a dog as soon as I promise to walk it five times a day, feed it, and clean up poopies." She giggles. "I told her I don't want to clean up poopies. She doesn't either. So we can't get one."

"Well, Princess has very small poopies," the woman says. "They aren't any trouble at all."

"Did you hear that?" Gigi says to me. "Maybe we could get a dog like Princess."

"We'd better be on our way now, Gigi."

"Bye, Princess."

Down the long aisle, Gigi keeps looking back at the dog until we're around the corner. We go to the flooring department, but I can't find what I'm looking for. I wait for an associate to help me, and then I tell him what I need.

"You mean adhesive?" the guy says. "What kind of flooring are you needing it for? Laminate? Engineered wood? Hardwood?"

"Laminate."

"And are you laying it over concrete or a subfloor?"

"It's on a second story. It's over wood. Listen, I'll know it when I see it if you can just point me in the direction—" My eyes sweep around, and I realize Gigi isn't next to me. "Gigi?" I look around the corner. "Did you see where the little girl went?"

"I, uh, no," the man says.

I race through the aisles. "Gigi. It's not nice to hide." Okay, this is serious. My heart is really pounding now. "Princess, come on out."

"Sir," a different associate says, "is everything okay?"

"No, everything is not okay. I was with a little girl, and she just disappeared. Red hair. Blue shirt. Five years old. You need to lock the doors until we find her."

"I'm sure she's around here. Little ones walk away all the time."

"Lock the fucking doors!" I yell. "Gigi!"

"I'll call a supervisor."

"Yeah, you do that," I say running away, looking down every aisle. "Have you seen a little girl?" I ask everyone I pass.

Everyone says no.

"Fuck."

Fuck. Fuck. Fuck.

"Gigi!"

My phone rings. I don't have time for it, so I let it roll. It rings again. I whip it out. It's Maddie. Jesus, what the hell do I say?

"Where are you?" she yells when I answer, her anger strangling me through the phone.

"At the hardware store," I say as calmly as I can.

"Down the street?"

"No. Home Depot."

"Home Depot?" she yells, the strain in her voice spearing me.

"I told you I was going to buy tack. You said it was okay if I brought Gigi."

I'm still running, looking down all the aisles. The associate from earlier catches my eye. "So?" I mouth to her. She shakes her head.

Fuck.

"I did no such thing," Maddie says. "And why are you out of breath? Tag, what's wrong? And where's Gigi?"

"Here, with me."

"Let me talk to her."

"I can't."

"Why can't you? Tag, you're scaring me."

Someone comes over the loudspeaker and a voice thunders throughout the store. "Code Adam. Code Adam. Code Adam. Female. Five years old. Red hair. Blue shirt."

"Tag, why did they just say *Code Adam* over the PA system? You know that's the signal for a missing child, don't you?"

"What? No. You're hearing things."

And you're a motherfucking liar who Maddie won't ever trust with her little girl again.

"Tag, damn it, what's going on? Tell me!"

"Okay, so I might have lost her."

Her pained cry echoes through the phone, breaking me to my core.

Chapter Thirty

Maddie

Expletives I never thought I'd hear myself say come spewing out of my mouth at the man I was convinced I was in love with a few minutes ago. The man who took my daughter and lost her.

He shouts at me to stop yelling at him. "I didn't lose her as much as she wandered away."

"You're blaming *her*—a five-year-old?" I turn to Patrick. "Call the police, then take me to the hardware store." He doesn't move. "Patrick! She's missing!"

"I'm sure she's somewhere in the store, Maddie."

"What is it with you men?"

"Do you think you could be overreacting just a little?" Tag says. Then I hear him shout her name, only it's muffled.

"Overreacting? You're kidding, right? And you just yelled for her. Don't sit there and tell me I'm overreacting when I can hear in your voice that you're scared."

"Okay, yeah. I'm fucking scared. But more about you biting my head off and feeding me a huge *I told you so* sandwich than anything actually happening to Gigi. We're in a store for Christ's sake."

"And there's the Tag Calloway I knew you were. Cocky. Uncaring. Not giving a shit about anyone but yourself. I knew he'd show up sooner or later."

"Maddie, come on."

"Don't *Maddie* me. You know who else goes to hardware stores? Murderers. Kidnappers. Especially kidnappers—they need supplies." I turn to Patrick. "Will you please call the fucking cops?"

"Oh, God. There she is. Gigi!" Tag yells.

My breath catches. "She's there? You see her?"

"She's good. She's fine. I've got her. It was the damn dog. She met this dog out fr—"

"Tag, I don't care about the dog. Put her on the phone. Right now."

"It's your mom," I hear him say. "She wants to talk to you."

"Mommy, Mommy, there's a doggie named Princess. And the nice lady said her poopies are small, and if I work really hard, I can take care of a doggie like her. And I like the name Princess. Tag calls me princess, but that's okay, we could still call a puppy Princess, right, Mommy?"

She's okay. She's okay. She's okay. Calm down.

"Why don't we talk about it later, baby? Right now, you and Tag need to come home. Can I talk to him again, please?"

"Okay."

"Everything's fine," he says. "I promise I won't let her out of my sight again. I'll pick up the tack, and we'll be on our way."

"Tag, I don't care about the goddamn tack or whatever. Walk my child to the car, strap her in the booster, drive like your life depends on it, and bring her home. Right fucking now."

Unlikely DATE

Patrick takes the phone from me. "Hey, Tag. It's Patrick. Maddie's a little shaken up right now, as you can imagine." I pace the floor while they talk. "No, I think it's just best if you come straight home." He smiles at me, reassuringly. "Yeah, okay. See you soon."

He hands me back my phone. Gran pours something in my coffee. "To calm your nerves."

"I don't need alcohol, Gran. I need my daughter."

"She's safe," Patrick says. "And she'll be home in ten minutes. Relax."

I walk to the front of the shop, lock it, and put up the CLOSED sign. "We're done for the day. You can all go. Thank you for helping with the wedding."

"Are you going to be okay, sweetie?" Gran asks.

I nod.

"Well, then. I have a date with a handsome man, a bottle of wine, and his Barcalounger."

Visions I don't want to be envisioning swim through my head. "Really, Gran?"

"You kids don't own the rights to all the fun. You should be so lucky to have an active sex life at my age."

"Gran!"

She giggles, picks up her flask, and walks to the back door. "Give that baby girl a big kiss for me and tell her I'll see her Tuesday."

Blake looks green in the face as he watches her leave. "Don't say it," I say. "We're all thinking it. Just go." I reach into the register and hand him and Lincoln each an extra forty dollars for putting up with each other and helping out today. "Bye, guys. Thanks again."

I tally today's receipts to pass the time. When the back doorbell rings, I race to it and throw the door open. I hug Gigi so hard. "Baby, go upstairs with Patrick. I'll be up soon."

"Paddy," she says. "I met a doggie today."

"Tell me all about it."

As soon as the door to my apartment closes, I storm toward Tag and hit his chest with my fists. "What were you thinking taking her like that?"

"I was thinking you said it was okay."

"Okay?" I feel flames of anger simmering in my eyes. "Why would you think it would be okay for you to take my daughter without my permission? It was irresponsible, and she could have been hurt. Or really lost. Or taken."

"She's fine. She wandered away. I'm sure it happens all the time."

He puts a gentle hand on my shoulder. I flinch and shrug it off.

"Not to Gigi, it doesn't. So much has already happened to her. I thought you understood that."

"It was hard to hear you over the band. I really did think you gave your approval."

"I am so mad I can't even look at you. You know how I am with her, and you go and do this? How can I ever trust you with her?"

"It was an honest mistake. *One second.* I was talking to a worker and took my eyes off her for one second. I guess she saw the dog and followed it."

I huff out a breath and throw my hands wide. "Do you know what could have happened in that second? Those minutes when you couldn't find her?"

"I know. I'm sorry."

"You *don't* know. That's the problem. You don't know what can happen in those precious seconds when you can't get to someone." My chest heaves and sobs threaten to bellow. I steady myself against the counter when my legs try to collapse under me. "When danger has engulfed you and you try and try but you can't reach her."

He steps closer. "Maddie."

I retreat. "No, Tag. You can't possibly understand why I keep her so close. So close that I'll never be far enough not to save her. Our bedrooms share a wall. Do you know I have an axe in my closet—one I can use to punch through the wall if I can't use the door? Also, three gallons of water I could use to wet down my clothes. And in case you haven't noticed, unless she's with Patrick, you taking her upstairs was the farthest I've been from her since she spent time with Cody's parents last year. Do you even realize what a huge step that was for me? And then you take her—you drive her across town. What if you'd been in an accident? What if the dog had bitten her? What if—"

"Are you serious?" His head shakes with a sharp jerk. "You're being ridiculous. What if she slips off the swing at the park and hurts her leg? Or if she falls down your stairs and breaks her neck, Maddie? What if a comet strikes the planet and kills us all? You can't protect her from everything."

"I can sure as hell try."

"Your way of thinking is approaching neurotic."

My entire body hums with fury. "You run off with my kid, but *I'm* the crazy one?"

"I did not run off with her. We went to the fucking hardware store." Frustrated hands rake through his hair. "I don't know how many times I can say I'm sorry. I'll be more careful next time. But,

Jesus, Maddie, she's five. Maybe it's time to loosen the tether and cut the umbilical cord already."

Bile rises in my throat, and the urge to throw a vase at him is overwhelming. I point to the door. "Maybe it's time for you to leave."

He throws up his hands. "Yeah, fine. I'll go. You need time to cool off. Once you calm down, you'll realize how much you blew this out of proportion." He opens the door. "Call me when you're ready to talk."

"I'm never going to be ready, Tag."

The look of shock on his face quickly turns to anger. "You're ending this?" He waves a finger between us. "This, what we have—you're ending it because Gigi followed a dog and was out of my sight for two fucking minutes?"

I clear my throat and look at the wall. "Looks like it."

"Lady, you *are* fucking crazy if you're going to throw away what we have over something as stupid as that."

"If I'm crazy, it's only because I believed you could change. But you're still the same person you always were. You were just pretending not to be. I tried to tell myself it wouldn't happen, but I knew you'd find a way to hurt me. Once an asshole, always an asshole." I swallow the huge lump impeding my voice. "Now get out."

He leaves. The door almost falls off the hinges with how hard he slams it. I crumble into a ball on the ground, my body heaving uncontrollably. I hear his tires spin as he races away, and then I cry. I cry over the piece of me I almost lost today—my daughter. And I cry for the part of me I know I'll never get back—my heart.

Chapter Thirty-one

Tag

Cooper lets Dad into the house, then goes back to the guest room he's been calling his own since he showed up almost a month ago.

Dad looks around my kitchen and living room. I don't have to follow his gaze to know what he sees. A flattened carton of cigarettes. A dozen old take-out containers. Smashed beer cans. Empty whiskey bottles. Ashy remnants of marijuana buds.

He goes to the fridge, takes out two beers, puts one on the coffee table in front of me, and sits. "Brody called me today."

I pop the tab on the Budweiser and chug half of it down. "Why would he do that?"

"Because if you keep this up much longer, your business will fail, son. CSM is yours to put on the map or run into the ground, and the decisions you make right now may determine which of those happens."

"I'm sick."

He opens the pizza box on the table. I'm sure mold is growing inside. "I can see that from all the food and booze."

"Is there a point to this visit?" I tap a cigarette out of a pack and light it.

I don't have to look up to see the disappointment. "We're worried about you, Tag."

"We?"

"Me. Mom. Hell, everyone."

"Yeah, I'm sure Mom is so torn up."

"Tag, I've about had it with your attitude toward her. She did nothing to you. What happened, happened between *us*, and more than a decade ago. I've forgiven her. Why can't you?"

"Maybe it's you I can't forgive."

"Me?"

"She cheated on you for a year. It wasn't a slip-up or some drunken mistake. She made a conscious decision to have an affair over a long period of time."

"We were going through rough times."

"Ha! Like we haven't gone through any since? Did she cheat on you again after Chaz died? What about after Addy's accident?"

"She didn't."

"As far as you know."

His voice sharpens. "She didn't, son. We both learned our lesson the first time."

"Both?"

"You were fourteen. I know you were almost a man, but we didn't want to burden you with details. You were so wrapped up in your sports and your friends and school. You all were. Addy was only six. We were trying to protect you."

"From what?"

"We fell on bad times. The construction industry came to a halt. Your mom got pregnant."

My eyes finally snap away from the beer can. "Mom got pregnant when Addy was six?"

He nods. "We already had the five of you, and no money was coming in. The bank was threatening to foreclose. We tried to be happy about the news, but we could barely take care of the kids we had."

"I remember. That was the year I had to get a job bagging groceries to pay for all the entry fees and sports equipment. You said it was because I was growing up and needed to show responsibility."

"We were ashamed to tell you anything else."

"Did she have an abortion?"

"No. No way. We were going to have that baby even if it meant moving and renting a two bedroom with air mattresses all over the place."

"But…"

"Your mom had a miscarriage the day before we were going to tell you kids. She was almost four months along. It devastated her. Between the stress of that and our finances, we pulled away from each other when we should have bonded together. It was my fault as much as it was hers."

"*You* didn't cheat."

"I didn't. But it might have been because of the lack of opportunity. For months, we passed in the night. I took odd jobs bartending. I did plumbing jobs on the side for a fraction of what the big companies were charging. I even got a job at CCU as a night janitor."

"Dad, really?"

"It was a rough year or two. Things didn't turn around until my cousin, Andrew Montana, sold off some of the land his father had bought from the McQuaids, using a good bit of the proceeds to purchase the failing country club. He hired me for all the plumbing renovations. I was working full time again, and we were able to save our house. I owe everything to him."

"You started the business after that."

"I did. And it's been smooth sailing ever since."

Disgusted, I say, "So she came back to you only when you made something of yourself?"

"No. She came back to me because I went after her."

"Went after her? But she never left."

"Not physically. She stayed for you kids. But mentally, emotionally, she was done with me. I had to fight for her."

"Why would you want to do that after what she'd done to you?"

"Because she was worth fighting for. And when you find that one thing in life that is, you shouldn't give up until you've done everything in your power to win back what's yours."

I down the rest of my beer and fetch another. I look out the kitchen window at the shed that's still filled with materials I was using to fix up Maddie's place. I close my eyes. "Maddie Foster was never mine."

Dad laughs softly. "I'd only seen the two of you together a few times, but it was pretty clear to everyone around you that she was. Hook, line, and sinker, Tag."

I shake my head and stare at the dirty pile of dishes in the sink. "No, she was never mine. She belongs to her daughter. And the memory of what happened the night of the fire."

"You think she believes she's better off without you?"

I nod.

"Perhaps it's time you call your mother."

"What does she have to do with this?"

"She regretted it," he says. "She regretted being with that man right from the start. But it was a decision she made, and she was stubborn enough to convince herself it was the right one. And I was too pigheaded to admit it was partly my fault."

"I told Maddie I was sorry, Dad."

"Yes, but did she really *hear* it?"

"She heard it all right, and then she told me to fuck off."

"She said it in the heat of the moment. Women say and do things they don't mean when they're in emotionally charged situations." He chuckles. "If I've learned anything from thirty-two years of marriage, that's it."

"I called her for four days. Left her voicemails. Sent her flowers." I walk to the trash and show him what's inside—the dead flowers that showed up on my doorstep. "It's been over a week now. It's over. She's done with me. I have to move on."

"And you're willing to settle for that? In a week, a month, a year, will you wonder if you did everything possible to get her back?" He waves his arm around my house. "Look at this. Your house is a dump, you haven't shaved in God knows how long, and you smell like the floor of Donovan's after a bachelor party. That is not a man who is ready to move on. That's a man who's in love."

I finish my beer, crush the can on the counter, and throw it across the room, missing the trash can by a few feet. "Are we done here?"

"There's someone outside who wants to talk to you."

I look at the front door, my stomach in knots. "Fuck, is she here?"

"It's Amber. She was out front when I got here. Said she'd been trying to talk to you all week."

"I'm surprised Coop didn't let *her* in, too."

"She said he tried, but she wouldn't come in unless you invited her." He starts for the door. "If you won't listen to your brothers or father, at least listen to your best friend."

"Fine. Send her in."

I get my last beer from the fridge, knowing I'll have to send Cooper out for more.

Words are spoken outside the front door. They're talking about me. Everyone in Cal Creek is. In a matter of weeks, I've gone from being the stud of the town to the pathetic loser who can't keep a decent girl.

"Hey," Amber says from the hallway.

I lift my beer.

She glances around the room. "Oh, my god, Tag."

"You're free to leave if you don't like my decorating."

She picks up the pizza box, some fast-food bags, and an empty bottle of booze, and takes them to the kitchen. Then she sits across from me after removing more trash from the chair and stares me down.

"What is it? Just spit it out. I've never known you to hold back on me."

Her nose turns up. "I'm not talking to you until you take a shower. You reek to high heaven."

I point. "There's the door."

"I'm not leaving. Sophie's got Josie. I have all day. I can out-sit you any day of the week, Tag. So either you go wash yourself, or deal with me being in your hair." She pulls out her phone and ignores me.

The thing is, I know she means it. One time in high school, Amber and I had a stare down that lasted three hours because I told Jake Ingman that she thought he had bad breath. She didn't want to be known as the girl who went around talking about guys' hygiene, so she came to my house, locked me in my room, sat in front of the door, and did absolutely nothing until I broke down and called him and told him it wasn't true.

I stand and stomp across the floor on the way to the bedroom. "I'm not shaving."

"Fine. But at least wash the crumbs out of your beard. You look like a homeless man who just ate a box of Thin Mints."

After showering in record time, I catch a glimpse of myself in the mirror. I run a hand along the scruff of my thickening beard, momentarily wondering if Maddie would like it. Amber's right. I look homeless. I get out the trimmer and shave my neck to neaten it up a bit. Then I wonder why the fuck I'm doing it and throw the appliance in the sink, breaking it into pieces.

Amber looks up from the couch when I return. "I'm digging the facial hair."

"Oh, good. Well, as long as *you're* okay with it." My words drip with sarcasm. I look around. I've been gone for ten minutes, and she's practically cleaned the entire place. "You didn't come here to be my maid."

"The kitchen still looks like a dump. I'm not touching those dishes. Food is cemented onto them. You might just want to throw them out and buy more."

"You didn't come here to talk about my plates either."

"Sit."

"*You* sit."

"I *am* sitting." She snorts. "Get over yourself, Tag. I mean, seriously, this is pathetic, even for a jerk like you. Your business is suffering. Your family is worried. People are talking. You need to pick yourself up and act like a man."

"You need to quit trying to fix me and just be my goddamn friend."

"She's hurting too, you know."

It's the one thing she's said to me that has my full attention. My eyes snap to hers.

"Oh, she's not wallowing in self-pity and ignoring the basic principles of hygiene, but she's obviously upset about your breakup."

"You've talked to her?"

"Not about you. I went to her shop yesterday. She wasn't her normal self. She looked sad. Hell, even Gigi looked sad. They miss you, Tag."

"If she missed me, she'd have returned my calls. Do you even know why she's mad at me?"

"There are a dozen rumors floating around, most having to do with you cheating on her."

"That's bullshit and you know it. She doesn't trust me around her kid, and Gigi is her life. And if she can't trust me, we have nothing to build on. I don't know what you heard, but I thought Maddie told me it was okay to take Gigi to the store. I took my eyes off her for two seconds. Literally. I'm not exaggerating. Two seconds and she was gone, chasing after a dog."

"I know. I talked to Patrick. And Mr. Kidman."

"Who's Mr. Kidman?"

"One of the managers at the hardware store. He said he saw the video of what happened. Told me you looked terrified and were running around the store trying to find her. Said she ran away the second she saw the dog when you stopped to talk to an associate."

"Why did you talk to him?"

"I know him. He's a client I placed there. When I was there picking up paint samples for the dining room, he asked how you were doing and then told me all about it."

Unlikely **DATE**

"So if you know what happened, you know she's being crazy about the whole thing."

"Please tell me you didn't call her crazy."

"I think neurotic was the word I might have used." My head meets the back of the couch. "And then there was something about her overreacting, being overprotective, and needing to cut the umbilical cord."

Fingers pinch her upper lip. "You didn't."

"I've never done this shit before, Amber."

"For future reference, there are two things you don't say to a woman. You don't call her crazy, and you don't comment on her parenting ability."

"Well, I did both. And now she won't take my calls." I nod to the trash. "Or my flowers."

She laughs. "Saw that. I like it."

"You find this funny?"

"I have to say, on some level, I do. This is you, Tag. Certified playboy. Asshole extraordinaire. The guy voted in high school as the least likely to ever get married. And here you are, smoking, drinking, and eating your way to a miserable life over a girl."

"There's nothing I can do."

"If there's nothing you can do, then why bother with the self-pity? I'm here to tell you it doesn't look good on you. Go to work. Get back out there. Sleep with a dozen women to get her out of your system if you must. Just do *something*."

"You think I should try to fuck her out of my head?"

"Could you?"

"Could you have with Quinn?"

"I didn't leave Quinn because I didn't love him. I left him because I loved him too much. And I loved Josie too much to watch what was going to happen to her."

"I'm not the one who left, she did. And not because she loved me too much. Because she was afraid of me and what might happen to her daughter."

"It's exactly the same, then."

"It's so not."

"Okay, it's different, but there are still kids involved. Kids we love. I could see it on your face, Tag; hear it in your voice—you loved Gigi even if you didn't want to. You still do. And you love Maddie."

"We were only together for three weeks."

"You think falling in love with someone has a timetable? Remember when you saw Quinn and me come down the elevator at JFK? We weren't even officially dating at the time. We were screwing around, passing the time until I was ready to come home. I couldn't admit it to myself back then, but I was in love with him. I may have fallen in love with him after the crash, when we were stranded for hours."

"Your point is?"

"My point is, Quinn told me much later that when he took you flying, you asked when he was planning on telling me he was in love with me. What is it with men and their inability to express their feelings?"

"If I recall, he's the one who said it first, and you didn't even say it back."

She ignores my comment, continuing with her monologue. "I talked to your dad yesterday. He told me everything that went on with your mom. Why she had the affair. How he took partial responsibility. How he waited until it was almost too late to get her back. Look around you, Tag. It's almost too late. So do yourself a favor and pick up the goddamn phone and be a fucking man."

Then, without another word, she walks out my front door.

Unlikely DATE

I sit and stare at the empty chair for an hour, contemplating my sorry-ass life. Then I pick up the phone and dial. She answers on the first ring.

"Hi, Mom."

Chapter Thirty-two

Maddie

I miss him. I miss him so much. But I look at Gigi across the lawn and know nothing is more important than she is.

Today is especially difficult, as I'm nauseatingly tired of explaining to everyone at this party that, no, Tag and I are no longer together, and no, it's not because he cheated on me.

Nobody but my friends believe me. And my friends aren't here. They don't have kids.

But I can see it on their faces. The other moms at Kara's fifth birthday party whisper to each other as they stare at me. I don't have to hear them to know what they're saying. That they knew it wouldn't work out. Not with a playboy like him. He can't be tamed. Nobody could land him, especially not someone like me.

After the three-legged race, the pin the tiara on the princess, and the water balloon toss Gigi insisted I do with her, I'm hot. I sit under a shady tree and fan myself.

Sierra's mother, Laney, otherwise known as queen bitch of the universe, is what a lot of young men would call a MILF. She struts around town in her skin-tight shirts, showing off her lacy push-up bras (yes, even here), wearing sky-high heels that sink deep into the earth with every step she takes (again, here). She reminds me of that woman they made a movie about, Erin Brockovich. Except comparing the two isn't really fair to Erin because if I recall, Erin was a nice person who actually fought for the underdog. Laney, on the other hand, is the type of mom who thinks her child is the best at everything, requires the most expensive of everything, and, like her, should never have to lift a finger for anything.

When she walks toward me, I know nothing good is going to happen.

"Maddie," she says, loud enough for anyone in earshot to overhear. "You poor thing. You're all sweaty. I'd let you use my powder, but I'm afraid with skin as pale as yours, it'd look horrid. You can remove your sweater, you know. We're all friends here. It's not like we'll take pictures and post them on the internet or anything."

I hear a few muffled giggles from her friends. I try to ignore them as my throat thickens. "I'm sure you wouldn't, Laney. And I'm fine the way I am, thank you."

"Suit yourself." She goes back to sitting with Jenn Marbaugh and Morgan Watney, also MILFs, but slightly less bitchy ones. "Do you think she takes off her sweaters during sex?" she asks her friends loudly. "I'll bet that's why he dumped her. Then again, maybe she did, and it was just too hideous for him to touch."

Her words sting like needles, and I swallow an upsurge of tears.

"Why was Sierra's mommy mean to you?" Gigi asks, plopping down next to me. "What did she say?"

If I could rip Laney's eyeballs out and stuff them down her throat, I would. How dare she talk about me like that with Gigi around. "Nothing, baby. She just thought I would be more comfortable without my sweater."

"But you told her you wear it to cover your quilt, right?"

"Something like that."

"Because you're different."

"Yes, baby. They're getting ready to cut Kara's cake. You don't want to miss it."

An hour later, her stomach filled with cake and her hands holding balloons, we make the quarter-mile walk home from the park.

"Remember to look both ways when we cross the street."

"Okay, Mommy."

I watch her do it. She's always good about being careful. She certainly takes after me.

"Parties are fun," she says as we cross.

"Yes, they are."

"Can I have a party for my birthday?"

"Sure. We can invite Kara and Tori and Patrick and Gran."

"That's only two girls. Kara had fifteen. Can I have that many?"

My heart sinks knowing there's no way I could make that happen. I might be able to wrangle up five or six (by bribing their mothers with margaritas), but we just don't know that many people. "We'll see."

"Yay! I can't wait to tell Kara I'm going to have a party." A balloon escapes her hand just as we make it to the sidewalk. "Oh, no!" she shouts and chases after it.

And then my world implodes.

In slow motion.

By the time I see what's happening, it's too late to stop it.

A boy careening down the sidewalk on a skateboard plows into Gigi as she's running for the balloon, sending both of them crashing through the front plate glass window of the bakery. I lunge for her, but she's too far gone.

"Gigi!" My scream pierces the air.

Glass and blood are all over her. Is it hers? The boy's?

"Someone call 911!" a lady yells.

The boy gets up, stunned, blood running down the side of his face. But Gigi isn't moving. He fell on top of her. Please, God, let her be okay.

"Gigi." I kneel next to her, glass crunching under my knees and digging into my skin.

"Don't move her!" someone inside the bakery shouts.

Tears stream down my face and drop onto hers. Her face and arms are covered in blood, and the wetness from my tears streaks the blood down the side of her face. Her face is cut. I scream again. I've never felt so helpless in my life.

That's not true. This is the second time in my life I've felt this helpless.

"She's only five." I want to pull her into my lap. "She's my daughter. I have to help her."

"Don't," the man repeats, standing over me. "Hear the sirens? They're coming. If you move her and she has a spine injury, you could further injure her. We can't move her neck."

The man removes his shirt, rolls it up, and puts it around her head.

I take her little, bloody, lifeless hand into mine. "Gigi, baby, wake up."

People gather around. I hear gasps, muffled cries, pained whispers.

"Is she dead?" someone shouts behind me.

Unlikely DATE

My heart stops. *Is she?*

The man puts his fingers on her neck. "She has a strong heartbeat."

"Maddie," someone says behind me—Ava, I think. "Oh, my god, Maddie. What can I do?"

"Stand back," the man says. "The ambulance is here."

I don't move away. I can't let go of her hand.

"Ma'am, you need to move and let us do our jobs."

Finally, I look up. It's Jessica from Patrick's firehouse.

She puts her hands on my shoulders when she recognizes me. Her partner is already on the ground with Gigi. "Maddie, we've got her. She's in good hands. We need to put a neck brace on her and then transport her to the hospital. You can help her by letting us do our jobs."

Ava pulls me up from behind. "It's okay. She's going to be okay. She's strong, Maddie. You'll see."

Firefighters surround Gigi, making me stand back even further. They're moving the larger shards of glass out of the way. "Ma'am, you're injured," one says.

Blood is trickling from my knees. "I don't care."

He gets something from the ambulance. He hands me some gauze. "Here, to stop the bleeding. You can ride with her."

"Can you call Patrick Kelsey?" I ask him.

"You bet."

Someone brings a gurney, and they lift Gigi up on a backboard, her neck in a brace and her forehead taped all the way around. They put an oxygen mask over her nose and mouth, and there's an IV in her arm, with someone holding a bag above her. I'm standing here watching, Ava holding me up, and I realize I'm inside a nightmare. Again.

Only this time, there isn't anyone to cradle her and protect her. She's hurt. She's not moving. She might be dying. I grab on to Ava. "What's happening?"

I momentarily notice the boy, sitting on the curb, being treated by another firefighter. He's talking. And crying. And bloody.

But not as bloody as my daughter.

"I'm sorry," I hear him say. "I'm so sorry."

"Maddie?"

I look up.

"Time to go." A paramedic holds out his hand and helps me into the back. Jessica is inside, hovering over Gigi.

"I'll call everyone," Ava promises as the doors shut.

Someone pounds on the back of the ambulance, and we start moving, sirens blasting. Patrick says they only use sirens if it's really bad. "Why isn't she talking?" I ask. "Why isn't she moving?"

"We're going to find that out," Jessica says. "Her vitals are strong. Your little girl is a fighter. But I can feel a bump on the back of her head. Could just be a concussion."

"Her face," I cry. "Her arms."

"We won't know the extent of her injuries until we can get her scanned and make sure there isn't any glass inside her that we can't see."

My heart completely stops beating. "Inside her?"

"It may look worse than it is, Maddie. The body holds a lot of blood. We're giving her fluids to compensate. She hasn't lost as much as you think."

We're at the hospital in two minutes. I could have practically carried her myself if they'd allowed me to move her. It's around the corner and down a street that feeds into McQuaid Circle.

They whisk her into the emergency department, making me stand back. But I can see her. A doctor wearing blue scrubs feels around her head and neck, and the thing holding her head in place is removed. A large machine is wheeled past me by a woman wearing a lead apron. People stand back while they hover it over her in several places. Her mask is removed and someone waves something under her nose.

She doesn't wake.

A different, younger doctor walks over to me and introduces himself, even though I forget his name within two seconds. "You're Gigi's mother?" he asks.

"Yes. Maddie Foster."

"Well, Ms. Foster, we need to run more tests. The X-rays are showing superficial wounds only. Glass did not enter any organs or her bloodstream. However, she does have some fairly extensive lacerations, especially along her right arm. Her face will require multiple sutures as well."

My hands cover my mouth as I absorb his words.

"But, Ms. Foster, she hasn't regained consciousness yet."

"Is that bad?"

Of course it's bad.

"We'll know more soon. We're sending her up for a CT scan to check for a possible brain bleed."

"Brain bleed?" I double over and feel like vomiting. I glance back at her and see her eyes open. "Look! She's awake! Her hand is moving."

"That's good news. Wait here. I'll be back."

My legs are shaking, and I hold on to the counter as I watch them work over her. She cries, and I swear I don't know if I should be happy or sad. Crying means she's aware of what's happening.

But it also means she feels pain. "Gigi, I'm here, baby!" I shout, hoping she can hear me.

The young doctor comes out again. "She's confused and dizzy, which may indicate a concussion. We've given her pain medicine that should calm her. She's aware, but we're still sending her for the scan. She was out for more than ten minutes, so we need to rule out more extensive injuries."

"Can I see her?"

"For a minute, yes. But we really need to get her over to CT as quickly as possible. Come."

I wipe my eyes, knowing mascara has probably streaked down to my chin. I walk to the side of her bed and take her hand. It's still bloody. "Gigi, baby, Mommy's here."

She looks at me. Her eyes are hazy and distant. "What happened to the balloon, Mommy?"

I smile. She's still Gigi. "I'm going to buy you a hundred balloons, baby."

Her eyes flutter closed.

"Gigi!" I tap her hand. "Gigi!"

"It's the pain medication," a nurse says. "It works fast. Come with me, Ms. Foster. I'll take you to a waiting area while she gets her CT scan."

Patrick bursts through the emergency room doors. "Maddie!"

I go to him and collapse in his arms.

Chapter Thirty-three

Tag

There's pounding on my front door. Who the fuck is it now? Is Amber back for another pound of flesh? My father? I open it, ready to let whoever it is know I'm not in the mood for visitors.

Ava Criss is standing on my front porch. Her hands are in her pockets, her head low, her eyes red. She looks like she's been put through the wringer.

Something is very wrong.

Dread forms a painful knot in my gut. "What happened? Is Maddie okay?"

Tears come to her eyes, and she fails to speak.

"Fucking tell me, Ava. What's going on?"

"Gigi's in the hospital."

My heart lodges somewhere in the vicinity of my throat. "Oh, fuck."

"She fell through the front window of the bakery when a kid barreled into her on his skateboard."

"Jesus Christ, how bad is it?"

"Bad, I think, but I'm not sure." She hiccups and her voice cracks. "Tag, it was so horrible. Blood was everywhere and she wasn't moving. I think she took the brunt of the impact. The boy who ran into her walked away with cuts and scrapes. They took Gigi away in an ambulance. I promised Maddie I'd tell everyone."

"She asked you to tell *me?*"

She averts her eyes. "Not you specifically. But I knew you'd want to know."

I grab my keys and cross the threshold.

"Where are you going?"

"To the hospital."

"They won't let you see her. Family only."

"I'm going anyway."

The whole way over, horrible visions run through my head. Gigi lying in a pool of blood. Maddie standing over a tiny grave. The woman I'm in love with wanting to die along with her daughter.

I park illegally and run into the emergency department. Helen, the woman behind the desk, is a friend of my mother's. She knows exactly why I'm here. She stands. "Tag, you can't go back there."

I stride for the door. "The fuck I can't."

She puts herself between me and it. "Do I need to call security?"

Nervously, I run a hand through my hair. "Gigi's back there, and she could be dying for all I know."

Helen puts a motherly hand on my shoulder and guides me to the seating area. "You're welcome to wait out here."

"You must know something," I say. "How is she?"

Her head shakes from side to side. "I can't tell you that."

I punch the wall next to me. "I should be back there. I swear to God, if that little girl dies and I'm not there for Maddie, I'll never forgive myself."

Helen looks over her shoulder and then says quietly. "She's not dying, Tag."

I look into her eyes, searching for more. "But it's bad, isn't it?"

"That's all I can say, and I really don't know much more anyway. Sit. Can I bring you a coffee?"

"No."

"Is there anyone you'd like me to call to sit with you?"

Yeah, Maddie.

"No."

I pull out my phone and start about a dozen texts to her. But what do I say to the woman who dumped me, whose daughter could be severely injured? Hearing from me might make things worse at this point. So I text someone else.

Me: I'm in the waiting room of the ED. I know you're with her. Nobody will tell me anything. I need to know.

Ten minutes later, as I'm pacing the front sidewalk puffing on my third cigarette, Patrick walks out the door. I flick my smoke into the street and run over. "How is she?"

"Gigi woke up shortly after they brought her in."

A weight is lifted. However, the look on his face tells me there's more. "But…"

"But she has multiple injuries."

"How bad?"

"She's getting a CT scan now to make sure there isn't any bleeding or swelling in her brain."

"Jesus."

He holds up a hand. "It's just a precaution. They don't think she does, but she hit her head pretty badly when she fell, so they're covering all the bases."

"What else? Ava said there was a lot of blood."

"The good news is the X-rays showed no glass inside her body. There's no damage to her internal organs, and she most likely won't need surgery."

"The good news," I say flatly. "What's the bad news?"

"She fell into a plate glass window, Tag. She's cut up pretty badly. They'll know more after the CT scan when they get her all cleaned up."

I light up again, feeling as worthless as a condom at a baby shower.

Patrick raises a brow at my Marlboro.

"You going to lecture me about smoking? She fucking dumped me and now her kid is hanging on by a thread."

"Nah, man. Not my place."

"How is she?"

"You mean other than the fact that her daughter is getting a brain scan and is caked in blood?"

"You know what I mean."

"You're asking if she misses you? Now, when all this is happening, you want to know if she's still torn up over you?"

"Would she see me?"

"If you think now is the appropriate time to try and win her back, you're stupider than I thought."

"You think I'm stupid?"

"To let her go—yeah, I do."

Unlikely DATE

"I didn't let her go. She broke up with me."

"And you let her."

"I called. I sent flowers. What the hell else was I supposed to do?"

"I don't know. More."

"More? What do you expect? Was I supposed to force myself on her? She's a grown goddamn woman, who I get the feeling no one can tell what to do."

"You got that right. But you bailed, man."

"Damn it, I didn't bail. I fucking love her." I look through the doors. "I even love her kid."

He steps back as swiftly as if I'd punched him in the chest. "Does *she* know that?"

"Yeah, of course. We spent every day together for almost a month."

"Did you say the words, Tag?"

A hundred times in my head.

"No. But she had to know."

He laughs. "My point has been proven. Stupid."

"What does that matter anyway if she doesn't trust me with Gigi?"

"I guess you'll never know then, huh?" He thumbs to the door. "Listen, I have to get back in there."

"You'll let me know how Gigi is?"

"Yeah."

"And you'll tell Maddie I was here?"

"Don't think I have to." He nods through the doors. I follow his gaze and see Maddie watching us from the doorway behind Helen.

She wipes her eyes and walks away.

"Wait." I call him back before he goes inside. "Do you have a key to Maddie's apartment?"

"Why?"

"The floors, they're only half-done. And I can't just sit around and do nothing. Cooper and I will go finish them."

He grins and reaches in his pocket. He removes a key from his ring and tosses it to me. "Maybe you're not so stupid after all."

"How's that?"

"Looks like you're doing more."

Chapter Thirty-four

Maddie

"Right this way, Ms. Foster," a nurse says. "Gigi's CT is done, and she's been moved to another floor."

"Is she okay? Did they see anything bad?"

"The doctor is waiting to speak with you."

Patrick takes my hand, and we follow. We're quiet in the elevator to the third, and top, floor of the hospital. He was here. Tag came to check on Gigi. I wanted to go to him, but I couldn't. After all, I'm a hypocrite now, aren't I? My daughter is lying in a bed in this hospital because of me, when just last week I yelled at him because she walked away and followed a dog.

The elevator doors open. The nurse guides us to a counter. "Wait here."

I stare down the hallway, wondering which room Gigi is in. I've been to this hospital before, more times than I care to remember. The first time I was here was over five years ago. I was in the maternity ward, and it was the best day of my life. The next time I was here was the worst. I pray this time doesn't overshadow that one.

A man wearing scrubs walks over. He extends his hand. "I'm Dr. Yelton, Gigi's doctor."

"Maddie," I say. "And this is my friend, Patrick."

"You and I actually met years ago, Maddie. I was Gigi's doctor when she came in to be treated for smoke inhalation. I spoke to you back then. You were obviously dealing with your own injuries." His eyes quickly assess my exposed skin. "You're looking well."

He's making small talk. Does that mean Gigi's okay, or is he hesitating?

He opens a chart. "So, Gigi's CT scan is normal. We assume she has a concussion, but there's no test for that. We base it on her symptoms. Is she dizzy, does she have memory loss, is she nauseous—things like that. Since she's still sleeping, we can't assess her quite yet."

"She remembered the balloon," I say. "When she woke up in the emergency room, she asked me about the balloon she was chasing when the accident happened."

"That's a good sign. It probably means if she does have a concussion, it's not a bad one."

"What else?" I ask, terrified of his answer. "There was so much blood, and the ER doctor said she had cuts on her arm and face."

"She does. The nurses have cleaned her up, and we're waiting on a plastics consult."

"What does that mean?"

"Well, her arm has an extensive laceration, but that's not what concerns us. She has several smaller lacerations on her face. We want to make sure those are sutured in a way that offers minimal scarring."

Unlikely DATE

My hand flies to my mouth, covering a torturous sigh. "Her face will be scarred?"

Patrick pulls me tightly against his side.

"Most likely, yes. Don't be alarmed when you see her," Dr. Yelton says. "Her face is bandaged up. But she was lucky. The glass didn't get near her eyes or mouth. The worst cuts are on her forehead and left cheek. We'll know more once Dr. Granniss has seen her. You're welcome to sit with her. She's still asleep and probably will be until after she's sutured."

"Yes, please."

"We'll talk more later. And I'd like to keep her overnight for observation." He nods down the hallway. "Room 314."

"Thank you."

I grip Patrick's hand knowing I'm squeezing it to the bone. What am I going to see when I walk in there?

I stop in the open doorway. I half expect her to be hooked up to machines. She's not. She has an IV in her left arm, and it looks like she's sleeping peacefully. Tears stream down my face as I stifle a pained sob. She probably can't hear me, but in case she can, I can't have her knowing I'm horrified at what I see. My daughter is a mummy. All I can see of her face are her eyes, nose, and mouth. And her right arm is completely covered in a bandage that is tinted pink from her blood. Her hands have smaller bandages on them. The rest of her is under a blanket. I can only pray there aren't more bandages elsewhere.

"I promise the dressings make it look worse than it really is," Patrick says.

I cross the room and carefully take one of her hands. I don't want to hurt her. "Mommy's here," I say softly. "You're going to be fine, baby. Remember what I always say about going to the doctor? You get ice cream after. Well, you're going to get gallons and gallons. You can eat it for breakfast if you want."

Patrick sits in the corner, watching as I talk to her until Dr. Granniss comes in and introduces himself as the head of pediatric plastic surgery.

"Surgery?" My hand covers my heart. "She's going to need an operation?"

"No, no. But with the injuries to her face, we want to make sure her quality of life isn't impacted."

I tug on my sleeve, knowing exactly what he means.

We stand back as he unwraps her arm. She has a gash extending from her wrist to her elbow. "Lucky girl," he says. "Missed her radial artery by centimeters."

Lucky? I want to shout at him. Patrick knows what I'm thinking. He squeezes my shoulder.

When he unwraps the bandages on her face, I try not to scream. My baby looks like she's been butchered. The pain piercing through my heart at the sight of her is a white-hot bolt of agony.

Dr. Granniss points to her forehead. "This one here will suture nicely, and as she grows older, the scar will blend into the glabella lines above her brow. While she's young, her bangs can cover it." He touches the edge of her face near her right eye. "This one is a bit more difficult, but it'll only require three or four stitches and shouldn't leave as bad a scar." His eyes focus on her cheek. He gets lost in thought, studying her as he cocks his head from side to side. "All of the lacerations will leave some sort of scar. They'll be red at first, then fade to pink. Some will be more visible than others. But this one here on the cheek will be the one that bothers her the most. It doesn't follow the contour of her face or fall in any natural facial creases. Normally, we use six SPI, that's sutures per inch, but on her face, we'll use more and they'll be

Unlikely DATE

smaller. This jagged part here will require some extra attention to make sure the edges come together nicely."

He turns to me. I'm sure he sees the blood has drained from my face. "Breathe, Mom. Kids are resilient. She's going to be fine. Yes, it will appear daunting at first, until she gets the stitches removed. But all in all, things could have been worse. Her eyes were spared. She'll have a beautiful smile." He glances at her. "I can tell she's a gorgeous child. And she still will be."

I nod, unable to speak.

"Thank you, Doctor," Patrick says.

"I'll be back in a few minutes to get started. You might not want to watch. It can be unsettling seeing your child get so many stitches. Go get a cup of coffee. Don't worry, she won't feel anything. We're giving her enough pain meds to keep her asleep, and I'll use a local anesthetic. Someone will come get you as soon as we're done."

Patrick takes my elbow. "Come on."

I break away from him and go over and kiss Gigi's left arm. Her perfect, unblemished arm. Then I follow Patrick to the cafeteria and cry.

"Are you the little girl's mother?" a woman asks. "From the accident at the bakery?"

I look up from my cold coffee. "Yes."

"I'm Ginny Ashford. My son, RC, was the one on the skateboard." Her voice grows thick. "He's so, so sorry. I can't tell you how broken up he is over it."

"I'm Maddie. Gigi is my daughter's name." I suddenly realize that if she's here, her son must be as well. "Is your son here? I'm sorry, everything happened so fast I didn't know what happened to him after I saw him sitting on the curb."

"In the back. He has a few cuts they needed to stitch up. Nothing as bad as Gigi's. I heard reports of what people were saying. All that glass." A tear escapes her eye. "I can't imagine what you must be going through. Is she going to be okay? I know how fast he rides the skateboard. I've told him he needs to slow down. He never listens. I won't blame you if you sue us."

I'm totally caught off guard. "Sue you? It was my fault, not his."

"Your fault?" she and Patrick say at the same time.

"How in the hell was it *your* fault," Patrick says in a scolding tone.

"I'm her mother. I should have had her hand, but she was holding the balloons. One got away from her and she ran. She ran right into him. If anyone should be suing anyone, you should be suing me."

Ginny sits on the other side of me and pats my leg. "Oh, Maddie. Stop it right this second. You can't blame yourself. Kids will be kids. Accidents happen. Believe me, I have three boys. You want to bubble wrap them and protect them from this cruel world, but you can't. No one can."

I nod. "I'm starting to realize that."

She gets up and pulls something from her pocket. "RC wanted me to give this to your daughter. It's a buffalo head nickel he carries around for luck. He never goes anywhere without it."

"Oh, no. I couldn't."

"Take it, please. He really wants Gigi to have it."

I let her put it in my hand. "Thank you. I hope RC will be okay."

She hands me a slip of paper. "Please let me know how Gigi is. And if there is anything we can do. Anything. Please let us know." She starts away, then turns. "Your daughter wouldn't happen to be the Gigi from Gigi's Flower Shop on McQuaid Circle, would she?"

"Sort of. I mean, it was named after my grandmother, but yeah. I own the shop."

"Hmm. Well, bye now."

"Ms. Foster?" a nurse says, holding the door to the hallway open. "We're ready for you."

~ ~ ~

"Mommy?"

I lift my head off her bed and blink sleep from my eyes. It's morning. And she's awake.

"Hey, baby."

She looks around. "Where are we?"

"We're at the hospital. Remember yesterday and the balloon? You had an accident."

"My face feels funny."

Bandages still adorn most of her head, keeping her stitches dry and covered. "Does it hurt?"

"A little."

"I'll ask the nurse for something so it won't hurt."

Gigi was in and out of it all night, waking when Gran came to see her, and for a few minutes here and there, but obviously she doesn't remember being here.

"The doctor said you can go home today. But you have a bump on your head and some cuts, so you'll have to be very careful, okay?"

She looks past me to the doorway. "Who's that?" She squints. "Is that Grammy and Papa?"

I turn to see Cody's parents standing at the entrance to her room. I remove my hand from Gigi's. "I'll be back in a few minutes."

I walk out and wait for one of them to say something.

"We heard about Gigi," Ellen says. "Is there somewhere we can talk?"

"There's a lounge at the end of the hall."

I ask a nurse to sit with Gigi, then lead the way to the lounge and take a seat in the corner. They don't sit. Evan hands me an envelope. It looks official.

"What's this?"

When he doesn't answer, I open it. It's a summons to appear in court. They're filing for custody. Again. "You have some nerve coming here and giving me this right now."

"Gigi being here is exactly why we're doing it," Ellen says. "You're clearly an unfit mother. First, we hear about her getting lost in the hardware store with some stranger, and now this. I'm sure the judge will reconsider his earlier ruling and award custody to us."

I sink into the chair, a lump clogging my throat. Am I going to just sit back and let them do this again? Four years ago, I was sure Gigi would be taken from me. I even thought it might be best for her. The fire was my fault, after all.

The fire. It's the first time I've allowed myself to think of it as anything but The Incident.

But last night, when I sat up and watched my baby all night long, I remembered everything Ginny Ashford said. Everything Tag said. And I know they're both right. Evan and Ellen couldn't have prevented what happened yesterday. God himself may not have been able to intervene. Gigi is a kid. She ran after a balloon. Just like she ran after a puppy.

I sigh. What have I done? I ruined one of the best things that ever happened to me—Tag.

I wish he were here with me right now. I know for a fact he'd stand up to the Jamisons. He wouldn't allow them to walk all over me and take my daughter away. What would he say if he were here?

Suddenly, I have a moment of clarity. I realize that although my heart will always ache for Cody, I've had enough of the hollow agony raging inside me.

I take a breath, channeling my inner Tag, then I stand and rip the envelope to shreds. "You should be ashamed of yourselves. I knew Cody well. He used to tell me all kinds of stories. Like how he got the scar on his knee when he fell off his scooter. And how he spent two days in the hospital after he nearly drowned in a pond." I shoot Evan a pointed look. "Oh, and what about the burn on his calf from the muffler of *your* motorcycle when you took him riding when he was ten?"

I don't know why they seem so surprised that I know all this. Cody and I were together for over three years.

"Do you think Cody's grandparents should have sued you for custody? What gives you the right to think you can parent Gigi any better than I can? Nobody, and I mean *no one,* could love that little girl more than I do. She is my life. Every thought I have is about her. Every breath I take is for her. So you go ahead and file your papers. I promise you, this time I'll show up fighting. It may have taken me a while to realize it, but I've done nothing wrong. I'm not perfect. I make mistakes like every other human. Like *you.* And if I were you, I'd think long and hard about this. Because you need to decide if hating me is more important than ever having a relationship with your granddaughter."

I walk past them, not looking back. I turn the corner and slump against the wall, finally letting anxiety overcome me.

Clapping echoes behind me. "There's the hardass I knew was hidden inside somewhere."

"You heard that?" I ask Patrick.

"I did indeed. And you nailed it, Maddie. Now come on, the nurse is looking for you."

I put the Jamisons out of my head—it's a problem for another day. When I go back to Gigi's room, I stop dead. Gigi's bandages are off. Three black rows of stitches cross her face. One long trail of sutures runs up her right arm, as if a zipper could open up her delicate skin. Smaller patches of stiches are on her hands. I have to hold in my sobs at the sight of her.

Gigi holds up her right arm. "Mommy, look! Now I'm different, too. Just like you."

Bile rises in my throat. Gigi's life flashes before my eyes. Her future is full of sweaters, body makeup, self-loathing, and shame. I study her face behind my tears. I swallow them, refusing to let her see me cry, because I know that, unlike me, she won't be able to hide her scars. Oh, my god. I'm a terrible mother. What kind of message have I been sending her? Will she think she is hideous because that's what I've taught her by hiding my scars?

I make a split-second decision. I won't let the Jamisons win. I will be the best mother I can, even if it means facing my fears and teaching my daughter to face hers. I can't hide anymore. I'm the only one who can set an example for her.

I shed my sweater and throw it into the trash can by the door.

Patrick's jaw drops. And then he smiles. "You go, Mom."

I walk to her bedside. Despite the wounds, the stitches, the future scars, she's still the most gorgeous creature I've ever known.

"You dropped your sweater, Mommy."

"Mommy's not going to wear sweaters anymore, baby. Not unless it's cold out."

She cocks her head. "You're not?"

I smile. "Nope. And as soon as the doctor says it's okay, I'm taking you swimming. And you know what else? We're going to the beach. I'm going to save up all my money, and next summer you and I are going to Florida. We're going to splash in the waves and dig our toes into the sand."

"And build sandcastles?"

"Yes, baby. We're going to build sandcastles."

"Are you okay, Mommy? Why are you crying?"

"I guess because I'm so happy."

"Because we're going to the beach?"

"Yes. Because we're going to the beach." I lean over and hug her, vowing to tell her how beautiful she is every day of her life.

"I'm sorry," I tell the nurse. "You were asking for me?"

She sniffs back her own emotions. "I wanted to show you how to care for her wounds. It might be best to keep the ones on her arm and hands covered until the stitches come out. Kids play hard and they need to stay clean and dry. But you can leave her face exposed. If she starts picking at the sutures, you can cover them with a thin layer of petroleum jelly and a non-stick bandage."

She explains everything to me and gives me some literature as a reminder.

"I'll get her discharge papers going, and you should be out of here later this afternoon. We'll send you with a prescription for liquid painkillers. It'll help her sleep the first few nights."

"Thank you."

She leaves the three of us alone. Patrick nods to the trash can. "Dang, girl. Lots of changes going on with you today."

I look out the window, knowing I'm really wishing for one more. I finally ask, "What did he say when he was here yesterday?"

"Why don't you ask *him?*"

"I was so mean to him, Patrick. I said horrible things."

"Somehow I get the feeling that's all water under the bridge."

There's a knock at the door. My heart leaps thinking it could be Tag. It's not.

"May we come in?" Evan Jamison asks. "I promise we'll be quick."

"Only if you don't say anything to upset them," Patrick asserts.

Evan shows me the pieces of the torn envelope and then deposits them where I'd put my sweater. "We thought about what you said, and you're right. We want a relationship with Gigi."

"I want that too," I say. "I've always wanted it. But I can't have you turning her against me."

"We won't," Ellen says. "We promise." She looks at Gigi with glistening eyes. "Maybe the four of us could have a picnic or something when she's feeling up to it."

I nod and can almost feel Cody smiling. "I'd like that. We both would. Would you like to come say hello?"

Several hours later, Gigi is being wheeled to the entrance. Patrick and I flank her sides.

"I'll go out and pull the car around," Patrick says, running ahead. He looks back with a huge smile. I guess he's as happy as I am to be getting Gigi out of here.

Outside, I thank the wheelchair escort and help Gigi onto the bench. Then we sit and wait for Patrick.

Someone pulls up. But it's not him. It's a Range Rover.

Chapter Thirty-five

Tag

I turn off the engine and take a deep breath, swallowing my feelings. Gigi's face. Her fucking beautiful face. I paste on a smile and pull my shotgun passenger out of the SUV.

"Tag!" Gigi sings.

I stride over and set the giant teddy bear, which is bigger than Gigi, next to her.

She hugs it and then me. "Thank you. Thank you."

"Anything for you, princess."

I reach on the floor of the back seat and pull out something else. I hand Maddie the flowers. "And these are for you."

She smiles. She recognizes the wrap. I bought them twenty minutes ago from her grandmother.

"I'm so sorry," I say. I glance at Gigi. "For everything."

"Me too."

"Can I take you home to your apartment?"

"Well, Patrick was—"

A car horn sounds, and when I look over, Patrick waves. Then Maddie's phone pings with a text. I glance down and read it.

Patrick: See you at your place.

"That's a yes, then?" I ask.

"Yes. Wait. Her booster."

I open the back door. It's already in there.

"A conspiracy?" she asks.

"Something like that." I lean down and carefully pick up Gigi. "Come on, let's get you in."

"Be caref—" Maddie starts, then shakes her head. "You're good. You got her."

Wow. I stare. Something's changed. I belatedly notice her sweater is missing. Maybe it got left behind. "Did you forget something?" I ask, nodding to her arm.

"Nope."

She doesn't look squeamish, or shy, or self-conscious when she says it. She just grabs the bear and stuffs it in next to Gigi.

Gigi falls asleep almost instantly. I glance at her in the rearview. "Is she okay?"

"The nurse said she'd be drowsy," Maddie assures me.

The trip to their place is quick. Patrick's car is around back when we get there. And Maddie's grandmother is standing in the doorway.

"Gran!" Gigi says when she wakes as Maddie gets her out of the back.

Rose kisses her on her good cheek. "My Lord, it's good to have you back home."

"Wait till you see, Gran," Gigi says. "My arm looks like your needlepoint." She giggles sleepily. "Mommy has her quilt, and now I have my needlepoint."

Rose and Maddie lock eyes and share a sad look.

Patrick carries Gigi inside. She calls back. "Don't forget Smokey."

"Hey," I say. "I thought you were calling me Tag now."

"My bear. I named him Smokey."

I chuckle and get him out of the back while Maddie gets the flowers.

"Business has been real good today, Maddie," Rose says.

"That's good," Maddie replies with a sad smile. "We've got hospital bills to pay."

"I don't think that will be a problem."

Maddie stops walking. "Really? Why not?" She looks at me and then the flowers. "You didn't shove a bunch of money in here, did you?"

"Me? No."

"Wait here," Rose says when we step inside.

"I wonder what she's talking about," Maddie asks.

"You won't believe it," Rose says, handing Maddie some receipts. "Ginny Ashford came in and asked if we could send a huge arrangement of flowers to both the emergency department and the pediatric wing of the hospital to thank them for their wonderful care of Gigi. Also, her niece is getting married, so she'll need us to do her shower and wedding. Additionally, she's in charge of the altar flowers at her church, and she placed a standing order for a very pricey arrangement to be delivered to the sanctuary every week."

The more Rose talks, the further Maddie's mouth slackens. "Oh, my gosh. She didn't have to do all that. I knew they had money, but this is too much. I don't hold her son accountable."

"I'm not sure you quite understand the extent of the Ashford's wealth," I say. "Ginny is my second cousin. Her husband, Wyatt, owns a financial consulting business that has a shit-ton of rich clients. So believe me when I say, you shouldn't feel one ounce of guilt accepting their business."

"Well, okay then." A sense of relief visibly washes over her, and it makes me hate the fact that above everything else, she was worried about money.

"I hope you don't mind I closed up early." Rose rubs her hands together. "These old hands aren't what they used to be. Besides, if you're all good here, I've got a date with—"

"A Barcalounger?" Maddie says with a wry grin.

Man, it's nice to see her smile.

Then Maddie looks troubled. "I have to get up there before Gigi uses the bathroom."

"Why, do you think she needs help?" I glance at the bear in my arms. "And, do you mind if I bring this guy up?"

She doesn't protest, so I follow her up the stairs. She stops at the top before going inside. "She still hasn't seen her face yet. Five-year-olds don't normally go around looking in mirrors. And she had the bandages on her face until just a little while ago. I'm scared of what she'll think when she sees herself for the first time. How am I supposed to tell her she's most likely going to be scarred for life?"

"I'd like to help if I can."

"How could you possibly help?"

I shrug. "Because I see you differently than you see yourself."

She looks confused, then walks through the door.

"Mommy! Mommy!" Gigi cries from the back.

Shit. The bathroom.

We race down the hall. Patrick's standing in the doorway looking distraught. "I didn't know she hadn't seen them yet."

"Baby, it's going to be okay." Maddie drops to the floor and turns Gigi around. "You've got cuts on your face, but it looks worse than it is. They used the stitches to fix your skin, like on your arm."

"My face will be needlepoint, too?"

Maddie locks eyes with me in the mirror. I don't envy her this talk. "Not always. Remember the nurse said your stiches will come out next week? After that, it will look better. But baby, it's going to take a long time for the scars to fade."

"Scars?" She looks at Maddie's bare arm. "Like you have?"

"Not exactly like mine. Yours will be more like little lines instead of patches. And over time, they will disappear a little but not completely."

It seems like Gigi understands, but she looks back in the mirror, and her bottom lip quivers.

"Come here, princess," I say, lifting her up. "I want to tell you something." I walk her out to the living room and sit her on my lap. "You're just like your mom now, and you know what? That's a good thing, because she is a superhero, and now you have superpowers like she does."

"Superpowers?" Gigi asks excitedly. "Like flying and being invisible?"

"Not exactly. More like X-ray vision."

"What's X-ray vision?"

"Well, let me tell you. Your mom here can see what others can't. She saw something in me that nobody else has ever seen. And you know what other superpower she has that you have now?"

"What?"

"Kindness."

"That's not a superpower."

"I think it is. And you know how I know? Because your mom has been kinder to me than anyone in my whole life. The scars she has make her special and allow her to see the world differently. They let her look past the surface of things and see what's underneath. And now you will be able to do that too. So whenever you look at yourself in the mirror, I don't want you to see scars, I want you to see what I see. Kindness. Beauty. Imperfect perfection."

"Mommy, I have superpowers too!"

"You sure do, baby." Maddie has tears in her eyes. "Thank you," she mouths.

I set Gigi on the couch and stand. "Now, what do my two superheroes want for dinner?"

"Was there ever any question?" Maddie says.

"Goodwin's mac and cheese it is."

"And ice cream," Maddie says. "I promised her lots of it. Rainbow sherbet and mint chocolate chip."

"Seriously?" I cringe. "Together?"

She laughs. "It's better than you think." She looks down. "Oh, my gosh, the floors. *You* did this?"

"I hope you don't mind. Patrick loaned me his key. Cooper and I finished it up earlier. We also did a few other things."

"What other things?"

"Don't worry about it." I thumb to the door. "Right now, I've got to go get food for the princess."

Gigi is already closing her eyes on the couch. I tuck Smokey up next to her and ruffle her hair.

I run across the street to the diner and the ice cream shop, the whole time wondering where we stand. Where I stand. She said she was sorry. But sometimes that's just what you say. And what was she going to say in front of Gigi anyway? Go eat shit and die?

Maybe this whole afternoon was about making Gigi as comfortable as possible. On my way back across the street, the urge to smoke is strong. I pull out my pack. There's only one cigarette left. I look up at Maddie's window, then I toss the pack into the trash can on the sidewalk.

My dad told me to fight for her, and that's exactly what I plan to do.

Back at her place, Patrick opens the door. "They're in Gigi's room reading a book."

I stand in the doorway and listen. I recognize the story Maddie is reading to her. I have to hold in my laughter, because she does the voices really well. Beast is injured and he's dying. Belle is slumped on top of him, crying. And just as the last petal of the rose falls, she declares her love for him, saving him from a lifetime of ugliness and solitude.

It's a children's book. A fairy tale. But fuck, how art imitates life. Maddie has no idea how much she has saved me. From everything. From myself. From a pitiful future of douchebaggary and loneliness. But our story isn't over. She hasn't said the words. I need to hear them. I need to hear them more than I've needed anything ever.

Gigi's eyes close and she drifts off. Maddie finally looks up and sees me staring. I back away and go to the kitchen, where Patrick is spooning out dinner.

Maddie joins us, eyeing the food on the table. "I'm sorry you went through the trouble. I think she might be down for the night after I gave her the pain meds."

"It wasn't any trouble at all. Do you think now that she's asleep we could talk?"

Patrick busies himself putting away the ice cream.

"It's just not a good time with Gigi and all."

"Yeah, of course. I understand. Some other time, then. I'm just going to take off."

"But you brought all this food."

"You guys enjoy."

Maddie looks torn, like maybe she wants to beg me to stay but can't bring herself to say the words.

Beg me.

A piece of her hair has come loose. I want so badly to push it behind her ear and then pull her into my arms. To tell her how this last week has been torture, hell, how living my life without her makes it not worth living.

Beg me.

"Thanks," she says instead. "For the food, the bear, the flowers. Everything. I… guess I'll see you around."

Her words are like a dagger to my heart. A death to the dream that, until a few weeks ago, I didn't know I wanted. "Anytime. You just take care of her."

I go down the stairs, defeated, wondering if the last petal just fell.

Chapter Thirty-six

Maddie

"You stupid bitch," Patrick says as soon as Tag is out the door.

I whip around. "Excuse me?"

"I wasn't clear enough? How about these: foolish, ignorant, dense, brainless. Need I go on? Girl, did you not see how that man was looking at you? What he did for Gigi? What he *said* to her? I may not have been on the Tag train at first, but I'm telling you, that's one ride you need to take. And I'm not just talking about his delicious body. You need to ride that one all the way to the station."

I roll my eyes. "You can stop with the metaphors."

"I'm serious. The dude is majorly into you. You have to go talk to him."

"*You're* the brainless one if you think I'm going to leave Gigi here after everything."

"You heard what the nurse said. She's going to sleep all night after giving her the meds. She's out like a light, Maddie. She's not going to wake up. And you know what you're going to do? You're going to sit here and brood over the fact that you're in love with the guy, and he's there and you're here and both of you are miserable." He turns me around and points me in the direction of the door. "I'm here. And you know I'm well trained to handle anything. You'll be two minutes away. Do something for yourself for once, Maddie."

As he pushes me toward the door, I realize it's not the old, peeling, rotting door that was there yesterday.

"He replaced my *door?*"

"If you'd open your eyes, you'd see he replaced a lot more than that."

I let my gaze wander the living room and kitchen. And that's when I see the changes. I'd been so wrapped up in Gigi, I hadn't noticed anything but the floors. The light fixtures have all been replaced. There is a new ceiling fan. And, wow, a subway tile backsplash.

"He did all this in one day?"

"Guess the man was determined. It's amazing what we do for the people we—" He cuts himself off.

"The people we what, Patrick?"

"The people we want to fuck, Maddie. Now get out of here and go get your man."

I hold up my phone. "Text me. Like every thirty minutes. I have to know she's okay." I break away from him and reach for the sweater draped over the back of the kitchen chair. It's a habit; something I've done a thousand times. As I put it on, visions of Gigi flash in my head. Patrick smiles when I toss it on the couch.

Second thoughts bombard me. I slump my head into my hands. "Am I a terrible mother for leaving her at a time like this?"

Unlikely DATE

"You're an incredible mother, Maddie. Part of that is taking care of your own needs and showing your daughter there is more to life than flowers, Disney books, and gay best friends. If she doesn't see you taking risks and going after what you want, how will you ever expect the same of her?"

"Fine. Every thirty minutes."

"I got it. Now go."

At the bottom of the stairs, I think how I should have changed. I'm wearing the same clothes I had on yesterday. I haven't showered either. But I know if I go back up, it will be that much harder to leave again.

I take the car, even though Tag's house is only a ten-minute walk. Suddenly my heart is racing. What am I going to say? What is he?

At his house, there's a van parked out front. He's got company. This was a bad idea. My phone pings with a text.

Patrick: If you chicken out and come back, I will lock you out of your own house. You know I'll do it, girl. And Gigi is fine, BTW, even though it's only been three minutes.

I park and look at myself in the mirror. I take my hair down from the ponytail and fluff it, hoping it improves my disheveled appearance. I run a wet finger under my eyes to clean up yesterday's makeup. I pinch my cheeks to give them needed color. Then I go to the door.

When Tag opens it, he stands there like he's not sure I'm real.

"Last week, after the hardware store, *I* was the asshole," I say.

"Not true," he says. "It was me. I said hurtful things to you. Things I shouldn't have said."

"They may have been hurtful, but they were also true. And I needed to hear them. I guess they just didn't sink in until this happened."

He opens the door. "Can you come in, or did you just come to argue over who's the bigger asshole?"

I laugh. "I can come in. Patrick promised to text me with updates, but she should be out all night."

Cooper walks into the room. He looks between us, then thumbs at the door. "Yeah, so, I'm gonna go."

"Please don't leave on my account," I say.

"I'm not." He gets his keys. "Okay, so I am."

Tag and I watch in silence as he leaves, then we stare at each other. There's so much more to say. I'm just not sure how to say it.

Turns out, I don't have to.

"I'm not going to beat around the bush or play games with you," he says nervously.

I toss him a smirk. "I thought you liked games."

"Not with you." He paces behind the couch and runs a hand through his hair. He stops and locks eyes with me. "Listen, there are a million things I want to say to you, but really, there's only one thing that matters." He points at the door. "That little girl, I fucking love her. And I love you too."

Air leaves my lungs. Blood echoes through my ears. Tears fill my eyes as light overflows my soul. "What?" I ask, needing to be sure my mind isn't playing tricks on me.

"You need me to say it again?"

I swallow and nod.

He walks toward me, pinning me in place with his eyes. "I love you, Flower Girl. This past week has been miserable without you. I couldn't work, I couldn't even leave my damn house. I couldn't leave because I knew you were out there, and if I saw you, it would hurt so damn bad. You're like a freight train that came barreling at me, ran me over, and spit me out, transforming me into someone I never knew I could be."

I chuckle.

"What's so funny?" he asks.

"Nothing. Just a lot of train metaphors tonight."

"Is that all you have to say?" He cups my face in his hands. "Because I swear if you don't say you love me right fucking now, I might run away and cry like a damn baby."

I look directly into his eyes. "I love you right fucking now."

He laughs. Then heat from his eyes devours me. "Do you have any idea what it does to me when you cuss?"

I shimmy against him. "Maybe you should show me."

"Oh, I plan to, but first, I need you to say it again."

I smile. It's hard to believe that I could be feeling anything but sad after what happened to Gigi. But in this moment, just for a second, I've never felt happier. I say the words I've never before said to a man. And I mean them from the bottom of my heart to the core of my soul. "I love you, Tag Calloway."

He sweeps me into his arms. "You should be sainted, Maddie Foster, because you just performed a miracle."

My phone pings. Concern crosses his face as he puts me down. "Check it," he says.

I look. "It's Patrick. Everything's fine." I put away my phone and jump into his arms, wrapping my legs around him. "We have thirty minutes. What are you going to do with me?"

"Only thirty? Then I guess you'll just have to settle for three orgasms."

He carries me to his bedroom and puts me on the bed. He stares at my arm. "You're not wearing a sweater."

I look at his arm. "You *are* wearing a patch."

"I fell off the wagon. I'm back on it now. What's *your* excuse?"

"I'm not wearing them anymore."

He looks pleased. "Really? Since when?"

"Since earlier today when they unwrapped Gigi's face, and I saw her future flash before me. Since I realized what a terrible example I've set by shaming my own body because it's not perfect. Since I knew I didn't want her growing up like me, with zero self-confidence, always wondering what people think of her. She's not a freak, Tag. Her scars won't define her. And the pathetic thing is, all this had to happen to show me that mine don't define me either."

"Holy shit, Maddie."

"What is it?"

He rubs a hand over his chest, gripping his shirt over his heart. "I didn't think I could love you more."

He reaches out, his thumb brushing over my lower lip. The small gesture sends a rush of sensations crawling across my body. When he leans down and his lips touch mine, it's like coming home. And I know for sure it's a place I always want to come home to.

His kiss is gentle, almost unbearably fragile, but it's not gentleness I want right now, not after being without him. I weave fingers into his hair and pull him forcibly against me, my tongue spearing between his lips as if something inside me is awakening with feral need. My tongue moves with untamed urgency and is met with a sound echoing from the back of his throat, something between a moan and a growl.

I get a hold of his shirt, needing to feel his skin against me. He breaks away long enough to pull it over his head and toss it aside. Then his lips are on my throat. I inhale his shampoo, the minty fragrance of recently chewed gum, and that extra scent that's just… him. It's everything I thought I'd never smell again.

Unlikely DATE

I push him away, quickly removing my shirt and bra.

"So beautiful," he says, taking me in under the remnants of the sunset shining through the west window.

For the first time in my life, I don't feel exposed. I'm not vulnerable under his heated perusal. I'm something else.

I'm powerful.

His hand hovers above my stomach, over the side near my scars. "I want to feel you," he says, his words laced with hunger. "I want to feel every inch of you."

Never has a man looked at me the way he is right now, with such tenderness, sweetness, and unbridled passion. The air crackles between us, and it's as if our very souls collide. If hearts could explode, mine would detonate this very instant.

I don't think. I just take his hand and place it on me, closing my eyes at the overwhelming feeling of another person's hands on my sensitive flesh that, until now, was explicitly off-limits. He touches me as if he's been given a gift to cherish—one that's only for him—and instantly we become bonded on a level I didn't know existed.

The feel of his body on top of me is everything. I feel him—all of him—pressed against me. "Thank you," he mumbles against my lips. He laces his fingers with mine and stretches our arms outward on the bed. I hold on tight as his mouth claims my breasts as if he'll never get the chance again. His soft, dark hair tickles my chest, and I arch into him.

"I can't wait," he says. "I have to have you."

When I smile in agreement, he peels down my pants and underwear and then sheds his own.

His heated stare holds mine. "Where do you want me to touch you, Flower Girl?"

"Anywhere," I say. "Everywhere."

Inch by inch, he crawls down me. He spreads my legs wide and puts his tongue on me. In me. Around me. His teasing is both a punishment and a reward. When his fingers find the right place inside me, I hear nothing but the sound of my moans as he plays me like a finely tuned instrument. My fists knot in his hair, pulling him against me, telling him what I need without words.

I fall apart under him in the most perfect way.

He climbs my body and sinks into me. When he kisses me, I taste myself on his lips. It's dirty. Provocative. Sexy. It's all the things I didn't know I wanted.

I'm flipped over. He's beneath me and I'm straddling him; we're still connected in every way. He grips my sides, not giving a single thought to what he's touching, and thrusts up into me. I lean over, my breasts bobbing onto his chest and my hair cascading around us, slipping between our lips when I kiss him.

I tug on his nipple rings, and he groans. His fingers sink into the skin of my back, my hips, my ass, with a mind of their own, his touch wild and hungry. His thrusts become more demanding. I rock back and forth, matching his greed with my own.

When his fingers pinch my nipples and then rub my clit, my head becomes fuzzy, my vision blurred. Fireworks dance before my eyes as I come on top of him, rubbing out every last quiver as I lean back and fist the comforter on his bed.

He grunts and thrusts once more, holding me still as he joins my ecstasy.

I collapse down on top of him, languid and unable to move. He gently rolls me to his side and rises on an elbow as he traces a finger along the edge of my face. "I love you, Flower Girl."

A text on my phone ends our post-coital bliss. I scramble to the side of the bed and dig into the pocket of my jeans. Patrick says she's still sleeping. Thank goodness he was a few minutes late with his text.

"How long can you stay?" Tag asks. "I know you want to get back to her."

"A little bit," I say, not wanting this feeling to end.

"Can I see you tomorrow?"

I inhale and then blow out a long breath. Then I say out loud something that's been bouncing around in my head all afternoon. Something that terrifies me. Something in my heart I know is right. "After I get back from the elementary school. I've decided to enroll Gigi in kindergarten."

He cocks an astonished brow. "She's going to be thrilled," he says, his face beaming.

"I hope so."

"And can I see you every day after that?"

"I think that can be arranged. Good thing we live so close, huh?"

"What did you think of the renovations?"

My head settles onto his chest. The feel of his heartbeat is calming. "I love them. You've done so much. It looks great. I don't know how to thank you."

"It does look great. I knew it would. My guess is you could ask at least eight hundred a month for it."

I lift my head. "What are you talking about? Why would I want to do that?"

"I've decided I want my mattress back."

My hand is still on his chest, and his heart is now pounding. I pull away, confused. "Oh, okay, sure."

He secures me back to him. "I don't think you understand. I want my mattress back, and I want you to come along with it. Both of you."

Surprised, I sit. I look around. "You want us to move in with you? But it's only been—"

He puts fingers to my lips. "Were you lying when you said you loved me?"

"No."

"Were you not being truthful when you said you'd like to see me every day?"

"Well, no."

"Then what's the issue? Is it Rose?" He takes my hand. "Because if you need me to put a ring on this finger for her, I will."

"Tag, are you crazy? We're nowhere near that."

"Do you mean to tell me if I asked, you wouldn't say yes?"

In a flash, every fairy tale I've ever read to Gigi runs through my head. This man, this self-centered beast of a man has somehow become my prince. And I'm Cinderella, Fiona, and Belle all rolled into one.

"Relax," he says, running a finger down my arm. "I'm not actually asking you to marry me, Flower Girl. I'm just asking if you'd say yes if I did."

"Well, if you're not actually asking, then I don't really have to answer."

He laughs. "No, I guess you don't. Not today anyway." He climbs on top of me, both his stare and his body trapping me under him. When I gaze into his eyes, they tell me everything I need to know, that I'm his forever. Then his words tell me he's mine.

And suddenly, I'm as certain as the scars on my body that he'll be getting his mattress back.

His mattress, his princess, and his whole world.

Epilogue

Maddie

One month later...

Little kisses tickle my arm, my neck, my face. My eyes fly open, and I start laughing at the small furry tan-and-brown creature jumping around me. I fully wake from where I nodded off on the couch and pick up the puppy. "You got her!"

"I called the breeder," Tag says. "I thought we should pick her up a few days early. You know, in case things didn't go so well today."

"She's beautiful." I pull the miniature Goldendoodle into my lap. "Gigi will love her."

"How did drop-off go?"

My head slumps. "Oh, Tag, I'm so nervous. Some of her classmates were really staring. You know how mean kids can be."

"Did anyone say anything?" he says defensively. "Because if they did, I'll stalk them to their houses, thump their fucking parents, and tell them how to raise a proper child."

"Says the man who's been co-parenting one for all of three weeks now."

He sits down and ruffles the puppy's tuft. "Best damn three weeks of my life."

I kiss him. "Mine too."

"So, how bad was it?"

"A boy flat out asked what was wrong with her face. *And* my arm."

"What did you say?"

"I didn't say anything, Gigi did. And a whole lot more politely than I would have."

"She's amazing."

"She is."

"Because she has an amazing mom."

I check my phone. "It's almost time to pick her up. The first day is just a half day." My stomach turns. "What if I made the wrong decision? Maybe it was too soon. We should have waited longer, until she healed more."

"Stop second-guessing yourself. Sending her to kindergarten is one of the bravest things you've ever done. It's going to be what's best for her in the long run. You'll see."

The puppy worms her way between us, wanting more attention. I see something on her collar. Something sparkly. "What's this?"

"Just something else I picked up this morning. I was never going to work today. You just thought I was."

My heart does flips. My body hums. My world stands still. My mind reels. It's an engagement ring. I take a closer look—it's *two*, actually.

I look at him, confused. "Two?"

Unlikely DATE

"You don't think I'd marry you without Gigi's permission, do you? The other one is for her."

Now my heart doesn't just flip, it cartwheels right out of my body and collides with his. A happy tear falls. He captures it with his thumb. "Hey, now. I haven't even asked you yet. You're not allowed to cry until it becomes official."

He pulls the puppy onto his lap and unbuckles her collar. The rings slide off into his hand. They're identical, one a smaller version of the other.

"Tag, they're beautiful."

His fingers press against my lips. "Shhh. No fucking talking," he says, his voice cracking with emotion. "Otherwise, I'm not sure I'll get through this."

My glistening eyes fight to hold back tears as I nod in silence.

He puts the puppy in my lap and gets down on a knee. *Tag Calloway is down on a knee.* The world has definitely shifted on its axis. I wait in disbelief as he works to gather his thoughts. And I wonder how, in a matter of months, after one unlikely date, my life turned into a fairy tale, complete with my own trash-talking prince.

He sighs. "I didn't think this would be so hard."

My gaze falls to the floor. Maybe he doesn't want to do this after all.

A finger under my chin raises my head so I'm looking at him. "You don't get it, Flower Girl." He clears his throat. "It's hard because I'm not good with words, and I want to do this right. But I'm just not sure how to beg you to spend your life with me and have our future children without completely fucking it up."

I have to suppress a giggle, because Tag Calloway couldn't propose any other way.

"Okay, here it goes." He takes my left hand in his. "I'm a fake. A fraud. Everyone thinks I'm this big, strong guy, when in reality, it's just the opposite. I'm weak. Or I was until you. *You* make me strong. Before you, both of us were afraid. You were hiding your body. I was hiding my heart. Both of us were scared of being hurt in different ways. And you know how I know we're perfect together? Because we love each other enough to risk everything. You risked it all by trusting me with your body. I'm risking it all by pledging my love to you."

Tears are actively streaming down my face now. Who knew Tag was a romantic?

"You can talk now," he says.

"Was there a question somewhere in there?"

"Oh shit, yeah. Will you marry me, Flower Girl?"

A smile the size of Texas overtakes me. "I've never wanted anything more."

He slips the bigger of the two rings on my finger and pulls me in for a kiss, squishing the puppy between us. She licks our chins from underneath, wanting in on the excitement.

Tag pulls away. "Assuming all this is good with Gigi, of course."

"I'm fairly certain you won't have a problem convincing her. She asked me last week if she would ever be able to call you *Daddy*."

He does a good job at hiding it, but I can tell he's choking up on the inside.

"I can't believe I'm going to say this," he says, shaking his head in disbelief. "But nothing would make me happier."

The alarm on my phone goes off.

Tag laughs. "Thank God that didn't go off two minutes ago. It would have seriously messed up my mojo."

Unlikely **DATE**

I swallow hard, holding my hand out to see how the ring looks on me. "No matter what happens when we pick her up, I'm telling you right now, today is the best day of my life."

He tucks a piece of hair behind my ear. "No, it isn't. There are going to be so many best days in our lives that you won't be able to choose." He puts Gigi's ring back on the collar and buckles it onto the puppy. "Now let's put this little furball in the car and go get our kid."

Our kid. It's been three weeks since we moved in with Tag, and he's already treating her as his own.

I admire my ring once more and pick up the puppy, reeling over what the future holds.

At Calloway Creek Elementary, we leave Gigi's surprise in the car (both of them). I don't need a bunch of five-year-olds fawning over the puppy. She's Gigi's puppy, the one she's been wanting for more than a month. The one she has no idea she's getting. It looks like both our dreams will come true on the very same day.

Tag grabs my hand as we approach the entrance and wait with all the other kindergarten parents. "Stop tapping," he says, trapping my thumb. "She'll be fine."

"Oh, please, like you haven't been squeezing the blood from my hand."

"Fine, I have to admit, I'm kind of terrified. If anyone made her cry today, I'm not sure what I'll do, Maddie."

I blow out a deep, troubled sigh and send up a prayer.

Little kids stream out of the school. I crane my neck but can't find her. Where is she? Did they keep her back because she's so upset? Because she got bullied and is crying?

"Tag, where is she?"

"Maddie," he says with a lift of his chin. "Look."

I glance around but still don't see her. All I see are other people's kids. And they're filthy with black, red, blue, and green marks all over their arms and faces.

"That poor teacher," I say. "Looks like it was pure chaos in there. Oh, my gosh, there she is."

My heart stops beating. I stop breathing. Gigi's teacher is holding her hand, walking her out to us. Why is my daughter being escorted by Mrs. Petrozzi?

"Mommy! Tag!"

I get down on her level and hug her so hard that I'm sure I squeeze the air right out of her.

"She's a wonderful little girl," Mrs. Petrozzi says.

I look up at her teacher. "Thank you. I think so. But it looks like you had your hands full today."

Her eyes sweep across the seventeen other students. "What, that? No, they were no trouble at all."

"But they're all filthy," I say, then belatedly notice Gigi is not.

Tag puts a knowing hand on my shoulder. His eyes mist. He picks up Gigi in his arms.

"I've never had a student like her before," her teacher says. "She taught them more today than I've ever taught any student in my eight years at this school."

"What? How?"

"Tell her, Gigi," she says. "Tell your mom about the markers."

Gigi giggles. "All my new friends wanted to be like me, Mommy. Now we're *all* superheroes."

Acknowledgements

As always, there are so many people to thank. Without my incredible team of supporters, experts, editors, and beta readers, book number twenty-two wouldn't be possible.

First off, thank you to my amazing assistant, Julie Collier, who I swear never sleeps and answers my texts even late at night. She gives me advice, encouragement, and fluffs my ego as needed.

To my copy editor, Amanda Cuff—your notes in the margins make me smile. You never tear me down; you just build me up for which I'm grateful.

To my beta readers, Shauna Salley, Joelle Yates, Laura Conley, Heather Carver, and Ann Peters—most of whom have been with me for some time now—you guys keep me going with your Facebook posts, constant reminders of your love of my characters, and ongoing pimping of my books.

Tag may be one of the most enjoyable characters I've written to date. I write so many 'nice' guys, it was fun to step out of my box and get into the mind of an 'alphahole'. Be on the lookout for more of those in future books!

About the author

Samantha Christy's passion for writing started long before her first novel was published. Graduating from the University of Nebraska with a degree in Criminal Justice, she held the title of Computer Systems Analyst for The Supreme Court of Wisconsin and several major universities around the United States. Raised mainly in Indianapolis, she holds the Midwest and its homegrown values dear to her heart and upon the birth of her third child devoted herself to raising her family full time. While it took time to get from there to here, writing has remained her utmost passion and being a stay-at-home mom facilitated her ability to follow that dream. When she is not writing, she keeps busy cruising to every Caribbean island where ships sail. Samantha Christy currently resides in St. Augustine, Florida with her husband and four children.

You can reach Samantha Christy at any of these wonderful places:

Website: www.samanthachristy.com

Facebook: https://www.facebook.com/SamanthaChristyAuthor

Instagram: @authorsamanthachristy

E-mail: samanthachristy@comcast.net

Printed in Great Britain
by Amazon